Noah

Trying to Forget Lost Love

Gary Hope

"Noah: Trying to Forget Lost Love," by Gary Hope. ISBN 978-1-951985-58-5 (softcover).

Published 2020 by Virtualbookworm.com Publishing Inc., P.O. Box 9949, College Station, TX , 77842, US.

Who cares if you find true gold or only fool's gold. The adventure lies in the search.

1.

"NOAH, THANKS FOR COMING IN. As editor of the paper, it's my duty to counsel any employees who may be having problems."

"But I'm not having any problems, sir."

"Maybe you're not, Noah, but our readers are. The complaints have nearly doubled over the last six months. The tone in the column you write is often surly and downright mean at times. What's going on? Has something happened in the last year? We can't keep going like this, Noah."

Noah took a deep breath, then stared out the window at the Salt Lake City skyline. He'd driven up from his home in Moab to the Salt Lake City Tribune editor's office to take this warning in person. He knew his attitude had somewhat changed because of some setbacks in his personal life, but he didn't think it was affecting his work as a columnist for the paper. He answered all kinds of questions from readers in the Salt Lake area, usually with informative, funny, insightful answers; however, he had let his personal misfortunes affect his answers lately and his readers were taking offense. Example in case:

"Noah: I wrote you a question last week and instead of answering my question, you insulted me! You really disgust me, Noah! Signed, Andy."

"Andy: I never discussed you at all."

The editor read several more of these complaints to make his point, ending with this one:

"Noah: Can you help me? I bought some of that new, hard, red candy; I heard it may be bad for my teeth. Is it? Signed, Shirley."

"Dear Shirley: You know what's really red and bad for your teeth? A brick!"

● ● ●

"Noah, this type of attitude has to stop. You represent the paper, not just yourself. I have to know that you can control yourself and act professionally. If not, we'll have to address this entire situation more permanently. You really need to get your personal life on track and not let it affect yourself like you have been. Do I make myself clear?"

Noah kept staring out the window, wondering if he should lie to his boss and tell him what he wanted to hear, or just drive back to Moab and hike out into the wilderness and stare into the sun until he went blind and died. "Yes, sir. I'm sorry for the trouble. Everything will be back to normal. You can trust me."

"I'm glad to hear that, Noah. Your column has always been one of the most popular parts of our entire paper. I'd hate to lose that. Keep in touch with me, if you don't mind. And, of course, you know we'll be looking at the column for a while to monitor things . . . you understand that, right?"

"Yes, sir. Don't worry. Everything will be fine." Noah stood up, smiled, and shook hands with his boss. He exchanged pleasantries with the secretary, stopped and spoke with several old acquaintances, then went outside, got in his car, and cried like a baby. After a few minutes, when he could control his emotions, he drove out of town and stopped at the nearest roadside bar. He ordered an Iron Maiden and found a corner table away from the other few people sitting there on a Monday afternoon. He had some questions he had to answer if he was going to continue with the paper, and in fact, continue with life.

Noah's entire existence came tumbling down when he lost the two loves of his life on one tragic day. Tragic for him, apparently not for anyone else. He had fallen head-over-heels in love with a woman he met online. Ana was her name. He loved her brain, her wit, her charm, her conversations, and everything else about her, even though he had never actually met her. Not only had he never met her but he didn't even know where she lived, where she worked, how old she was, or hardly anything else about her—except that he loved her.

At the same time, he had met a park ranger from Canyonlands National Park, down near Moab, who had captivated him as well. The more he saw her, the more enchanted he became. He had almost convinced himself that he was also in love with her as well. If it hadn't been for the hope of Ana, he would have chased her to the end of the earth and back. Dorothy was her name and she was a true beauty who Noah bonded with almost immediately.

Then, one fateful day, Noah had almost convinced himself that Ana and Dorothy could be, might be, had to be . . . the same person. He tried to prove that point but failed miserably. Almost immediately after his failure, Ana stopped emailing him and Dorothy transferred to Death Valley National Park in California. Which was indeed death for Noah. He felt like dying. His world collapsed and from that point forward the tone with his column and his readers became worse and worse until the editor called for the meeting today. He had to change: He knew it but just didn't know how to do it.

Ana was gone. Dorothy was gone. His felt like his life was over. Something had to change. What? He guzzled his Iron Maiden quickly and ordered another one while he thought about his predicament. With Ana, he had no alternatives. Her email address had been deactivated since that fateful day. Every email he'd sent had been "return to sender." It was impossible to contact her.

He knew Dorothy had moved to Death Valley in California and he had tried calling the office there but she wouldn't take his calls. Finally, a co-worker of hers told Noah to stop harassing her or she would notify the authorities. He reviewed both of these scenarios as he half-chugged and half-sipped his second Iron Maiden and ordered his third. After his fourth drink, he was slurring his words and his thoughts became totally random and abstract. After his fifth drink, the bar manager stopped serving him and he staggered out to his Jeep and collapsed in the back seat.

He woke up Tuesday morning with a raging headache and the realization that he had vomited and peed all over himself. It was going to be a long four-hour drive home. He spotted a Goodwill near the highway and stopped there to buy some new clothes. He went into the restroom and changed, throwing his old soiled clothes in the dumpster. He stopped again and bought some Extra-Strength Excedrin, which didn't help his headache at all.

He finally made it to Moab and almost stopped at the Moab Brewery but wisely kept going and pulled in his driveway tired, sick, and without hope. He knew he had to answer some emails from work in the morning, and he knew the editor would be monitoring his responses. He hoped he would not be himself, he hoped he could be a kinder, gentler Noah than the person he had evolved into. While he lay in his bed thinking these thoughts, he let his mind wander.

As long as he was hoping and dreaming, he might as well dream for great things. He picked up an arrowhead from his nightstand, the same arrowhead that Dorothy had given him once on a hike they did together one rainy day in the past. He held it for the millionth time, or was it the two-millionth? Then he picked up a picture he had of Ana, one taken from the rear, where he couldn't see her face. He'd held it so many times that the paper was starting to disintegrate. Dorothy and the arrowhead in one hand; Ana and the picture in his other hand . . . dreams floating in his mind like clouds across the desert landscape. Unreachable and unrealistic.

Noah

Incredibly enough, he woke in the morning with the arrowhead and picture still in his hands. At least the hangover was gone. Now, all he had to do was get up and breathe. C'mon, Noah, you can do it. The good people from Salt Lake City are anxiously waiting to hear from you.

2.

"Noah: Who are you voting for in the city councilman race? Signed, Jack."

"Jack: If voting changed anything, they'd make it illegal."

Noah read his response, then thought about his editor reading it and quickly deleted that answer and gave a more politically correct response. He took a deep breath and said to himself, "Please, dude, be nice . . . you need this job."

"Noah: Why are men so obsessed with breasts? They don't care if a woman is tall or short, or smart or dumb, or rich or broke . . . all they care about is how big her boobs are. Am I right? Signed, Becky."

"Becky: I will answer this question the only way I know how: as a man who has researched this issue extensively. I have found that the primary biological function of breasts is to make men stupid. And with that, they are a great success."

Noah thought about deleting this answer as well but then thought, *I can't keep deleting every answer! I have to be me. Just a nicer version. I'll try my best, I'll really, really try; but in the end, if they don't like it, they'll just*

have to fire me. Finally, he had some peace of mind. That decision helped him—not with Ana or Dorothy—it just helped him breathe and continue to exist.

"Noah: Sometimes I feel like I just want to get away from it all. Just leave it all behind and go! Is this abnormal? Have you ever felt like this? Signed, Emily."

"Emily: Here lately, nearly every day, I recite this poem by Mr. WB Yeats to myself: *'Come fairies, take me out of this dull world, for I would ride with you upon the wind and dance upon the mountains like a flame!'* Yes, Emily, we all feel like that at times."

"Noah: I like to do my Christmas shopping early and beat the rush. I'm looking for suggestions for my husband this year. What did you get for Christmas last year? Signed, Susan."

"Susan: You know what I got for Christmas? Fat! I got fat!!"

Noah finished up his morning work, as politically correct and kind as he was currently capable of, then picked up his arrowhead and picture and sat outside to gaze into the distance at the snow-capped La Sal Mountain range. He had stared at these beautiful mountains for years but had never actually been up into them. Time for a change! He couldn't continue to sit here and mope around; if so, he'd lose his job and his sanity. He had to move forward. A night camping in the La Sals would be a perfect start.

All week he was careful in his responses with the column, hoping that his editor would take him off the "watch list." Saturday morning he packed up his little tent, dusted off his sleeping bag, stocked his cooler, and bagged up some food to get him through the night. It was a beautiful day in Moab and Noah couldn't wait to get started.

He drove his jeep up toward Mt. Tukuhnikivatz, the closest of the peaks--hard to pronounce but gorgeous beyond description. The little two-lane road soon turned into one lane, then it turned into a gravel path, before becoming two barely visible ruts with knee-high grass growing between the ruts. Finally, he came to the end of the rutted pathway and that's where he parked. He unloaded half of his equipment and headed off into the trees. He didn't want to go too far because he had to come back and get the rest of his gear.

There were large patches of snow in the shadows and under the trees, everywhere out of the direct sunlight. He heard the sound of rushing water and walked in that direction. He found a small stream, no more than six feet in width, and this is where he made his camp. He hurried back to the Jeep and brought back the rest of his equipment and started setting up his camp. There were no signs anywhere prohibiting a campfire, so the first thing he did was start a fire. There were so many twigs and small limbs lying around that it would be easy to keep the fire burning.

The tent behind him, the stream in front of him, and the fire beside him. He should be the happiest guy in Moab. He should be the most contented man on the mountain. He should be . . . none of those things. Why? He couldn't forget; that's why. He couldn't forget the way Ana made him feel when he read her emails. Nor could he forget the way Dorothy made him feel when he saw her walking down a pathway with him on some remote hike in the back of beyond. He just couldn't forget.

However, there was one thing that was easy for him to forget . . . his coat! When the sun went down, it got cold and it got cold fast. Noah ate his meager dinner wrapped in his sleeping bag and he was still freezing. He thought, *How can it be so warm down in Moab and so drastically cold up here?* Well, several thousand feet in elevation change answered that question pretty quickly. It wasn't even 9:00, yet and he was freezing. The little fire only helped if he got within two feet of it. By 10:00 he realized he'd never make it.

8

Fortunately for him, there was a three-quarter moon which helped him pack up his stuff and hike back to the Jeep. He only tripped once and only got scared once when he heard a noise directly in front of him. He stopped and hoped his heart wouldn't explode. He waited a minute or two and didn't hear anything else, so he kept going. After the second trip and packing the Jeep, he started the motor, locked the doors, and turned on the heat. His seven-hour camping expedition had been a total disaster, exactly like his love life had been. What's a guy to do?

The trip down the mountain didn't take long. He went from the heater going full blast, to rolling down all windows and reveling in the warmth of the desert. He unpacked the Jeep and thought about visiting the Moab Brewery, which was just down the road, but instead, he turned on his computer, hoping against all despair, that a message from Ana might magically be there. It was not.

"Noah: I've made some terrible mistakes in the past; things I can never undo. I know I've hurt some people close to me, especially some who used to be my friends. But I've changed . . . I really have. How do I get those people to trust me again? Can you help me? Signed, Mary."

"Dearest Mary: Your future does not equal your past. The two most important days of your life, Mary, are one, when you're born, and two, when you figure out why you were born. Seems like you're figuring that out now. Good luck with everything."

Noah really thought this last response might get his editor off his back and let things return to normal again. In fact, his editor had only called him on that day so he could show the Human Resources Department that he was handling the complaints the paper received. He had no intention in the world of ever firing him. Noah's column was the most popular feature in the paper, after the daily Mormon devotionals. Sure, sometimes he made people mad, but that's what made his column popular. He told the truth and called out people who thought they were holier than thou. People loved Noah. And most importantly, Noah sold newspapers.

"Noah: My parents are in their sixties and they're worrying me. They are out nearly every night doing something. I don't think they can afford to live like that, not to mention their health. Don't you think I should step in and try to help them? Signed, Monica."

"Monica: Make someone happy today. Mind your own business."

"Noah: A bunch of my friends wanted me to invite you to join our weightlifting club. You might like it. We get together and bench press three times a week. It's a blast! How about it? Signed, Craig."

"Craig: I want you to check out this statistic on Google: In the last 11 years, 115 people have died from weightlifting accidents in the gym; however, in that same 11 years, only 1 person has died from eating from a doughnut. Make good choices!"

Noah thought, *The editor should be okay with those answers. He just doesn't understand that the hardest work I'm doing right now is trying to appear normal.* He turned off most of the lights in his condo and sat in front of the computer, begging it, pleading with it to somehow, someway, send him a text from Ana.

Computers are so mean!

3.

AT DEATH VALLEY NATIONAL PARK, Dorothy worked inside her office, doing all the paperwork a good, faithful government employee should do. She smiled at the visitors, she said "Yes, sir" and "No, sir" to her boss, and she did everything that was required of her with no complaints. She was the perfect employee . . . and she hated every minute of it.

The average high temperatures at Death Valley ranged from highs of 67 degrees in January to 116 and above in July, frequently exceeding 120 degrees. She was used to intense heat from growing up in southeastern North Carolina. They told her it wasn't that bad in Death Valley; they told her it was a "dry heat" and didn't really feel that hot. They lied to her. Even the hottest of days back in Lumberton, North Carolina, were never like this.

Dorothy grew up in Lumberton to a poor family, in poor conditions, and it never improved. Her father was a poor, white tobacco farming drunk. Her mother was a poor, textile working Lumbee Indian, who birthed Dorothy when she was only fourteen years old. She didn't know how to be a mother; heck, she didn't even know how to be a teenager. Dorothy's dad died from drunkenness when she was in high school. Her mother basically ignored her as she tried to live her own life. Dorothy never had anything. She was never truly "white" and she was never truly "Indian." Not to her peers anyway.

In high school, her guidance counselor told her of a college in Missouri named College of the Ozarks. It was a college that was free! All students had jobs through the college that paid for everything. Dorothy jumped at that opportunity, she applied and was accepted. She never looked back. She only returned to Lumberton for the funerals of her mother and her grandmother. Her Indian heritage gave her a beautiful skin tone that appeared to be a smooth tan year-round. Her father's heritage gave her his features, which she would have declined if she'd had the chance.

Dorothy grew into herself after college. During her school years, she certainly wasn't ugly, but she wasn't what the boys called pretty either. But she evolved. Working with the National Park Service afforded her the opportunity to move around and grow . . . and she did. By the time she met Noah in Utah, she was at her peak. She was the type of woman who looked considerably better with no makeup on whatsoever. But she never believed that. She always thought she should be using mascara and rouge and lipstick and eyeliners like all the other women. Someone should have told her—she didn't need any of that stuff—she was beautiful as is. Noah knew it. He knew it very well.

From the first hike they took together with a group of other people, her skin tone, the shape of her legs, her face, and her hair had Noah infatuated. If he hadn't been totally enamored with Ana at the time, he would have followed Dorothy off the highest cliff in Canyonlands. But he was entirely smitten with Ana and couldn't help himself.

Dorothy and Noah ended up on the same Colorado River rafting trip as well, with about a dozen others. One lonely, dark, drinking night, everyone stripped and swam in the Colorado, and Dorothy and Noah saw each other au naturel. They never discussed that night, but they also never forgot that night.

Then, the hike in the rain, where Dorothy gave him the arrowhead . . . Noah was hooked. That's when he began to question his feelings for Ana versus his feelings for Dorothy. That's when he started to also question if these two women could somehow be the same woman. A test he failed at proving.

During the time they had known each other, Dorothy had convinced herself that Noah could never be interested in someone like her. He deserved better than her. Noah wanted someone prettier than her. Someone who knew how to wear makeup. Someone who wasn't a park ranger. She knew he wanted Ana, not her. From her hikes with him, and the river trip with him, and the rainy hike with him, she knew . . . he had all the opportunity in the world to do something. To say something. But he didn't. She had convinced herself, *He doesn't want me. He wants some phantom, email goddess that exists only in his mind.*

What Noah suspected, but never knew, was that Ana and Dorothy were indeed the same person.

Dorothy was so convinced that Noah could never be attracted to someone like her that she emailed him using the pen name Ana, just so she could have that closeness with him. It was the only way she knew to have contact with him. And it was now the thing that was making her miserable as she sat in a hot office, wasting away in Death Valley National Park. A truly apt name for her state of affairs.

Every evening after work, Dorothy would go to her apartment on the outskirts of nowhere and wash clothes, clean the carpet, do the dishes, and have a glass of wine, all before sitting in front of her computer and writing a long, amorous email to Noah. She never sent any of them but they made her feel better. Thinking of him. Writing to him. Remembering the night on the river. Remembering the hike in the rain where she gave him the arrowhead . . . she wondered if he kept the arrowhead or threw it away.

She went on a few dates with other lonely rangers who were stuck out here in this lonely place. She was hit on by lustful young men during tourist season, all hot with passion as well as temperatures. And she wondered how long it would take to get over Noah if she could ever get over him? What was the solution?

She looked at various job postings for other jobs in the park service. There were always openings at the so-called cannonball parks in the east: Gettysburg, Appomattox, Fort Sumter, and the likes. But she wanted to stay out west where she could breathe, where the scenery was undeniable, and where she was close to where Noah lived. She just couldn't let go. When she transferred to Death Valley she had to sign a waiver stating she'd stay a certain length of time; that time was nearly up. She would soon be free to transfer to another park if she so desired. Everyone who worked at Death Valley so desired. One year was enough!

Even though Dorothy didn't email Noah any longer, she still read his columns online and wished she could respond to some of them. She, too, along with Noah's editor, could see a difference in his tone. She wondered if it had anything to do with him losing the phantom Ana. One morning she read his response to a question: "You're not who you think you are, but who you think you are."

At first, it made no sense to her. But after reading and re-reading it over and over, she almost convinced herself that Noah was writing to her, not to someone named Harriett in Salt Lake City. Love can do those things to you. In her case, it made her submit a question to the paper for Noah using a fake name. She wrote,

"Noah: Where can I find love? Signed, Lost & Lonely."

"Dear Lost & Lonely: Look to where love is going to be, not where it has been. And when you find it, please let me know, so I can find it too."

When Dorothy read that response, she burst out crying. Unfortunately, she happened to be in her office at the time and her boss thought he must've said something to her that caused her to be so upset. He tried to apologize, but Dorothy convinced him it was only "that time of month." That response always assuaged men's feelings and eased the tension. She made it home that evening and re-read the email several more times while crying into her wine glass. Fortunately, wine always understood.

Dorothy checked the park service websites for job openings and almost fainted when she saw an opening at Arches National Park. Why? Because Arches is located just north of Moab, Utah, the town where Noah lives. This was a junior position as a ranger checking cars in and out of the entrance and exits to the park. It was meant for newcomers to the park service, not an experienced employee like Dorothy. But she didn't care. The decrease in salary bothered her a little, however, the thoughts of being in Moab, near Noah, overwhelmed any other feelings she had. She filled out the online application and sent it off. Finally, a smile returned to her face for a short time; then she remembered she had to go to work today and face another 114-degree inferno of a day.

4.

NOAH HAD NOT RECEIVED ANY COMPLAINTS from his editor since the fateful meeting that day, so he stopped worrying about his responses and hoped he had enough common sense to avert any further damage.

"Noah: I'm thinking of retiring. It scares me a little bit, though, having nothing to do all day. Do you think people actually have fun retiring? Signed, Allen."

"Allen: There is no pleasure in having nothing to do; the fun is in having lots to do and not doing it. Good luck, though."

"Noah: I'm a pretty successful businesswoman here in town. I have a nice house, a great car, and I vacation all over the world . . . all by myself. I know a lot of women are envious of what I have achieved. Why, then, am I not happy? Signed, Kathryn."

"My dear Kathryn: I wish I knew you better to honestly answer that question; however, I've always found that it's not what we have in our life that matters, but who we have in our life that matters."

When Dorothy read this response from Noah, sitting at her desk in Death Valley National Park, she quickly got up and went outside to walk down one of the paths into the desert. If she started to cry again, surely the dry, intense heat would dry up the tears before anyone suspected anything. She walked about a half-mile into the heat then turned and came back. She decided to write Noah another anonymous question for him to answer in his column:

"Noah: We're interested in you. Please tell us readers something personal about yourself. Are you in love with anyone right now? Signed, Anna."

Dorothy used the name Anna as a way to hopefully jog Noah's memory. Not spelled like his Ana, but close enough to hopefully make him think.

When Noah read this question the following morning, it did jog his memory. At first, he didn't want to answer it . . . he was afraid to. Then he thought, "What if this message actually is from Ana and she's testing me to see how I feel?" He typed a response which he didn't like. He deleted that one then typed another one which he also deleted. Seven more responses, seven more deletions. Finally, he went back to his first answer and retyped it:

"Anna: Yes. And just so I don't get a million emails asking who she is, here's my answer to that as well: She knows who she is and that's all that matters."

He finished up his work for the day but couldn't get the email from Anna out of his mind. There was something about the question itself and the name "Anna" that swirled around his head. He decided to sit outside for a bit and stare off into the La Sal Mountains and remember how cold he got up there last week. After dark, he changed clothes and drove into town to the Moab Brewery for a liquid refreshment and hopefully to meet a few of the locals for some conversation.

The brewery was a popular destination for a lot of the tourists, but it was also a favorite hangout with the local mountain bikers, river guides, and townspeople. As soon as he walked in the door he heard someone calling him. It was Sandy, the river guide. Sandy was a fairly attractive woman in her mid-thirties, although it was hard to be certain because life on the river was hard on one's complexion. Plus, Sandy didn't care. She appeared exactly as she looked—take it or leave it. As was her choice of sexual partners, she didn't care . . . male or female made no difference to Sandy.

She was at the bar and was saving a stool next to her for Noah. He and Sandy had a shady history of sorts. On a river trip they took together, Sandy had once gotten drunk and kissed Noah before he realized who she was. Then she promptly puked in the river and passed out. Neither of them ever brought up that incident after the trip. Noah was unsure if she even remembered it.

When he came over, she ordered him a Black Raven Stout, which was his favorite. She said, "Noah, dude, where have you been? I heard you went up to Salt Lake last week."

"Only for a couple of days . . . work stuff. How's the river guide business going?"

Sandy grinned, but Noah quickly realized she wasn't grinning at him, but rather at a swarthy-looking guy across the bar. Noah elbowed her and she said, "Huh?"

"How's the river guide business going?"

She still didn't look at him, but asked, "Do you know that guy over there?" Meaning the swarthy-looking guy.

Noah answered, "No. Do you know him?"

"I think I shacked up with him once but I can't remember."

Noah looked over at the guy who was now raising his glass of beer towards Sandy and motioning for her to come over. "I think he wants you to come over there."

Sandy didn't hear Noah but was nodding slowly at the guy. Then she turned towards Noah and said, "Can you kiss me real quick? I want to make him jealous."

"No, I'm not going to kiss you, Sandy. Just go over there and talk to him."

"Aww, c'mon Noah. What's it gonna hurt?"

Noah stood up and waved at the guy and yelled out, "She wants to talk to you." Then he grabbed his beer and walked away. The guy immediately came over and within five minutes he and Sandy were headed out the door. Noah didn't know anyone else in the bar; too many tourists tonight. He finished his beer and drove back home. He got a bottle of water from the fridge and wrote a long email to Ana telling her how much he missed her, how much he needed her, and begging her to come back into his life. He hit send and waited thirty seconds for the message to come back: "Recipient unknown." Then he went to bed and held his arrowhead from Dorothy in one hand and his picture of Ana in the other. Another long, restless night.

"Noah: I'm dating a new guy who has a college degree. I didn't go to college, but we seem to be having a good time with each other. Usually, by the third date, most guys have tried to . . . well, you know what they all try to do; but this guy hasn't tried anything. I've never dated an intellectual type before. Is this normal for them? Signed, Lydia."

"Lydia, my dear: Beware! An intellectual is someone who has found something more interesting than sex."

"Noah: My son plays on the little league baseball team and I go to every game. I never miss one—never! Last week the umpire blew an easy play and called my son OUT on a play at first when it was clearly evident that my son was safe. I let him have it! I told him how blind he was and that he needed glasses, and a few other things. Guess what? They threw me out of the park just for stating my opinion. This wasn't fair, was it? I mean, a guy has a right to be himself and stick up for his family, doesn't he? Signed, Jerry."

"Jerry, Jerry, Jerry: Yes, you should always be yourself. Unless you suck."

●●●

"Noah: I have a professional cooking tip I want to share with your readers, if it's okay: I lightly roast a bit of parsley and kale, then dip them in a light oil before mixing them over some roasted potatoes. It makes a world of difference. I hope your readers will enjoy the advice. Signed, Gloria."

"Gloria: Thanks so much for sharing that! I also have a pro tip: If you stir coconut oil into your kale, it makes it easier to scrape into the trash."

5.

DOROTHY DIDN'T GET THE JOB AT ARCHES NATIONAL PARK. She
was so upset that after work that evening, she put on her shortest skirt,
with fishnet stockings; her lowest cut blouse, with no bra; and applied
more makeup than she'd ever worn in her life. Then she went to the
nearest cowboy bar at the closest podunk town near the park. But her
luck was so bad that all she got was drunk and sick while passing out
on a stool with her head lying in a wet spot on the bar. She was finally
awakened by the park superintendent who had stopped in after a
meeting with another park official. He shook Dorothy and asked if
she alright. She promptly puked on his pants and shoes. He had the
bartender call Uber and helped put Dorothy in the backseat.

She woke up in the morning on her couch, unable to remember how
she got to her couch, and unable to remember how the top two buttons
of the four buttons on her low-cut blouse were unbuttoned. She
quickly checked to see if she was still wearing her underwear—she
was. She thought of Noah. Then she thought of not getting the job at
Arches National Park. Then she tried to remember which cabinet the
Extra-Strength Tylenol was in. What's a girl supposed to do? The
only man she's ever loved is two states away and completely, totally
unaware of her existence. She's stuck in a nowhere job, in a nowhere
park, in a natural furnace, with nobody to blame but herself. She
swallowed four Tylenol, sat on the bed, and thought, *It ain't easy being
me.*

After her head eased up a bit, she decided she had to punish herself for being so stupid the night before. What was she thinking? She's not that sort of girl. That sort of girl stayed in Lumberton, North Carolina, worked in a textile mill, had four kids before she was twenty-three years old, and married the first man she could find who could keep a regular job more than six months.

So, she took a personal day from work and drove into the outback. Where? She didn't know; there were no signs out here in the middle of nowhere. She found an abandoned dirt road and took it until it dead-ended in a pile of rocks. She put on a hat and her sunglasses, then made sure she took her compass and a backpack with snacks and water before heading due north on her hike into the abyss. North seemed to be the most remote of the four directions and that's what she wanted . . . remoteness, loneliness, and solitude.

She was rewarded. There was nothing to see, nothing to remember, and nothing to curse at—only nothingness. However, she wasn't mad at the landscape: She was mad and disappointed at herself. How could she have let this happen? How could she have deceived and mislead Noah so badly? Someone she loved? Someone she wanted to give everything to: her soul, her body, her mind, and all her entire being. This wasn't how you treated someone you loved. You didn't lie to them and lead them on. How did she end up like this? No one else to blame, she did it all to herself.

She finally found a rock large enough to sit on while she ate some almonds and drank some water. Then, she resumed her march into the void. Soon, her mind became blank, no more thoughts of Noah, no more thoughts of anything. Tromp, tromp, tromp . . . step after useless step. Concentrating on nothing more than where her next footstep would land. After some unknown time, she started thinking again: She thought about her family home, her parents, her grandparents. She remembered a boy she met in school. She thought of her college years and how busy and fun they were.

Noah

At another water break, she looked up and saw several buzzards floating about a thousand feet above her. Had they located a meal? Or were they waiting on her to make a mistake? Hard to tell. She hadn't seen another living creature on the entire hike. No snakes, no rabbits, no mice, not even any bugs. Most sensible creatures would be out of the sun, waiting for the cooler part of the day before venturing out. Eventually, Dorothy decided to turn back. She checked the compass and headed south. At this point, she didn't really care if she found her car or not. But she did. She wasn't really looking for it, she just walked upon it. Too much experience in the wilderness for her to get lost. But she did accomplish her most important goal which was to punish herself: She was tired, hot, thirsty, hungry, and exhausted. And it all felt great.

●●●

Noah's luck was beginning to change. He met a young lady from a new mountain biking company in town. Vicki, with no "e" at the end, was the part-owner of the biking company, along with her ex-husband. A little strange but very lucrative. Her ex had developed ties with the minor celebrity crowd in Los Angeles and mountain biking was now one of the "in" things to do on your time between shooting commercials and making minor, B movies. All their customers had perfect hair, abnormally white teeth, incredible bodies, and no brains or talent whatsoever. They thought nothing of paying Vicki's company $5,000 a week for an exclusive trip into the Utah wilderness. A normal person would bring their own bike, or rent one for a couple of hundred dollars, and ride the same trails for free. But fortunately for Vicki, these weren't normal people.

Vicki was very athletic, with great legs and a lean body from years of riding bikes. She was attractive, but not pretty in a beauty contest sort of way. She was the kind of woman that all men noticed when she walked in the bar, mostly because of her short bicycle pants and tight t-shirt. Noah noticed her immediately. For some reason, Vicki was wearing a shirt with a picture of an owl on the front when Noah first saw her. He left his beer on a table and walked up to the bar next to

Vicki to order another beer, just so he could talk to her. He brushed lightly against her and she turned to look at him. He looked down at the picture of the owl and said, "What's he looking at?"

At first, Vicki didn't understand what Noah meant, then she remembered the picture of the owl on her shirt and answered, "Most women don't care what a man looks like, and it's a good thing too." Noah didn't know if he should be insulted or impressed. But the picture of the owl was very hard to look away from, especially when both of its eyes seemed to protrude a little as she spoke. Vicki continued, "What's wrong? Cat got your tongue?"

Noah, who had just started on his third Black Raven Stout, when two was his limit, answered, "I'd never let a cat get my tongue. But I love it when owls grab my tongue." He was expecting to either get slapped or cursed at.

Instead, Vicki smiled and said, "Maybe later . . . but I seldom hang around tourists from Encino."

He answered, "Encino? Is that anywhere near Paris? I'm sorry ma'am, but I ain't never been out of Grand County here in Moab."

That started it. Vicki finished it back in Noah's bedroom early the next morning. Even though they'd been in bed all night, they were both thoroughly exhausted, drained, wasted, and yet exhilarated beyond memory. He wanted to find out more about this voluptuous woman he'd met. He had a hundred questions he wanted to ask. But the only question Vicki wanted to ask was, "Again?"

Eventually, Vicki had to leave and lead a group of bikers up the Slickrock Trail later that morning. Her ex had gone back to LA to sign up their next excursion group, all looking to prove they could pay the $5,000 a week to be with the "in-crowd." The business might not last too many years, but at twelve to fifteen people per tour each week, at $5,000 each, it didn't need to last very long to ensure a healthy, lasting bank account.

Noah

After she left, Noah was completely drained, yet happy. He checked out her company online and found they had been in business for nearly four years and had just recently expanded into the Moab area. He started figuring: four years, even if they only did tours half the year, $5,000 per person, an average of twelve people per tour—that's $60,000 per week! At only twenty-six weeks per year, that's over a million and a half dollars a year! For riding bikes!! And they've been doing this for nearly four years. No wonder Vicki's owl was smiling.

Vicki and Noah met each night for the next two tour groups. Fourteen consecutive nights and Noah was beginning to question his stamina. Typing emails for a living left him a little behind the eight ball, compared to Vicki's physical endurance from riding bikes all year. But he tried. He also tried to talk with Vicki. However, unless it was about a new trail, a new type of bike, a new sexual position, or a new actor she'd just met, she just wasn't interested.

Noah missed talking. He missed listening. He missed the intellectual interaction. He missed what Ana used to give him. Don't misunderstand . . . he loved the sex and Vicki was excellent in that area. But he started questioning whether he liked the sex with Vicki as much as he liked the non-sex with Ana back in their email days. Ana flooded his mind, exploded his senses, and exhilarated his emotions as much or more than physical sex with Vicki. When Vicki would go to work, Noah would re-read all the emails he'd ever received from Ana. He kept them in a file on his computer. He would never delete them. Never. He would catch himself reading the emails from Ana, yet daydreaming of Dorothy's face and legs.

He kept trying to engage Vicki intellectually: "Vicki, who is your favorite author?"

"Mmm, we had this one guy last year who wrote comic books. He was great, a little snooty, but he was loaded."

"What did you study in school?"

"Well, Jon and I-- he's my ex-- we sort of ran off after our junior year and started bumming up and down the coast. So I guess I just studied how to get by."

"You never went back to graduate? Wow, one more year and you could get your college degree."

"College? No, Noah, we ran off during high school. We were both sick of it . . . so boring."

Before Noah could respond, Vicki was under the covers and doing her best to make him completely forget about high school, college, and authors. She was good at that. But ever-increasingly, it was more and more difficult for him to forget his past and what it was that really made him happy.

After Vicki left that morning, Noah found it hard to concentrate on his work. He had piles of emails to answer but simply couldn't think. Was sex with Vicki draining his mental capacity? Were orgasms clouding his mind? He looked over the first pile of emails, which was nearly two weeks old, and still couldn't figure out how to answer them. And he knew his emergency stockpile of answers was running down quickly and he'd have to send something in or risk getting in trouble with the editor again.

He kept flipping through the questions and finally found a few that made sense to him:

"Noah: I'm on my own now and I'm thinking of trying to get a college education but college is so expensive. Any advice? Signed, David."

"David: If you think education is expensive, try ignorance."

●●●

"Noah: I think I have a problem. I maxed out all my credit cards but it wasn't my fault. I was only trying to keep up with my girlfriends; they've all got money. Then, I took out a loan for a high-interest rate and I can't pay it back. I just need some help! And, please, don't say I'm stupid or anything, cause I'M NOT! Signed, Eileen."

"Eileen: I'm not saying you're stupid. I'm just saying you've got bad luck when it comes to thinking."

"Noah: I broke up with my boyfriend a while back and I sort of let myself go. I gained a little weight and made some bad decisions and other stuff. That's all understandable, isn't it? Signed, Janice."

"Janice: It's alright letting yourself go as long as you can get yourself back."

It seemed to Noah like the dam had burst. He was thinking again. He quickly filled out enough questions and answers to get back on track. It felt good. Now . . . what was he going to do?

6.

NOAH AND VICKI CAME TO A QUICK UNDERSTANDING: physical relationship only. Vicki only wanted physical intimacy during her outings in Moab, she had "other" interests back in Los Angeles and elsewhere. He was happy with that. She was an interesting diversion for a week or two during the biking excursions but when she left the area, he was a little relieved, both physically and mentally. During his "off" weeks from Vicki, he usually did some hiking on weekends and met a few male friends for drinks occasionally and dreamed of Ana and Dorothy. He couldn't help himself.

Nearly every night, after the sun went down and his loneliness set it, he would write another long email to Ana's old address, telling her how much he missed her. Then he would wait for it to be returned. During that short period of waiting, he would think about Dorothy and the hikes they took together. He distinctly remembered the one time his hand accidentally brushed against her leg. And, he would never forget the night he saw her without clothes on, swimming in the river during their river trip together. Oh, Dorothy . . . what happened?

This is exactly what Dorothy was thinking in the hot confines of Death Valley National Park: what happened? She was extremely happy emailing Noah as the phantom Ana. She could be honest with him about how she felt, what she liked, what her interests were, just about everything except . . . who she was. She missed that intimacy she once had with him. She missed the daily emails, the sharing of

28

thoughts, lusts, and dreams. She wanted it back. But like us all, who for one reason or another, fool ourselves into thinking or not thinking clearly, she too had convinced herself that Noah was not interested in her "real" self—Dorothy. She was convinced he was only interested in Ana—her alter-ego, dreamlike, phantom email persona. But don't we all do that to ourselves? We aren't good enough. We aren't pretty enough. We aren't smart enough, rich enough, clever enough; on and on and on it goes, until we find ourselves exactly in the same predicament that Dorothy finds herself right now. She wants to tell herself: *Dorothy, worry is a waste of energy! It can't change the past. It can't control the future. It only makes you miserable today.*

Meanwhile, Noah was hard at work reading and answering emails from the good people of Salt Lake City.

"Noah: What am I doing wrong? I always let my friends have their way. I let them make all the decisions on where we go, what we do, everything! I always compliment them on their makeup, their shoes, their clothes, their hair, everything about them; and yet, I heard the rumor that one of my friends thinks I'm fake and doesn't like me. What's a girl to do? Signed, Ava."

"Ava, Ava, Ava: You can be the ripest, juiciest peach in the world and there's still going to be someone who hates peaches."

"Noah, dude: Us guys were having an argument about good-looking girls. Some like big boobs, some like nice legs, and others like a shapely butt. What curves on a woman's body turns you on, dude? Signed, Bill."

"Bill . . . dude: For me, a smile is the most beautiful curve on a woman's body."

"Noah: Have you seen some of the city/county resolutions that are now up for vote? It's downright scary what these councilmen are trying to push on us. Can you please address some of these issues as a voice of reason for your readers? Thank you, signed, Doris."

"Doris, my dear: If we're ever in a situation where I am the 'voice of reason' then we are in a very bad state of affairs."

The day's work was done so his editor should be happy, the tourists were spending money in town, the national parks were full, and Noah was empty. Vicki was with a tour group up at the Escalante River and wouldn't be in Moab for a couple of weeks. Noah's friend Sandy was spending all her time with her new "swarthy-looking" friend, Dorothy was somewhere in California, and Ana had vanished. And to top it all off, when he opened his refrigerator for a cold beverage, all he had left was a half-empty bottle of red wine that Vicki had left. When it rains, it pours.

He figured if he put enough ice in the wine he could probably drink it. He sat out on his patio and stared at the mountains while watching a rabbit run from bush to bush. He took a sip of the wine then poured the rest of it on the ground. He hated to poison the ants, but better them than himself. He left the picture of Ana on his bed stand but clutched the arrowhead from Dorothy tightly in his left hand, where his ring finger was. Before he felt too gloomy, he got up and started walking out in the barrenness of the desert beyond his property. The sun had nearly set but there was still a nice glow for him to see his way amongst the sagebrush, prickly pear, and pinyon pine trees.

About seventy-five yards from his patio he heard a slight buzzing sound. He stopped walking and the buzzing stopped. He started walking again and the buzzing returned. The evening glow was fading fast, which meant his vision was severely limited. He'd never actually heard a rattlesnake before. He'd seen a few of them out in the desert, but they always slithered away silently. Whatever this was, wasn't slithering away silently. He was a little concerned because all he had on were his flip flops, making his toes, feet, and ankles prime targets for any upset rattlers.

He turned to come back home, staying in the open and away from any bushes and cactus as much as possible. He was pretty sure he'd left, whatever it was making that noise, behind him in the desert. Then, BOOM! Something bit his left big toe. Noah kicked his leg out and the snake flew into the air, landed, and slithered away before he could react or tell what kind of snake it was. He looked down and could see a few drops of blood oozing from his toe—a definite bite. He hurried back, grabbed his keys and took off for the local clinic. His toe was throbbing!

He hobbled into the office to find it completely packed with all sorts of tourists wanting attention for sprained ankles, upset stomachs, and cactus puncture wounds. There were four others in line waiting on the receptionist but Noah's toe was throbbing and bleeding. One overweight lady sitting in a chair saw his foot and screamed. All the others in line looked back and motioned Noah forward. The receptionist asked, "Name?"

Noah lifted his foot in the air and said, "I've been bitten by a snake."

All the other tourists immediately shied away from him, as if it were contagious. The receptionist said again, "Name?"

Noah yelled out, "A rattlesnake. A rattlesnake bit me!"

"Sir, what is your name?"

Noah yelled again, "Can't you see I'm dying here?"

"You're not dying, sir. If that bite was from a rattlesnake it would be swollen and would have turned blue by now. Your toe is only bleeding a little. You probably got bit by a garter snake, or a whip snake, or a king snake; they're all pretty common around here and none of them are poisonous. So just calm down and tell me what your name is."

Noah yelled again, "Don't tell me . . . "and that's the last he remembered before fainting and falling on the floor. He woke up later on a small cot in the hallway. His toe was bandaged and throbbing as a nurse came up to him and told him he'd be fine. Just stay off his feet for the next day or two and change the bandage twice a day. They offered him crutches but he declined and just hobbled out to his car to drive home. At least he had an automatic and wouldn't have to use his left foot on a clutch.

All his friends were gone, all he had to drink was red wine, and a snake had bitten his toe. What else could happen to him? He hobbled into his condo and plopped down in his chair in front of the computer. He was going to write his editor and tell him what happened; however, when he turned the computer on, his world exploded! A starburst shone in his living room and a rainbow burst across the carpet . . . he had an email from Ana.

7.

DOROTHY WAS BACK AT WORK in Death Valley National Park, dutifully filling out forms, checking manifests, ordering supplies, and taking care of the paperwork resulting from tourist emergencies that happened almost every week. Last week, two old men were out hiking and forgot to take any water with them. Their car was spotted at a trailhead as the park was closing, so the ranger investigated and found the two guys sitting on the ground, leaning against a rock wall, totally dehydrated and disoriented. He called an ambulance and got them some water and eventually, they were okay. This episode took Dorothy all morning to fill out the forms and document everything.

Two days ago, a couple of teenage boys were roaming out beyond the campground and came upon a newly-born bighorn sheep. They futilely tried to catch it and never saw the mother bighorn sheep as she charged at them and rammed them both repeatedly as she protected her offspring. The boys were bruised and bloodied but nothing was broken. Their parents wanted to sue the park service and this caused Dorothy two complete days of filling out forms and taking statements and all sorts of menial madness.

This morning, as she was finishing up all the documents and forms, her boss came by and asked how she was doing with everything—he's the guy who found her passed out in the bar that night. Dorothy answered, "Fine, sir. Everything is under control."

Her boss looked down at her, smiled, and replied, "Dorothy, if everything seems under control, you're just not going fast enough."

She didn't really understand what he meant but didn't want him to know that she didn't understand, so she asked, "Sir, do you have any advice that might help me?"

He tilted his head a little and answered, "Dorothy, from my experience, advice is what we ask for when we already know the answer but wish we didn't."

That was the precise moment in time Dorothy decided to email Noah again. She was so nervous and fidgety the rest of the day it was almost unbearable. She skipped lunch and walked around a path in the desert to burn off some energy—it didn't help. All afternoon her mind wandered and the clock moved as if in slow motion. She dreamed of a hundred different opening lines she would write to Noah —and rejected all of them. The only thing she was certain of was that she would indeed write to him, but only as Ana, not as herself. She had convinced herself that Noah was not attracted to her at all. He'd had many opportunities to act if he had been interested, but he never did. But he was interested in the elusive, unknown, unseen, beguiling Ana, her alter ego.

Dorothy had convinced herself that if she couldn't have a physical relationship with Noah, then she would settle for the online kind. At least she would be in his life again and she could talk with him and communicate with him and dream . . .

She knew this was crazy. She knew it would only cause her pain. She knew it would only lead to heartache, but she couldn't help herself. Usually, when she got home, she would take a cool shower to wash off the hot, dusty grim from a day at the park. Then, she would make herself some dinner and usually have a glass of wine. Not today. She went immediately to her computer and activated her old email account to make it operable again. Then she started typing so fast that "spell check" was underlining every other word. She corrected everything, then read it seven times, then changed a few words, then deleted all the commas because she didn't want to think, and then she sent it:

"Noah, I hope you remember me. It's Ana. I wouldn't blame you if you deleted this message immediately. I wouldn't blame you at all. I've missed you and I apologize for abandoning you the way I did. I was confused. I still am but I would like to have you in my life again—such as it is. I understand if you don't want to write me back. You certainly have that right. But I hope you will.

Ana"

After sending the message, Dorothy ran a tub full of hot bubbly water and got herself a glass of white wine. She lit three candles and laid down in her tub wondering what Noah would do when he saw her email. She tried to think about work but she couldn't. She tried to think about Moab but she couldn't. She tried to think about her friends, her likes, her dislikes, her dog that she used to have a dozen years ago—but the only thing her mind kept returning to was that night on the river trip when Noah saw her naked, then she saw him kissing Sandy. Sandy . . . of all the people in the world, why was he kissing Sandy? Her mind was so confused, she got out of the bathtub and went to get another glass of wine without drying off. She left a wet trail from the bathroom to the record player to the kitchen. She didn't even notice it until she returned to the bathroom and saw the wet spots. It might be a three-glass night. She laid back in the tub and listened to the Carol King song she just put on the record player:

> So far away
> Doesn't anybody stay in one place anymore
> It would be so fine to see your face at my door
> Doesn't help to know you're just time away
>
> Long ago I reached for you and there you stood
> Holding you again could only do me good

Oh, how I wish I could
But you're so far away

One more song about moving along the highway
Can't say much of anything that's new
If I could only work this life out my way
I'd rather spend it being close to you.

But you're so far away

●●●

Noah saw the old email address from Ana and completely froze. He was unsure how long he sat there motionless and thoughtless. He kept half-expecting the email to magically disappear and vanish before his eyes. Initially, he couldn't bring himself to actually click on the email and read it. His mind was racing. Was Ana telling him to leave her alone? That she had found someone else? That he should move on with his life and find another woman? Certainly, after all this time, she wasn't coming back into his life. That would be impossible! Then, the little voice in his head yelled at him, *Open it, Noah!*

He always listened to the little voice in his head. It had saved him many times, but now he was questioning his little voice. Then, his little voice spoke again, *Noah, the worst thing that happens to you may be the best thing for you if you don't let it get the best of you.* Before he could understand that statement or change his mind, he clicked on the email.

He read Ana's email eleven times, then hobbled to his refrigerator and poured the last of the red wine into a glass. He took a big drink, thought he was going to throw up, then hobbled back to the computer where he read the email seven more times. Even though this was a dream come true for him, he couldn't help but visualize Dorothy as he read the email from Ana. Whenever he thought of Ana, his mind saw Dorothy—her face, her legs, her body, the vision of her nude in the Colorado River that night so long ago.

Noah

He finally reasoned, *What difference does it make? I'll never see Dorothy again. She's gone. Hopefully, one day Ana will agree to meet me and I can put a face to the images in my mind. Maybe she'll even look like Dorothy. A man can dream, can't he?*

So he wrote, "Ana, my dear sweet Ana, I've missed you terribly. If I did anything to hurt you or drive you away, then I apologize. Please don't leave my life again . . . I need you. Always yours, Noah."

Sure, he had Vicki every few weeks but that was only a slight physical diversion; something to pass away the idle time. He wanted Dorothy but she was gone into the depths and void that is Californication, never to return. If he could have Ana back in his life, his mind, his emotions, his thoughts, dreams, and essence . . . he'd be happy. He was sure of it.

He sat in front of the computer in a daze after he'd sent the email to Ana. He wasn't sure how long he sat there waiting on a reply but he grew hungry and his toe was killing him. He had to take some medicine and get something to eat. Dorothy read his email and smiled until her mouth started to cramp. She just finished her third glass of wine, yet was clear-headed enough to know that she should wait until morning to type Noah another message. She wanted her mind to be clear and focused when she emailed him again.

The pain medicine made Noah groggy, but a happy kind of groggy. He flopped on the bed and had sweet illusions floating in his mind of Ana, with Dorothy's face, filling all his dreams and desires. He clutched the arrowhead tightly in his left hand as he drifted away into the night.

8.

THE FOLLOWING MORNING, NOAH'S TOE STILL HURT but the bleeding had stopped. He needed to get caught up on some work emails and questions and he even had a slight change in attitude as he answered questions from Salt Lake City's finest citizens.

"Noah: Please be honest and tell me what you think. I want to get a tattoo of a teardrop under my left eye and a silver nose ring. I think it'll be cute—don't you? Signed, Ruth."

He wanted to answer, "Ruth: If I ever say to you 'Do you want me to be honest?' Please say NO."

But because of his change in attitude due to Ana's email, he answered,

"Ruth: Be a caterpillar. Eat a lot. Sleep a lot. Wake up beautiful."

"Noah: I'm a sophomore in college, majoring in education. I've always wanted to be a teacher—it's been my dream job. But now, I'm in love! My boyfriend wants us to get married and travel around for a year or two. He says I can finish my education later. If I've found my soulmate, then I should make him happy, shouldn't I? Signed, Jackie."

"Jackie: Don't give up what you want most for what you want now."

Noah

"Noah: My husband and I are very successful. We're both at the top of our professions and we have a big house, new cars, and all the things that should make us happy. Why aren't we? Signed, Empty."

"Empty: The things that matter most are not things."

9.

WHEN DOROTHY WOKE UP THE NEXT MORNING, the wine was paying her back for abusing it the night before. She hadn't sipped it as a good, little socialite should. Instead, she had guzzled it as though she were a traveler stranded in the desert at a lonely watering hole. One moment she was regretting sending him the email; the next moment she was glad she did send it. Half of her wanted to turn on the computer to see if he had replied to her email yet, and the other half was scared to turn it on in case he hadn't replied.

She wasn't really hungry but knew she should eat something. The problem was that she felt like she might start crying at any moment. She opened her refrigerator and saw the last piece of peach pie sitting there in a pan. She realized that you rarely see a person crying and eating pie at the same time . . . so she took it out. The pie satisfied her and a cup of coffee settled her down, but she still didn't want to turn on the computer yet. It was her off day so she started her chores: cleaning, washing, wishing for an email, dusting, and thinking about Noah.

She decided to go into town and do a little shopping while she thought about the computer. She drove into the little desert town and parked on Main Street. She was starting to feel better about everything until she got out of the car and saw that she had parked in front of a thrift store called Noah's Ark Consignment Shop. If that wasn't bad enough, two stores down was a café named Ana's. She got back in her car and drove home.

Noah

She walked into her place and opened the computer. There it was . . . the email from Noah. Unlike Noah, she only read his email three times. She wished she had another piece of peach pie to keep her from crying, but she didn't. So, she wept tears of joy. She thought of a thousand things she wanted to say to him. She was looking forward to their daily emails again—she missed them so much. Since she knew she could never actually have Noah, she would gladly settle for the next best thing: being his online lover. Maybe after a year or two, she might get the nerve to . . . no! She could never meet him. He didn't want her—she knew it. But she could be happy with emails. She was sure of it. So she typed:

"My dearest Noah, how I've missed you. I promise I'll never abandon you again. I hope you're well and happy and will continue to write to me. Nothing has changed in my life; I still feel the same as I've always felt. I hope you do too. Write me back and tell me that you still do . . . please!

Always, your Ana"

She was hoping to pick up where they left off before: two or three or four emails each day. Flirting with each other, dreaming with each other, living each other's passions. She was totally excited when her computer dinged with a message. It was from Noah. He had written her back in less than ten minutes. She was so excited she could hardly click on the right spot to open the email.

"Ana, tell me where you are. If you're still in North Carolina, tell me where and I'll come there. If you've moved, tell me where and I'll come there. I don't care where it is, just tell me and I'll be there. Enough emails! I must see you now. I need to see you, Ana, to find out if this is going to work. I must see you, Ana. I'm waiting.

Anxiously, Noah"

When she read his response, she lost the concept of time, space, and relevance. This was not what she expected, not what she wanted, not what she thought would work. No . . . this was terrible! Noah thinks she lives in North Carolina. Noah thinks she's someone else. Noah doesn't know she's actually Dorothy. What is she going to do now? This and a hundred other questions flooded her mind.

●●●

As soon as Noah sent the email, he felt a sense of relief and closure. Now he would know if Ana wanted him in her life or not. He would know if she was only playing with him, or if she was serious about a relationship with him. He'd lost Dorothy, he did not want to lose Ana. Wherever she was, he would go there. He had a great sense of relief with his decision. He wanted to get outside now and move around and breathe but his toe prevented him from walking. So, he put on his flip flops and hopped in the Jeep.

He headed south toward Canyonlands National Park, where Dorothy used to work as a ranger before she moved to California. It was a beautiful place and . . . it's where Dorothy used to work. It took about an hour to get there and a lifetime to see all that was there. He first drove out to the Island in the Sky and pulled off every overlook to gaze into the depths of the back of beyond. He thought of a few hikes he'd taken with Dorothy. He remembered sharing a water bottle with her once. And he recalled another time when they were leaning against a rock wall together trying to stay out of the rain, their shoulders and arms close together, her legs next to his, her hair gently falling onto his arm as they sat together. Yes, he loved the wilderness.

He drove over to the exit for the Maze, which was a remote district that required much more time and self-reliance to explore. But he could dream. He could dream of camping out in the vast expanse of nothingness and waking up in the tent next to Dorothy. He could dream of skinny-dipping in the river each morning and evening— washing the dust off each other from the day's adventures. He could dream of them sitting on a ledge in a canyon and watching a lonely buzzard float by below them, riding on the currents and thermals, never having to flap a wing. He could dream . . .

Noah

As he started the car, he came to reality and wondered to himself why he was dreaming about Dorothy—she was gone! Why wasn't he dreaming about Ana whom he might meet soon? He kept wondering about that as he drove back towards Moab. His thoughts were only broken as a deer ran across the road in front of him, startling him back to consciousness. It took an hour to drive out, but it seemed as though it only took fifteen minutes to drive back.

Instead of going home, he pulled in at the Moab Brewery to have a drink and be around some humans—such as they were. What they were was mostly tourists. He didn't mind them; they were mostly nice and pleasant and didn't act too weird. He sat at the bar next to a couple from King of Prussia, Pennsylvania. They were nice and even explained to him why their city was named King of Prussia—very interesting.

As he started on his second, and last, Black Raven Stout, his old friend Sandy walked in the bar with an older lady who looked rather weather-beaten. They sat at a small table near the window and soon Sandy saw Noah at the bar and came over to say hello. "Noah, what's up dude?"

"Not much Sandy. Who's your friend over there?

"Aw, she's some old girl I hook up with every now and then. You know how it is."

Noah had no idea how it was, but he let that thought dissipate. He asked, "How's your other friend doing? The guy you met up with a couple of weeks ago?"

Sandy looked a little puzzled and asked, "What guy?"

"You know, the swarthy-looking guy you met when we were here that night."

She thought for a moment, then remembered, "Oh, him. He was just passing through. He lives in Reno and we just meet up for fun every now and then. He's really a nice guy but Reno's just too far."

Sandy ordered two beers, gave Noah a hug, and then kissed him right on the lips before he knew what was happening. He figured it was just Sandy's way of trying to make her girlfriend a little jealous. He didn't mind too much. Well, it was too late now anyway. She went back to her girlfriend as Noah finished his drink and limped out to his Jeep. As he closed the door, he wondered if he might have an email from Ana waiting on him, but he thought of Dorothy on the short drive home.

He didn't have an email from Ana, but he did have several emails from work. He needed to get these answered tonight before he went to bed. He took a long shower, changed the bandage on his toe, took some Extra-Strength Tylenol, and sat in front of the computer in his boxers. Time for work.

10.

"NOAH: I'VE BEEN READING YOUR COLUMN for quite some time now. I don't know if you're lying to yourself or lying to everyone else. Which is it? Signed, Eric."

"Eric: I lie to myself all the time. But I never believe me."

"Noah: I love my grandparents, but every time I go visit them, all they do is give me advice on how to live, who to like, what to do. I know they mean well but it gets a little old. Sorry to sound like this, I guess I'm just a little frustrated. Signed, Ronnie."

"Ronnie: Sorry, man. I'm sure they mean well. A lot of old people love to give advice; it compensates for their inability to set a bad example."

"Noah: I'm a single woman in my late 30's and I'm not unhappy with that. Almost every other woman my age is married. They think I want to be married, but so far, I don't. Sometimes I want to be cuddled, but I also want to be left the heck alone. Does this seem crazy to you? Signed, Carleen."

"Carleen: No, it does not seem crazy. Be yourself. Until you are happy with who you are, you will never be happy with what you have."

"Noah: Sometimes you sound like an idiot with the advice you give people. Do you realize that? Signed, Gary."

"Gary: Of course I talk like an idiot. How else could you understand me?"

11.

DOROTHY DIDN'T WANT TO LIE TO NOAH ANY LONGER but she didn't know how to tell him the truth either. If she was ever going to have a relationship with the man she was in love with, she'd have to come clean and tell him who she was: Ana and Dorothy. She needed time to figure this out so she decided to stall while trying to keep Noah interested, so she wrote:

"Noah, I think you're right, we should meet. I have some vacation time in two months and I would like to come and visit you if that's okay. Please let me know.

Always, your Ana"

When Noah read this email he couldn't stop smiling. Finally, he was going to meet the girl of his dreams. The girl who excited him, stimulated him, and charmed him beyond belief . . . he was actually going to meet the girl he had been in love with but had never seen before. At least he had two months to prepare and hopefully clean his condo before she came. He quickly wrote back:

"Ana, I can hardly believe it's going to happen. I'll plan us a great adventure: We can hike into the wilderness, float down the Colorado River, gaze into the mountains, and revel in each other's company. Let me know the exact details and I'll make sure you'll have the best vacation ever.

Very excited, Noah"

Dorothy thought to herself, *Yes, Noah, you'll have two months to build your excitement, only to be disappointed when I, Dorothy, show up at your door instead of your imaginary Ana, whom you've fallen in love with.* Her next thought was, *Where's the wine?*

Noah was so excited he almost starting vacuuming his carpet, well . . . almost. As he was contemplating this situation, his doorbell rang. He looked out the peephole and saw his old friend Sandy. He opened the door and Sandy immediately began saying, "Noah, dude, I'm in big trouble. I need your help. I mean like NOW!"

"Sure, Sandy. C'mon in and tell me what's wrong." But Sandy never moved. Instead, she looked over her shoulder and started stammering incoherently. Noah stopped her and said, "Slow down, come in and explain it all to me."

"Noah, I'm in big trouble, I need help." Noah's mind started racing . . . did she shoot someone? Did she accidentally kill a tourist? Did somebody drown on one of her rafting trips? Sandy continued, "My parents are out in the car, they want to meet you."

"Why in the world would your parents want to meet me?" As he said this, he noticed two older people getting out of a car and walking towards him.

Sandy quickly looked back at them and then whispered, "They think we're getting married."

Before Noah could respond to that insanity, the older woman said, "Oh, Noah, we're so glad to finally meet you. We've heard so much about you, we feel like we already know you, don't we Herbert?" Herbert nodded but didn't say anything.

Sandy leaned in quickly and kissed Noah on the cheek and whispered, "Please, Noah, I'll make it up to you."

Noah looked at everyone, then smiled, and said, "Well, c'mon in, it's so nice to finally meet you as well."

Before he could say anything else, Herbert plopped down in Noah's lazy boy recliner, while Sandy took her mother's arm and said, "Let me show you around the place, Mom." They walked down the hall toward the bedroom, which had a picture of Ana on the nightstand and an unmade bed. Noah looked at Herbert who did nothing but stare back at him. There was an awkward silence that seemed to last about three years before Sandy and her mom came back into the den. Sandy said, "Mom loved the picture of your sister on the nightstand, Honey, but how many times do I have to warn you about making up the bed?"

Noah smiled and looked over at Herbert, who was not smiling. Sandy's mom said, "Show me the kitchen, Honey."

They walked away and Noah looked again at Herbert, who finally spoke, "I warned her about living in sin."

Since there was no answer on earth Noah could give to that statement, he remained silent. Fortunately, Sandy and her mom came back in and sat down. Noah offered them coffee or soft drinks but they declined. Then Sandy's mom said, "Will you two live here after the wedding?"

Sandy quickly jumped in, to keep Noah quiet about this subject, and answered, "Now, Mom, I told you not to bring that up. We have a lot to discuss and many decisions to make before we cross that bridge . . . right Honey?" She was looking at Noah, pleading with her facial expressions for him to please play along.

Noah was a good old boy; he knew Sandy was only trying to hide her lifestyle from her parents . . . "Right, we sure do. But you guys will be the first to know what we decide."

Sandy's mom giggled with delight as Herbert continued to try and stare a hole into Noah's brain. After several more minutes of excruciating small talk, Sandy finally said, "Well, we'd better be running or you'll miss the bus back to Salt Lake." Sandy's mom hugged Noah first, then Herbert shook Noah's hand while trying to break every bone he could while doing so.

Sandy and her mom hurried off to the car while Herbert hung back a few steps. He then turned and faced Noah and said, "I guess it could be worse . . . I actually thought she was gay." Then he turned and followed the two girls to the car.

They all got in the car and as they started to drive away, Sandy looked back at Noah and mouthed "I'm sorry. Thank you."

●●●

That entire weird episode left Noah's mind spinning. About an hour later, Sandy came back to see him, by herself. "Noah, I'm so sorry, thanks for helping me out, dude."

Noah looked sternly at her and replied, "What in the world was that all about, Sandy?"

She shook her head and answered, "My parents think I'm straight. They don't know that I sometimes . . . experiment."

"Experiment? Is that what you call it nowadays?"

"Look, Noah, my dad gives me this big allowance each month. You know I couldn't live on what I make from river-running! Heck, I drink up most of that pay. Without my dad financing me, I'd have to move back in with them; or worse, get a real job." Noah understood. He may not have liked being played like he was but he understood. Then Sandy continued, "It won't happen again . . . I promise." She hugged Noah's neck and then tried to kiss him, but he was expecting that and skillfully twisted away.

When Sandy left, he decided the best thing for him to do now was to answer some questions for his column and try to calm down a little. So, he settled down at the computer and began working.

Noah

"Noah: I'm a senior in high school and I don't understand why adults think we can't make our own decisions. My generation is entirely more knowledgeable in everything technological than the previous generations. We're probably smarter and care more about the environment, too. I just wanted to voice my opinion without having to hear some older person say, 'Back in my day . . . blah, blah, blah. Signed, Caden.'"

"Caden: It's hard for me to sympathize with you. You see, when I was your age I had to walk 10 feet through shag carpet just to change the TV channel."

The more questions from his readers that Noah answered, the better he felt. He finally shut his computer down and grabbed a beer to sit outside and gaze into the abyss. No more walking in the desert near sunset for him. The La Sal Mountain range still had snow capping all the ridges; and the majestic hue from the mountains, with the snow backed by the blue sky, made an epic scene to stare at and dream. When he went outside this time, he started to grab the arrowhead from Dorothy, as he always did, but instead, he left it sitting on his nightstand. Somehow, he must rid the memories of Dorothy from his mind. Ana was coming. Ana. The woman he had dreamed of all this time.

But still, as hard as he tried, his mind kept returning to the memories of Dorothy in the river, Dorothy on the trail, sitting next to her, accidentally touching her leg, pressing together under a rock ledge to get out of the rain. *Stop!* He told himself. *Ana is coming.* And still, his mind wandered. He again thought, *Life is trying to give me what I want; don't screw it up, stupid.*

Then his other voice answered, *Life is under no obligation to give you what you expect. Life doesn't see things as they are . . . life sees things as YOU are.* He suddenly stood up and grabbed a rock off the ground and threw it as hard as he could into the void. Then his other voice said, *Stop thinking so much; it's okay if you don't know all the answers.* He wanted to respond to this other voice but sometimes silence really is the best answer. So, he bent down, picked up another rock, and threw it at a clump of prickly pear cactuses in the distance. He missed.

12.

DOROTHY FINALLY DECIDED THERE WAS ONLY ONE THING she could do to keep her sanity. She would go back to Moab, meet with Noah, and tell him the entire truth. Let the chips fall where they may. At least he would know there was no fictional Ana . . . only her. If he liked her, fine. If not, she'd go back to Death Valley National Park and die her own slow death. At least she would know for sure.

She had two months before she was scheduled to visit Moab. The first thing she did was dye her hair a lighter shade. Most women would pay to have the radiant sheen and color of Dorothy's natural hair color, but when you're confused and scared, your mind tricks you into crazy things. At first, that initial evening, she liked the new color. When she woke in the morning, she hated it. It didn't match her eyebrows, it didn't match her eyes, and it made her look like a wannabe surfer girl.

She left the color on for two days to see if she would change her mind. She didn't. Then she changed it back to the original color. Next, she decided to go on a Keto diet and lose a few pounds. Somehow, all women think they need to lose a few pounds. Dorothy did not need to lose any weight. Oh, she could lose five or ten pounds and have the body of a runway model, but why? Lose her form, her shapeliness, and her figure in the hopes that Noah would find that more attractive? She quickly abandoned that idea as well. Either Noah would like her as she was or he wouldn't. She opened a bottle of wine and hoped she was making the right decision.

The next week at work was pure drudgery. The clock seemed as if it was in slow motion and temperatures hovered around 112 degrees most days. Most of the tourists lingered in the park offices and gift shop simply to get out of the heat. All day the tourists asked the same four or five questions. She felt like a wind-up doll always giving the same answers to the same questions. At times, she was tempted to make up stuff just to see if they were paying attention:

"Tourist: What's the hottest you've ever seen it here?"

"Dorothy: It got so hot one summer that the lizards would fry on the sidewalk when they tried to cross over to the other side. They'd become nice and crispy but the ravens and hawks couldn't eat them because if they landed on the sidewalk it would burn their feet."

"Tourist: Do you ever get bored out here in the middle of the desert?"

"Dorothy: Of course, I do. Last week I got so bored at work that I actually started doing my job."

"Tourist: I bet if you didn't know what you were doing and took a wrong turn, you could really get yourself into trouble out here, couldn't you, ranger?"

"Dorothy: It ain't what you don't know that gets you into trouble. It's what you know for sure that just ain't so."

"Tourist: Have you ever been lost or had trouble out here, ranger?"

"Dorothy: Sure . . . my life has been filled with terrible misfortune, most of which never happened."

Dorothy wished she could say things like that but she couldn't. She was too nice, too professional, too polite, and . . . she wasn't Noah. So, she filled out forms, helped out the other rangers, answered all the questions, and smiled like a good ranger is supposed to do. Each night she would turn the air conditioner on high, do some housework, wash some clothes, and eat a small dinner while she waited on the computer to ding and let her know that Noah had emailed.

Noah's email to her read:

"My dearest Ana, I wanted to let you know how much you mean to me. I've never connected with anyone the way I have with you, and even though we've never met in person, I can truly tell you that I have never met anyone else who compares with you. I can't wait until you visit. I promise we will a wonderful and exciting time together.

Always yours, Noah"

Dorothy wept as she read this message. Why? Because Noah had met her several times before and yet he truthfully admits in his email that he has "never met anyone else who compares with you." No one can compare to his dream girl, his fantasy girl, his . . . Ana. Dorothy was hoping the time they spent together on the rafting trip and all the hikes they took with each other would mean something to him. It hurt to feel rejected, not be wanted, to know that he would rather have some fantasy girl instead of her. So, she wept. What else is a girl supposed to do?

She moped around work for two days, then took Friday off as a vacation day and decided to take a long hike up in the mountains that surround Death Valley. She needed to be alone without having someone constantly asking her, "What's wrong?"

The Panamint Mountains border Death Valley on the western side and rise to over 11,000 feet. This makes quite a drastic change from the average below sea level elevations of Death Valley. Dorothy needed change. She set out before sunrise Friday morning with her backpack filled with water, food, and a small sleeping bag for her to spend the night staring at the stars from the top of the mountains. She arrived just after sunrise and started on a minor trail that was not clearly marked. Why this trail? She wanted to be alone and there was very little chance anyone else would ever take this path into the unknown.

She quickly left the tree line and was surrounded by rocks, a few scrub cactuses, and some local vegetation like the isolated monkey flowers. She could see Death Valley in the distance, with the heat waves shimmering up from the floor like some magical illusion. Dorothy was an experienced hiker but the drastic elevation changes still left her breathless as she continued to the summit. She climbed all morning, only stopping for water breaks and to catch her breath. The good news was that all the exertion from the climb took her mind off Noah and the impending doom she feared when they would meet in several weeks.

By mid-afternoon, she had long since left any trace of a trail and was simply picking her way up the slopes. She had finally arrived at a leveling off area and could actually see around her 360 degrees. She decided to make her little camp next to a large outcropping that gave her something to lean back against as she ate a few snacks. She had yet to see any type of wildlife or even any signs of wildlife, except for the ever-present vultures floating overhead, possibly waiting for Dorothy to make a mistake and provide them with lunch and dinner for the next few days.

Dorothy sat, leaning back against the rocks, and stared out into the distance. She was facing north so the sun wouldn't be in her eyes and she would be out of the main wind currents, which could be quite formidable on top of the mountains. She ate a few almonds and an orange as she tried her best to let her mind roam and think of anything else except Noah. She thought of her father who drank himself into an early death. And then of her mother, who she would always miss but was never close to. She owed her beautiful skin tone and luxurious hair color to her mother's Lumbee Indian heritage. Her facial features and size came mostly from her dad's side. She thought of growing up in Lumberton, North Carolina, and what life must still be like back there.

She did a great job of thinking about everything except what she tried so desperately to avoid. Until. Near dusk, she found a nice place for a bathroom break and as she wound her way back to her little camp, she came close to a ledge, or drop-off from the summit area. This ledge faced the sunset, so Dorothy walked near the edge to gaze at the last remnants of the sun's glow as it sank below the horizon for the evening. Dorothy stopped about five feet from the edge and stared. She was okay until the last rays of the sun tranquilized her. As many people do, she simply stared at that awesome scene and let her mind wander . . . wander to where it would go. To Noah.

The more she thought of him, the more she convinced herself that she'd never have him, that she would always be lonely and depressed. She convinced herself that Noah would never find a half-Lumbee, half-white girl attractive. She moved one step closer to the edge as she thought of the times she and Noah had spent together. Times that meant so much to her, yet so little to him (in her mind). She moved one step closer to the edge as she thought of the look that would probably be on his face when she told him that she and Ana were indeed the same girl. How disappointed and upset and furious he would be for misleading him all this time.

She finally moved to the very edge of the thousand-foot drop-off and thought of her life: a girl who has lied to the only man she ever loved; a girl in a dead-end job, in a dead-end park; a girl with no family and no one who even missed her. The sun had set and it was almost pitch black; no moon to light the way. No moon to hide the depths of despair or the vacuum of what lay below that last step beyond the edge. No one would ever miss her. No one would care. And her worries and troubles would be no more. Her mind suddenly seemed at ease. One more step and all her troubles would be gone. Nothing more to worry about.

Then, she heard a noise. She turned and saw a mountain goat standing directly behind her ten feet away. It wasn't moving. She turned to face it and said out loud, "C'mon, charge me. Knock me over the edge. Let's you and me get it all over with. C'mon!" But the mountain goat didn't charge her. After a minute or so, it simply turned away and disappeared beyond the rocks. A gust of wind suddenly made Dorothy step forward to balance herself. Only then did she realize she didn't want to go over the edge. She found her way back to her sleeping bag and crawled inside. Almost as if by magic, she closed her eyes and instantly went to sleep. No dreams of mountain goats, Noah, her parents, or the abyss.

13.

NOAH'S FOOT HAD HEALED FROM THE SNAKE BITE but he didn't
want to do any hiking—just in case. Since he really didn't have a nine-
to-five job, he could take off virtually any time he wanted, as long as
his column was up to date. He decided to take a short road trip up
north to a place he'd heard of but never visited. There was a little town
north of Moab named Boulder, in Utah—not Colorado—which he'd
heard was very remote, very old-fashioned, and very, very Mormon.

He programmed his GPS and left early Thursday morning to make
the two-hour drive back into history. The entire trip was scenic. Noah
could never quite understand why the general public didn't
understand or couldn't comprehend the beauty of back country Utah.
Boulder is near the Escalante National Monument and close to the
Escalante River, which provides magnificent views of remote canyon
settings. Near Boulder, he would stop all along Highway 12 and gaze
at wonders most people only dreamed of. Occasionally, he would walk
a little distance from his Jeep—but not far.

He eventually made his way into the little town itself and decided to
have a late lunch at a small place on the main street named Red Rock
& Llamas Café. The name "Llamas" had him hooked and he wanted
to investigate. It was nice inside and he was promptly seated by a
young girl wearing a floor-length dress with her hair tied in a bun on
top of her head. She smiled and handed him a menu and said, "Can I
bring you something to drink while you're looking at the menu?"

He was parched since he had forgotten to bring a bottle of water with him, so he answered, "Yes, please. I'll have a Bud Light."

The girl's smile instantly vanished as she replied, "We don't serve alcohol here, sir."

"Oh," said a disappointed Noah. "That's okay, I'll just have a Coke."

The girl then said, "We don't serve Cokes either, sir."

Noah asked, "Pepsi?"

"No, sir."

"Iced tea?" He was begging now.

"No, sir. No tea. How about a glass of milk?"

Noah wanted to be polite . . . but, milk? "I'll just have a cup of coffee."

She smiled again and replied, "Decaf coffee, great."

"Whoa . . . decaf?"

"Yes, sir, that's all we serve."

The young lady was suddenly not smiling again and Noah felt as if he were trapped. He finally asked, "Do you have any water?"

That answer brought a smile back to her face and relief to a flustered Noah. He then looked over the menu and was happy to find there was not a dish that contained llama. So, he ordered a country-fried steak and mashed potatoes. He sipped his water and began to notice that he was probably the only non-Mormon in the little café. The setting and scenery reminded him of a Norman Rockwell painting—except everyone was real.

Noah had been spoiled. Even though Moab was in the heart of Mormonism, it was never that evident due to all the tourists and businesses that catered to tourists. Boulder was not like that. Boulder was 99% Mormon. Only 99% because he had seen a one-room, very small building at the edge of town that had a sign out front identifying Canyon Baptist Church.

The meal was very good and the water was cold. When he went to the register to pay, he asked the older woman working there why the café was named Red Rock & Lamas Café. She explained that her husband ran a guide service that took tourists into the wilderness for a week's trip. He used llamas to carry the supplies into the red rock canyon country so the tourists wouldn't have to do anything but walk and take pictures. She smiled and told him that the tour business was booked up three months in advance. Somehow, that bit of news made him very happy. His waitress waved goodbye to him and the cashier gave him a pamphlet on the tour business and made him promise to come back. As he walked out the door he thought, *Ana would love something like this.*

After his lunch, he drove out of town and took a side road to investigate the countryside. He saw old-time farmhouses, men out plowing fields with mules, and once had to pull over to let a horse-drawn buggy turn in front of him. He felt like he was back in the 1880s. And he loved it. He kept thinking to himself, *Ana would love to see that. Ana would love to hike over there. Ana would love . . . everything.* Then, he woke from his reverie to realize he was lost. He had no idea where he was and he hadn't seen a road sign for over an hour. He had made several turns and didn't know if he could remember how to get back.

About a mile ahead, he saw an older man walking through a field, toward an old abandoned barn. He pulled over, got out of his Jeep, and walked near the man. When the man saw him coming, he stopped and put both his hands in his pockets and waited. Noah approached the man and said, "I'm a little lost and was hoping you could tell me how to get back to Boulder."

The old man smiled and said, "Sure. Just turn around and go back that way, then turn east at the crossroads for about five miles. When you pass the Johnson ranch, go south for a couple of miles and you should see a sign for Providence School. Then, you just go east again and you'll head right into Boulder." The old man patted him on the shoulder and said, "My wife's waiting on me. Good luck, son."

Noah watched him walk away and thought to himself, *East? South? What the . . . ?* He made a few more wrong turns, then found a sign pointing him in the right direction. Even though he never found Boulder again, he did manage to get back to Highway 12. He made it back to Moab a little after dark, just in time to visit the Moab Brewery and think about Ana and what he would tell her about his adventure today in the heart of Mormon country.

●●●

He didn't stay long at the Brewery: It was a little too crowded for him. Instead, he decided to go home and answer a few emails from his readers. If Ana was going to visit him for several days, he wanted to get ahead and build up a reserve he could quickly submit to the paper in case Ana required his presence and attention full-time.

"Noah: I was reading some of your columns online from a few months ago. You were discussing golf in one of them . . . did you ever take up that glorious sport? Signed, Eldrick."

"Eldrick: Hmm; I'm getting close. I've almost learned enough cuss words to start teeing it up."

●●●

"Noah: I've tried all the fad diets, I've tried drink supplements, I joined two gyms, and I've been ordering 'healthy food' online. None of it has worked for me. I'm almost at the point of giving up. Have you ever had success at trying to lose weight? If so, how? Signed, Nicky."

"Nicky: All of America feels your pain. One time I thought I was losing weight, but it turned out my sweatpants had come untied."

Noah

●●●

"Noah: I just turned twenty-one and am close to graduating from college. I'm looking forward to being on my own, getting a job, and turning into an official adult. I'd like to ask you, as an older person who has a lot of experience at adulting, what's the hardest part of actually being an adult? Signed, Danelle."

"Danelle: First, did you leave an 'i' out of your name somewhere? And second, through years of experience, I'm pretty sure the hardest part of being an adult is figuring out what to cook for dinner every single night for the rest of your life until you die. Or not."

●●●

"Noah: I know you've been asked this question a thousand times before, but let's try again and see if you can actually be serious for once in your life . . . okay? Tell us, what do women and men REALLY want from each other? Signed, Cathy."

"Cathy, Cathy, Cathy: Don't you understand, with matters of the heart, I'm ALWAYS serious. After extensive research and interviews, I have found that women truly want to be loved, to be listened to, to be desired, to be respected, to be needed, to be trusted, and sometimes, just to be held.

Men, however, just want tickets to the football game."

14.

HE HAD THREE EMAIL MESSAGES that quickly drew his attention: The first was from his editor at the paper saying that he was pleased with Noah's column and happy to see that his attitude with his readers had changed for the better. Noah wasn't aware that his attitude had changed but if his editor complimented him on it, then . . . great! The second email was from Vicki, telling him that she would be back in town later this week and was looking forward to "seeing" him. He knew what "seeing" meant and he had to let Vicki know there would be no more "seeing" since Ana was back in his life. The third email was from Ana.

"Noah, I'm counting down the days until my visit. I hope you're as excited as I am. I won't ask what you have planned for us but I know it will be grand and fun. Truthfully, though, I would be very happy just to sit under a cottonwood tree and talk to you. To see you and connect in person as we have online is the most important thing I want from our visit. Anything else will just be a bonus.

Very excited, Ana"

Noah read the "Very excited" part and instantly became very excited himself. But before he could be too overwhelmed, he started thinking of what he should email back to Vicki. He had to let her know that it was over between them. He knew there was nothing between them anyway except sex, but he needed to let her know that the sex was indeed over. He sent a long explanatory email to Vicki and tried to be as politically correct as possible while trying not to hurt her feelings. Just as he hit the send button, there was a knock on his door.

He looked through the peephole and almost fainted when he saw Vicki smiling back at him. She could see his shadow darken the little peephole and instantly started waving furiously at Noah. He opened the door and before he could say anything, she jumped into his arms and started kissing him passionately and deeply. With her arms around his neck, her legs around his waist, and her tongue down his throat, he was at a vast disadvantage in his attempt at breaking off the affair.

When Vicki finally loosened her leg grip, she started pulling him towards the bedroom. He tried pulling back but still couldn't say anything because she never stopped kissing him. At the entrance to the bedroom, he used the doorframe to brace himself and stop the momentum. Vicki said, "Stop, Noah, I don't have long; I have to get back to work."

He finally moved her arms from around his neck and said, "Vicki, we can't do this anymore."

"Yes, we can. It won't take long, you know how you are."

"No, Vicki, that's not what I meant. I mean we can't be together anymore. I've reconnected with a girl I used to know and we're trying to work things out."

Vicki looked a little stunned, then asked, "Is she here now?"

"No, not right now. But she will be soon."

Vicki brightened up again and said, "Well, we're okay then. It won't take long and I'll be gone. She'll never know I was here!"

"No, Vicki. I can't do that. I just can't do it. It was nice what we were doing. I loved it, but it's over now . . . okay?"

She looked at Noah and exclaimed, "It was nice? That's what it was to you, Noah? Nice?"

He knew in his heart of hearts that there was no answer on Earth that would make this situation any better, so he didn't say anything. Vicki stared at him for about fifteen seconds, then turned and stormed out the door, slamming it harder than Noah believed was possible for any human to slam a door.

He peeped out the window to make sure Vicki actually left, then he hurried out to his Jeep and decided to take a drive just in case she came back. He drove out of town about five minutes to the entrance into Arches National Park. The line of cars waiting to get into the park wasn't too bad so he pulled in behind an SUV from Modesto, California--at least that's what the sticker on the car said. Noah had been here many times in the past but one never really gets tired of beauty in the truest sense.

He thought about hiking up to Delicate Arch but changed his mind when he remembered it was about an hour to hike out and then an hour to hike back--his toe was still a little tender, plus he didn't bring any water with him. He settled on a fairly empty parking lot at the trailhead to Lost Gulch. He parked and walked about a hundred yards down the dusty trail and found a nice shaded area to sit in where he could lean back against a rock and not be noticed by any other tourists.

The first thing he did was fall asleep. He wasn't sleepy or tired or rundown, but within five minutes of leaning back against the rock wall, he was asleep. Since he didn't wear a watch, he didn't know how long he was out. He woke when he did only because an ant had crawled across his nose and started to go up one nostril. Then his mind started working.

Most men would immediately start thinking of the attractive woman who had just left his house trying to have sex with him. Or, he would start thinking about the woman he was in love with who was coming to visit him in several weeks. Not Noah. Without thinking at all, letting his subconscious take control of his thoughts, and abandoning all reasoning—he started thinking of Dorothy. He thought of her hair, her face, the way she smiled, the tiny little lines near her eyes, the way her neck connected so sublimely to her shoulders. And then of her hands and how her fingernails seemed to fit so perfectly at the end of each finger, not colored, but reflecting the beauty that was within her. He remembered sitting close to her before, when she was wearing shorts, and how he was mesmerized by the smoothness of her legs and the contours of each muscle from her knees to her ankles.

The spell was only broken as a raven squawked at him from the limb of a juniper tree and brought him back to reality. He hated that raven! Then he chastised himself for thinking of Dorothy when he knew his one and only Ana was coming to visit. Why was he thinking of Dorothy? Why wasn't he thinking of Ana? At least he wasn't thinking of Vicki. Sad consolation at this point in time. He got up and knocked off several other ants from his legs, dusted his pants off, and trudged back to the Jeep, trying not to think, not to remember, not to . . . anything.

On his way out of the park, he stopped and pulled over at the access road across the way from Balanced Rock, which is one of the most famous of all the spots in the park. He turned in the access road to get away from the tourists taking ten million pictures of the scene. The access road turned away from the Balanced Rock and led to a small storage area for unused porta-potties and recycling containers. But, it used to be the home of something else a long time ago. It used to be special, and it still is for those who know and can remember and dream dreams that most people are not aware of. Noah was aware. He knew. That's why he stopped the Jeep and got out and sat on a rock and stared into the late afternoon sun. He watched the entire horizon start to turn all sorts of reddish, amber hues. He saw a rabbit run under a bush about twenty yards away and quickly picked up a rock to throw at it. Why would he do that? Kill a rabbit? He didn't. He tossed the rock on the ground and got back into his Jeep. Time to go home.

When he was sure Vicki wasn't lurking in the shadows down the street, he went inside and turned on his computer. He typed in Ana's address and starting typing: "Ana, each day I wait for your arrival is harder than the day before. How many more weeks is it until you arrive? Whatever the answer is, it's too many. If you want to sit under a cottonwood tree and talk, then that's what we'll do, my dear. It'll be like that time we sat on a rock ledge, in the rain, and talked all afternoon . . . "

Then he thought, *No! Wait!! That wasn't Ana! That was Dorothy I was talking to on a rock ledge, in the rain!* He immediately deleted that message as his mind began spinning. He again thought, *Why am I getting Ana and Dorothy confused? What's going on here?* Again he asked himself, *Why am I thinking about Dorothy? She's gone!* He had no answers to those questions. He had no solutions, no explanations, and no conclusions. He walked into the bedroom and picked up the arrowhead from the nightstand, the one that Dorothy had given him. He walked outside to throw the arrowhead into the desert as far as he could throw it. He reared back and . . . couldn't throw it. He walked back inside and put the arrowhead back on the nightstand, then he cursed himself and went to the refrigerator to get an ice-cold beer. And all he had was a half-bottle of stale red wine. He pulled the wine out, smelled it, and poured it down the drain, hoping his life didn't follow that same pattern in the near future.

15.

AS SOON AS NOAH WOKE IN THE MORNING, he checked his email—nothing but work stuff—so he turned it off and drove into town. Usually, the tourists aren't up and about this early and he can sit in his favorite coffee shop and relax at a table next to the window. It was a small shop and he'd been coming here for several years and ordering the same thing each time: regular coffee and a blueberry muffin. Also, he usually had the same young waitress serve him but he'd never asked her name and she never wore a nametag. He'd watched her transform herself over the years from punk hairstyles to shaved-head, from blonde to black, and now blue-haired. He wanted to tell her she didn't need to do any of that—she was pretty as she was. But wisely, he just drank his coffee and kept his mouth shut.

Today turned out different. He walked in and took his favorite seat next to the window, so he could watch all the tourists walk by, as he waited for the blue-haired waitress to come and take his order. However, today when she came to his table she was carrying his coffee and blueberry muffin with her before he'd ordered it. She put his food down on the table and said, "You're welcome." He looked up at her and she smiled and walked away.

When she came back later to refill his cup, Noah asked, "How did you know that's what I wanted?"

She smiled again and answered, "Same order, two or three times a week, fifty-two weeks a year, over four years . . . or, maybe it was just a wild guess."

He thought, *Is she messing with me or trying to be nice?* So, after four years, he finally asked, "What's your name?"

She cocked her head a little to one side, smiled, and replied, "Why, after all this time, do you care what my name is?"

Noah, having no other alternative than to be himself, answered, "I don't really. I was just trying to be nice."

She continued smiling at him and said, "Kai."

"Excuse me?"

"I said my name is Kai."

"Kai?"

"Yes, Kai."

Noah took a sip of coffee and then asked, "Exactly how do you spell your name, Kai?"

"Just like it sounds."

Noah nodded and said, "Ki?"

"No, that's not how it sounds."

"That's how it sounds to me."

"If you were Welsh, you'd know it means 'keeper of the keys.'" And with that answer, Kai walked back into the kitchen.

He watched her walk away and thought, *She IS messing with me; or, is she truly weird?* Then he turned back to the window and saw a very heavy-set woman struggling to walk down the street with a dog on a leash that couldn't have weighed more than two pounds. He finished his muffin and his coffee and then waited for Kai to go back into the kitchen before he went to the counter to pay his bill. As he handed the money to the cashier, he asked, "The waitress told me her name but I couldn't understand what she said. What exactly is her name?"

The cashier, who was an older woman, said, "She told me you would come up here and ask that question. I didn't believe her, but here you are."

Noah was stunned. "She told you I would ask what her name is?"

"Yep."

"Well, what is it?"

The older woman smiled and replied, "She told me to tell you her name is Margaret."

Noah knew when he was beaten. He took his thirty-seven cents in change and went back to the table and left Kai/Margaret a five-dollar tip as he left. Life in Moab is seldom boring.

Noah opened his computer and still no answer from Ana, so he started his work for the day.

"Noah: I miss the old days. Things today are just not as fun as they used to be. I know that sounds old and boring, but wouldn't it be nice to have a dialogue with people who weren't staring into their phones all day? Maybe I should just move back to the 1950s. How about you, Noah? Signed, Cleve."

"Cleve: I know exactly what you mean. I really miss the old days when you could call a person on the phone 57 times and hang up, and they never knew it was you . . . good times!"

"Noah: I moved to Salt Lake City a few years ago from Windsor, England, and I just love it here. My question is why do you Americans love coffee so much? Being English, I was raised on tea and simply don't understand your country's fascination with coffee. Can you explain? Signed, Megan."

"Megan: I'm sure every American would probably give you a different answer to your question about coffee. I can only give you my definition of coffee: a warm delicious alternative to hating everybody, every morning, forever. Cheerio, Megan."

16.

IT WAS NOW LESS THAN SEVEN WEEKS before Dorothy promised Noah she would come and visit him. She could still change her mind and abandon the whole crazy idea, or she could go and face him and hope he wouldn't hate her too much for misleading him all this time. She was very confused and changed her mind at least a dozen times a day. She needed to talk with someone who could give her some unbiased advice and be honest with her, even if it hurt her feelings.

She looked at the website for the U.S. Government Human Relations department and found there are counselors available who will meet with any government employee, and that it was covered by her insurance, except for the co-pay. She called and found good news and bad news: good, in that she could have an appointment in two days; bad, because the appointment was in Escondido, which was a long drive away. She made the appointment.

Dorothy arrived at the HR department early and drank a cup of weak coffee from a vending machine as she waited. At exactly 10:00, a woman came down the hallway and summoned her. Dorothy thought this rather attractive woman in a short skirt was the secretary leading her to the counselor. She was wrong; this middle-aged woman with short, curly hair was indeed the counselor herself. She sat on an old couch and motioned Dorothy to sit in the chair across from her.

She said, "I'm Mrs. Hudgins, but just call me Shirley. What can I help you with, Dorothy?" As much as Dorothy wanted to talk about her problem and explain things to someone else, she just couldn't find the words to start with. After a few awkward moments, Mrs. Hudgins said, "It's about a man, right?" Before Dorothy could answer, Mrs. Hudgins asked, "Are you pregnant?"

"No! I mean, yes. It is about a man but I'm not pregnant."

Mrs. Hudgins nodded and replied, "Just take it easy. Trust me, I've heard it all, Dorothy. There's nothing you can tell me that I haven't heard a thousand times before . . . probably five thousand."

Dorothy thought, *Really?*

"Just explain it all to me and I'll tell you how to get your life back under control. We'll figure it out, Dorothy."

So Dorothy started from the beginning and told Mrs. Hudgins everything. She left out no details, not even the nude swimming in the Colorado River on the rafting trip. Mrs. Hudgins started out taking a few notes but quickly stopped to concentrate fully on Dorothy's story. When Dorothy completed her saga, Mrs. Hudgins was the one who was silent. After a few moments, she said, "I need a cup of coffee." She got up and walked out of her office, leaving Dorothy to wonder if Mrs. Hudgins had indeed heard this story five thousand times before.

Mrs. Hudgins came back in holding two cups of coffee and handed one to Dorothy. She sat down and took her glasses off, saying, "So, to recap, you are in love with this man, Noah, right?"

"Yes."

"But he doesn't know you are actually Dorothy, right?"

"Yes."

"He thinks you are his email friend, Ana?" Dorothy nodded and took a sip of her coffee. Mrs. Hudgins had yet to touch hers. "But you've spent time with him on some hikes and he's seen you naked?"

"Yes."

"But you've never had sex with him?"

"No, we've never even kissed."

"But you're in love with him?" Dorothy nodded again. "And he's in love with someone named Ana with whom he's never met. Is that correct?"

"Yes, ma'am."

"And now, you're going to meet him in a few weeks and tell him who you really are?"

"I think so. I don't know. I'm not sure." Dorothy took another sip of her coffee while Mrs. Hudgins sat staring at her with her mouth partially open, as if she wanted to say something but didn't know how to start. Dorothy regained eye contact and asked, "What do you think I should do, Shirley?"

Shirley finally took a sip of her coffee and made a sour face—her coffee was cold. She said, "Excuse me a minute." Dorothy thought Shirley was going to warm up her coffee, but instead, Shirley came back in the room with another older woman. They both sat on the couch in front of Dorothy and Shirley said, "This is Lib. I want her to hear your story before we offer any advice."

So, Dorothy retold the entire history with Noah as Lib listened intently and Shirley sat mesmerized. When she finished with everything, Lib said, "So . . . in summary, you met Noah online as the fictional Ana. And quickly, you two fell in love with each other online. Noah thinks you're Ana . . . correct?" Dorothy nodded, so Lib continued, "But you've met Noah on these hiking and river trips as yourself and you're pretty sure he's not interested in you as Dorothy . . . is that correct?"

Dorothy nodded again, so Lib concluded, "And now you've agreed to meet this Noah in person, but he thinks he's going to be meeting his fictional Ana . . . right?"

Dorothy answered, "Yes, ma'am."

Lib looked over at Shirley, then back at Dorothy, and said, "We've got a problem."

The three of them spent the rest of the morning discussing all the alternatives; however, when "love" is in the equation, common sense and sensibility often take a vacation. Lib volunteered to take them all out to lunch, where they enjoyed mimosas and white wine (since it was now after noontime). The two counselors wanted to hear the story of the online affair again and how it evolved as it did. Then they wanted intimate details of each time Dorothy and Noah spent on hikes together and especially the rafting trip. Dorothy had to tell the story of the skinny-dipping episode twice. After that, Shirley took her iPad out of her pocketbook and they looked up Noah's advice columns on the internet. Shirley and Lib took turns reading some of Noah's responses out loud to each other, as they all shared laughs and sighs.

When Shirley closed the iPad, they both looked at Dorothy and Dorothy said, "See?"

They both nodded and each took a healthy drink from their lunchtime beverages. After several refills, Shirley offered this rather clouded advice: "If it was me, I would've nailed him on that rafting trip, when we were all naked; I wouldn't have given him the chance of ever forgetting me!"

Lib was nodding furiously, in between sips of her mimosa, and offered her advice: "Honey, I'd knock on his door and jump his bones as soon as he opened it. He'd forget all about this Ana slut after I was through with him."

And so the stories went--a little more vivid and X-rated as the drinks flowed through the early afternoon. Fortunately, Dorothy stopped after her second glass of white wine, only because she had to drive the other two ladies back to the office, then drive back home that afternoon. At least she got a consensus from the other two: go see Noah, tell him the truth, tell him how you feel . . . then, jump his bones!

17.

WHEN DOROTHY ARRIVED BACK HOME, she had an email from Noah-- of course, it was addressed to Ana:

"My dearest Ana, I hope you are well and getting excited about visiting me in just over six weeks. I can hardly wait. I want to show you Moab and all the national parks and wilderness areas near here—we'll have a great time. We haven't discussed this, but I'd really like for you to stay with me and not at some motel when you visit. I'm not suggesting anything, mind you. I have a second bedroom for you, or you can sleep on the couch, or you can camp out in the back yard. If none of those suggestions is appropriate, I can always slide over a little and you can sleep on the other side of the bed from me.

P.S. I don't snore, but sometimes I might have erotic dreams about hiking and canoeing and wilderness stuff.

Can't wait to finally see you in person,

Noah"

Dorothy smiled and even giggled a little as she read his email. She thought to herself, *Why can't he love me as much as he does Ana?* She read the email twice more and then typed her reply:

"Noah, that is a very nice offer on the sleeping arrangements. I'll take them all under consideration; I've always wondered about camping out in the desert—it might be fun. But please don't go to any trouble on my behalf, anything will be fine with me. However, I must warn you, as a young girl growing up in North Carolina, during those hot summer nights, I grew accustomed to sleeping in the nude and have been used to doing that ever since. Please let me know if there are any laws that might prevent me from camping in your back yard in the nude.

Always, your Ana"

●●●

Noah read the email and daydreamed about the possibilities of Ana sleeping nude in his backyard. Better yet, sleeping nude in his bed. He typed a couple of replies to send back to her but deleted them both until he could think more clearly and not be influenced so much by erotic fantasies. He decided to go back into town to his favorite coffee shop, not so much for the coffee and muffin, but to find out exactly what Kai/Margaret's name really was. It was bugging him.

He'd waited too late in the morning and all the parking spots on Main St. were taken by the tourists. He ended up parking on a side street a couple of blocks away. It irritated him to have to walk two or three blocks to get to the little café, but he thought nothing of walking five or ten miles out in the desert. Funny how the mind works like that.

He walked in the café but his favorite table was taken by a man and woman dressed in hiking boots, hiking pants with zippers down the thighs and legs, wide-brimmed hiking hats, state-of-the-art hiking shirts that wick away moisture while still keeping them warm, with expensive thermal gloves lying on the table and hiking canes propped against the table. They were drinking lattes and eating a vegan-free breakfast while discussing the effects of global warming on the Antarctic sea lions. Noah sat next to them for a few moments but quickly switched tables.

Kai never appeared this morning. The older lady came to take his order shortly after he moved to a different table. She asked, "What can I get for you, sir?"

He looked up at her and asked, "Is Kai here today?"

She smiled and answered, "You mean Margaret?" Noah reluctantly nodded and she said, "No, she's off today." So, he ordered his coffee and blueberry muffin and wondered if he should pursue this any further, then the lady added, "But if you want to see her, she's playing at the Fiddlin' Fish tonight."

"Playing what?"

"Guitar. She usually plays there a couple of times a week . . . she's good." Noah had heard of Fiddlin' Fish but had never been there. It was a fairly new place on the outskirts of town that catered to the millennial crowd. Then, the lady added, "She's a good singer, too. You should go."

He waited on his muffin while switching his glances from the over-dressed hiking pair to the mass of tourists walking down the street going from one shop to the next. When the lady came back with his order, she caught Noah's eye and asked, "How come you've never asked me what my name is? All these years and you've never asked."

He was not prepared for that question. Before he could think of an answer, she turned and walked back to the kitchen. He started to take a bite of his muffin when he noticed the two hikers staring at him. They were obviously eavesdropping on the conversation and Noah had caught them, which disconcerted them a bit and caused the man to knock over one of his hiking canes.

He picked up his coffee and muffin and walked to the vacant cash register and laid a ten-dollar bill down and left without speaking to anyone else. He walked down the street and sat on a bench outside the Back of Beyond Bookstore. Halfway through his muffin, a man came walking down the street with a large, mutt-like looking dog and stopped at the other end of the bench and the dog urinated on the leg stand of the bench. The man didn't apologize or say anything or admonish the dog for peeing on the street, four feet away from a poor man who just been chastised by an older woman for ignoring her for over four years. Noah wished he would have stayed at home and eaten cereal.

He worked on his column some, but in his present state of mind, he was sensible enough not to say too many dangerous things. So, he washed some clothes, thought about vacuuming, then went to the grocery store. All to pass the time until he could sneak into Fiddlin' Fish that night to see Kai/Margaret play and sing. And just as importantly, to see if there was some kind of banner or poster announcing her performance that would have her name on it.

Once it got dark, Noah dressed in old blue jeans, with a plaid, slightly torn shirt, wore an old ratty-looking beanie cap, and topped it all off with sandals—he now looked like the ultimate, trying-too-hard millennial. Fiddlin' Fish was a micro-brewery which had several of its own brews available. Noah ordered an Ardmore Amber and found a table away from the area set up for the music because he didn't want Kai/Margaret to see him. He did not see any posters announcing who was playing music tonight but when he asked the bartender, he was told that Lulu was playing. Lulu?

The Ardmore Amber was okay, not as good as his regular Black Raven Stout, but okay. He nursed it as long as he could waiting on Lulu to come out and play. He eventually had to order a second one before the music finally commenced. Lulu came out, which was actually Kai/Margaret, and she played an acoustic version of "Blackbird" first, then she started playing and singing. The older waitress was right— she was good.

Noah watched and listened for over an hour until Lulu announced this would be her last song before a short intermission. He decided he would go home after this last song. Just before Lulu started the song, she adjusted her microphone and then turned to look directly into Noah's eyes. It was probably only three or four seconds, but it felt much longer to Noah. Then she played an old Toy Caldwell song:

Gary Hope

Well I'm ridin' along
Singin' the same ol' cowboy song
That's been sung a hundred times before

Ain't got nothin' but my name
And I'm the only woman I know to blame
But I'm livin' I'm happy and I'm free
Just listen to the wind blow
Let it blow let it blow
Sand over my trail
I got my saddle on the ground
And that ol' moon he can still be found
Hidin' in the desert sky

I like simple things in life
Like a prairie breeze
A good stout horse between my knees
Just bein' alone just bein' me
And when I die let me die
With a dream in my mind
A smile on my face and no trouble behind

I got my saddle on the ground
And that ol' moon he can still be found
Hidin' in the desert sky
Won't you bury me with my chaps on
And my six-gun strapped to my side
So I can watch the moon a-hidin'
In the desert sky

He hurried out the door as the applause started for Lulu after the song. He was unlocking the door to his Jeep when he heard someone behind him speak, "Well, did you enjoy the show?"

He turned to see Lulu/Kai/Margaret staring at him. He said, "You're very talented and I finally found out your real name after all these years."

She looked at him and asked, "What do you mean?"

Noah

Noah answered, "You told me your name was Kai. The other waitress told me your name was Margaret. And now I find that it's really Lulu."

She smiled at him and said, "Stage name." She then turned and walked back into the Fish, leaving poor old Noah looking like the dejected, neglected, deflected, and corrected ex-millennial that he was so trying not to be.

18.

"Noah: I was in the grocery store yesterday and these three kids were running around unsupervised and causing all sorts of mischief. What's wrong with people today? It wasn't like that when we were kids, was it? Signed, Ellen."

"Ellen: You might be right. When I was a kid . . . no wait, I still do that."

●●●

"Noah: I'm a high school senior and I want someone to tell me why the schools make us take math and English now. I mean, our iPhones do all the math we need and spellcheck corrects all our writings . . . so why do we need these courses any longer? Signed, Mickey."

"Mickey: I understand what you're saying; however, your iPhone does not always correct punctuation, which can be crucial at times; e.g., 'Let's eat, Grandpa.' vs. 'Let's eat Grandpa.'"

●●●

"Noah: A few of us at work meet for drinks a couple of times each week when we get off. It used to be fun until a new guy, who shall remain nameless, started coming with us. He thinks he knows everything and doesn't hesitate to answer every question about every subject. Should we kill him? Signed, Woody."

Noah

"Woody: Naw, don't kill him. It's not worth it. For most of us normal, intelligent people, life appears infinitely mysterious. But the stupid have an answer for every question . . . like your friend."

19.

IT WAS NOW JUST OVER TWO WEEKS before Dorothy had promised to go visit Noah. She was so scared she couldn't sleep at night. Noah was so excited that he couldn't sleep at night. Ana, his dream girl was finally coming to see him. He knew he loved her personality, her wit, her charm, her intelligence, and her being, but the question remained: Would he love her face? Her body? Her legs? Her figure? Her physical being? Could he "stay" in love with someone with whom he didn't find physically appealing? This was the question he carried around with him day and night. "Why couldn't she look like Dorothy?" This was the second question he carried around in his mind day and night.

Dorothy volunteered for any overtime and extra assignments at work simply to pass the time and get Noah off her mind. One day, the guy who collected all the trash from the containers throughout the park called in sick and Dorothy volunteered to do his job. Her boss wouldn't let her do it because he needed her in the park offices, but she wanted to . . . anything to get her mind off meeting Noah in two weeks.

Noah had the opposite feelings: He could hardly contain his excitement while he waited on her visit. Time seemed to creep so slowly that he searched for anything to fill the void. He went back to his favorite coffee shop most mornings to sip coffee and watch the tourists stroll down the street. Kai/Margaret and the other older lady seemed to take pleasure in withholding Kai's real name from him. However, he did ask the older lady what her name was and she answered truthfully: Luray. Not a name that Noah had heard before, but certainly a name he wouldn't forget.

Kai had been busy at other tables and Noah hadn't spoken to her this morning. As he went to pay the bill, Luray leaned in close to him and half-whispered, "Did you hear about Margaret?"

It took him a moment to understand that she was referring to Kai, "No, what about her?"

Luray looked back towards the kitchen, then said, "She's pregnant. Doesn't want anyone to know yet."

Noah nodded, then asked, "Is she married?"

"No. She's never been married."

"Do you know who the father is?"

Again, Luray looked back towards the kitchen before answering, "No, I have no idea and I don't think she does either!" Noah didn't respond to that statement; he didn't know how to respond to that statement. Luray then continued, "You know how young people are today, not like we used to be—that's for sure." He was hoping Luray wasn't including him in the statement when she said, ". . . not like WE used to be . . ." She was at least fifteen years older than him, maybe twenty.

Luray then handed Noah back his change and said, "You didn't hear this from me." Noah nodded and wished he hadn't heard this news at all. He barely knew Kai/Margaret but he did know that having a baby as a single mother, while working as a waitress during the daytime and singing in a bar at night, might not be the ideal environment for a new mom to cope with.

He went back home and tried to work on his column some but couldn't concentrate because of the news he had just heard. He finally went online and Googled the Fiddlin' Fish and learned that Lulu was playing there again that night. He couldn't explain to himself why, but he wanted to go listen to her again. He had a lot of questions whirling around his head, so he decided to take a nap and rest his thoughts, while he remembered something his dad once told him: "Life isn't as serious as the mind makes it out to be."

●●●

He went to the club a little later than he had the first time he went. This night, Lulu was already on stage singing when he arrived. She was sitting on a stool and playing her guitar while she sang an old Bobbie Gentry song. He remembered the song but doubted any of the millennial audience did. Again, he sat at the rear of the room and tried to be as invisible as possible. During Lulu's break, Noah ordered a Canyonland Stout from the waiter. But, much to his surprise, the young waiter didn't bring his drink back to him—Lulu did. Or, Kai, or Margaret, or whatever her name is.

She handed him the drink and asked, "What are you doing here?"

"Listening to you sing."

"Why?"

Noah sipped his beer and answered, "Because."

She didn't respond but stood there staring at him. Noah couldn't help himself as he casually looked down at her stomach to see if her pregnancy was apparent yet. She saw him look down and said, "Luray told you, didn't she?"

"Told me what?" Kai didn't appreciate his attempt at innocence and pursed her lips and rolled her eyes at him. So, he answered, "Okay, yeah she told me."

"What, exactly, did she say?"

"She said you were pregnant and that you weren't married."

Kai nodded, then asked, "Is that all?"

"What do you mean, 'Is that all?'"

Noah

"Did she tell you who the father is?"

Noah developed a couple of small beads of sweat on his forehead as he lied, "No, that subject never came up."

She started to walk away, then stopped and turned back to Noah and said, "Liar." She sang the rest of her set sitting on her stool facing away from Noah. At the end of her show, Kai stood up from the stool to sing her last song. She looked directly at him and started singing:

> *When the world is ready to fall on your little shoulders*
> *And when you're feeling lonely and small*
> *You need somebody there to hold you*
>
> *You can call out my name*
> *When you're only lonely*
> *Now don't you ever be ashamed*
> *You're only lonely*
>
> *When you need somebody around on the nights that try you*
> *Remember I was there when you were a king*
> *And I'll be the last one there beside you*
>
> *So you can call out my name*
> *When you're only lonely*
> *All you gotta do is call me*
> *When you're only lonely.*

He stayed until she finished and left the stage before he went outside to his car. He looked around but didn't see her anywhere in the parking lot, so he drove home. How did she know he was lonely?

He had two emails from Ana when he arrived. He read each of them three times, then sent her a long message back before he went to bed. After he brushed his teeth and took a shower, he laid in bed and thought of Ana. It was hard thinking of someone he'd never met. He just thought of HER. As he was doing this, he was absently holding the arrowhead Dorothy had given him . . . rubbing the smooth surface of it and feeling the sharp edges. It made him feel good, not so lonely.

In the morning, he started to stay home and work on his column at the paper, but he didn't. He went to the coffee shop for his blueberry muffin and coffee, hoping he'd run into Kai. Before he even sat down, the older woman, Luray, came over to him and said, "I thought you were going to keep our secret private? Last time I ever tell you anything!" Then she huffed away. He started to just turn around and leave . . . he should have.

He sat at his favorite window seat for about ten minutes before Kai finally came over. At least she was carrying his order, so he wouldn't have to wait any longer. She sat it on the table, never looked at him, never said a word, then turned and left. He watched her walk away towards the kitchen, then looked down to find a cup of tea and a plain bagel in front of him. Tea and a bagel! He thought, *Really?*

He tried to sip the tea but gave up after a couple of tastes. He didn't even attempt to taste the bland-looking bagel. He didn't know what tea and bagels cost, but he got out a five-dollar bill and laid it next to the cash register on his way out the door. Now he was forced to walk down the block to the local Starbucks and drink a cup of their five-dollar coffee, which he didn't even like, but what's a man to do?

Kai went into the kitchen and cried. Luray tried to comfort her, without success. Kai was not the type of girl to easily break down; she tended to hold everything inside and not depend on others. She had been supporting herself since she was sixteen and was kicked out of a foster home for playing her guitar too loud. Everything seemed to have settled down in her life after that. She lied about her age and told everyone she was eighteen and found jobs waitressing.

She moved to Moab with a young man who she thought loved her . . . and he may have for a while. He was also a guitar player and they played in bars and clubs making money on the side. For a few years,

Noah

Kai was truly enjoying life. Then she got pregnant. Her boyfriend bolted at the news and stole some money Kai had hidden in their apartment. He left without a word and she has no idea where he went. She did not want anyone taking pity on her, though; she was confident she would be fine. That's why she was upset that Luray told Noah about her pregnancy. She thought he only came to the club because he felt sorry for her: single, pregnant, and all alone. She started another pot of coffee brewing and thought to herself, *What's a girl to do?*

The exact same thought that Dorothy had, sitting in her office, at Death Valley National Park, *What's a girl to do?* The night before, she had made a to-do list of things to do before she went to meet Noah for the first time: have her nails done, get a pedicure, have her hair trimmed, put white-strips on her teeth, and not eat anything but stale, green, yucky, no-fat food for the next ten days. As she was studying her list, the park superintendent walked in her office and told her that he needed her to go to Las Vegas the coming weekend for a conference on global warming and how it was affecting the national parks.

Dorothy dutifully replied, "Yes, sir, no problem." While she thought to herself, *Global warming . . . in Death Valley? So what if it's 114 degrees or 116 degrees?* But she took all the information from her boss and told him she'd be there and represent their office. He knew she would . . . Dorothy would always do what was needed. She was a good girl. When he left her office, Dorothy thought, *Vegas? Yep, I'll go to Vegas and get Noah off my mind. I can do Sin City. I can have fun. I, Dorothy, can be bad!*

20.

DOROTHY'S BOSS GAVE HER THURSDAY AND FRIDAY OFF to drive over to Las Vegas for the convention, which was very nice since the convention didn't begin until Saturday morning. Plus, the park service paid for her room at Bally's Hotel and Casino and gave her vouchers for food. Dorothy had driven through Las Vegas before but had never stayed there overnight. She packed a business suit for the conference on Saturday, and she also packed the three shortest dresses she owned. She wanted to see Vegas and she wanted Vegas to see her.

She arrived late Thursday afternoon and was a little embarrassed giving the keys to her eight-year-old pickup truck to the valet attendant. She hadn't even washed it once this year. He didn't care; he just smiled and waited for his tip. Although he was a little disappointed with the $2 Dorothy left him, he did enjoy looking at her legs as she got out of the truck. She passed rows and rows of clinking and jingling slot machines on her way to the receptionist's desk. Vegas could easily overwhelm and astound a country girl from Robeson County, North Carolina.

She checked into her room and stood at the window on the seventeenth floor and took in the vista of the famous Las Vegas Strip. All the glamourous hotels were lined up: Caesar's Palace, Bellagio, MGM Grand, on and on they went, down to the end where the skyscraping Stratosphere Tower grabbed her attention. She made a mental note to go there and take the elevator to the top of that magnificent structure. But first, down to the casino and try her luck at the slots!

She soon found out the basic premise of slot machines: anyone can play, no one can win. It didn't take her long to lose her first twenty dollars in the quarter slots. Then she switched to the nickel slots and lost ten dollars more. At least she got two free drinks for her time there. She roamed around and took in all the sights of the hotel and casino, but the dress shoes she had on with her short skirt were killing her feet. She saw an open bar and took a seat at the end nearest the casino so she could gaze into the euphoric unknown.

She ordered a glass of white wine and figured she could sip it slowly enough to last until dinner time. All the card games, the slot machines, the roulette wheels . . . it all overwhelmed her. She could sit and people gaze all afternoon while slowly sipping her wine. She was so taken in with the scenery, she didn't even notice the average-looking, moderately-dressed, unassuming thief who sat two stools down from her. When he noticed her staring at the jingling sound of someone hitting a ten-dollar pot at a slot machine, he stole her pocketbook.

She didn't even notice it was missing until she wanted to order another glass of wine. By then, it was much too late. The $180 she brought with her was gone. Her credit card and driver's license were gone. The keys to her office and apartment—all gone. She couldn't even remember what sort of credit card she had so she couldn't call to cancel the card. All she could do was cry. The police tried to help but honestly, there wasn't much they could do. Dorothy filed a report and got a replacement room key from the hotel. She had no money, no credit card, and no truck keys. She went up to her room and stared out at the sun setting behind the Stratosphere tower as she thought, *What's a girl to do?*

About an hour later, she received a call from the police. They had found her pocketbook in an alley. It still contained her keys and driver's license, and incredibly enough, even her credit card. The money was gone. The police figured the thief knew it would be hard for him to buy anything with the card knowing it had Dorothy's name on it. At least she could drive her truck and buy gas and food now. She spent her first night in Vegas ordering room service and watching an old movie on Lifetime. She was really doing a pitiful job of being "bad."

●●●

She went to sleep thinking of Noah. Thinking of the look on his face when she tells him she is actually his elusive Ana. What he might say. What he might do. When she finally went to sleep, she slept until nearly 11:00 Friday morning. She drank some of the stale, bland coffee that was from the machine in her room. Then, she decided to get in her truck and explore. She realized the Las Vegas life was not for her. She didn't have any cash to pay the valet for getting her truck for her. She tried to explain her situation to him but he just shook his head and said, "Forget it, lady."

"Lady?" She was probably younger than he was. When did she become a "lady?" Anyway, he skulked off and she set her GPS for the Hoover Dam. This incredible piece of engineering is tucked away on the border of Arizona and Nevada in the depths of Black Canyon on the Colorado River. Dorothy had always read about it and now she was less than two hours away from seeing it.

The traffic thinned out as she left the city. It soon became just desert and cactus and low-level mountains—all beautiful to Dorothy. When she arrived at the dam there was a crowd already there. She parked next to a car from Marysville, Washington, then noticed nearly every car in the lot was from some other state in the Union. She walked across the gigantic dam and stopped midway across to gaze across Lake Powell on one side and down into the depths of Black Canyon on the other side. The dam itself is 726 feet tall, which is 171 feet taller than the Washington Monument.

Noah

She saw a sign for elevator rides to the bottom of the dam and bought a ticket for it. Arriving at the bottom, where the Colorado River rushes out on its way to a slow death somewhere in California, she and all the other tourists looked up to the top of the dam and hoped this mighty structure didn't cave in. After walking around and seeing the sights, just before she got back in the elevator, she thought to herself, "I wish Noah could see this."

She drove around some back roads, out in the wilderness, before starting back for Las Vegas. As she began entering civilization again, she saw a sign for a casino that didn't look any bigger than her office building at Death Valley. She pulled in and parked with about a dozen other cars. Upon entering, she found the place to be old but well kept. It was mostly all slot machines, with row after row of penny slots. Dorothy sat down and let her mind wander as she put in two dollars and played penny slots for the next three hours. Whenever thoughts of Noah would creep in, she'd play two pennies to build the excitement. She finally became hungry and thirsty, so she cashed out and had only lost seventy-three cents in three hours. Not bad.

She made it back to her room at Bally's but didn't have the same enthusiasm that she did before. She went to her room and ordered a pizza from room service, while she watched a love story on the local movie channel. It was a story of a boy and girl who eventually overcame all the odds and ended up together in a beautiful ending. She wondered if anything in real life ever ended like that. Then she wondered how her life would end with Noah. In less than two weeks, she would find out . . . and she was starting to dread it.

The next day she went to the conference and listened to some so-called experts tell the attendees how they could help influence the world's increasing heat index. She didn't pay any attention to most of it. She daydreamed throughout the morning, had lunch with some total strangers, made sure her name was filed on the guest list, and then faded out the back door the first chance she got. She packed her bags and didn't even stay her last night at Bally's. She drove out of town and bought a large coffee at a convenience store, then set out for Death Valley National Park. She wanted to go home.

21.

When Dorothy arrived back home, the first thing she did, after using the bathroom, was to turn on her computer. As she had hoped, there were three messages from Noah. The first one read:

"My dear Ana, I can hardly believe it! In about two weeks we will finally meet. I have about a thousand questions for you and another thousand things I want to show you around the beautiful canyonland country where I live. Do you have anything special you'd like to see? If not, don't worry, I'll make sure you see everything that is important. Can't wait to finally meet you.
Always, your Noah"

The second message read:

"Dear, beautiful Ana, I am so excited that I can hardly sleep at night. Are you excited as I am? Just think, in a matter of days now we'll be together and there'll be no more wondering about each other. I've had a thousand pictures of you in my mind, now I'll finally get to see the woman I know is as beautiful as I've always dreamed.
See you soon, Noah"

And the third message:

"Dearest Ana, I haven't heard from you lately. Is everything okay? Please, don't worry about anything. I'm positive everything will be as we always hope it would be-- fantastic!
Your one and only, Noah"

After reading the second email, Dorothy almost started crying. After reading the third email, she did start crying . . . and found it hard to stop. After unpacking her bags and putting everything away, she realized she had another email, though not from Noah. This last message was from the counselor she met a while back, over in California, Shirley Hudgins. It read:

"Dear Dorothy, I've been thinking a lot about you and your situation. Please feel free to call me anytime if you need to talk; my personal number is on the card I gave you. Lib and I have discussed your situation a thousand times over the last few weeks. We'd love to help if we can. Please let me know if there's anything I can do.
Your friend, Shirley"

This made Dorothy feel a lot better, knowing there was someone who knew the truth and wanted to help her. Someone who wanted things to turn out well for her. Someone who was on her side. Someone who she could fall back on when the bottom dropped out after she met Noah. This eased her mind and took some of the focus out of the dread that was building up inside her. Still, it was a long, restless night.

● ● ●

Noah was so excited that he could barely go to sleep at night. In a few short days, he was finally going to meet Ana, the woman of his dreams. He woke early, yearning for his daily muffin and coffee from the shop downtown; however, he decided it might be prudent to avoid the coffee shop for a few days and let Kai/Margaret and Luray cool off a bit. He decided to visit Starbucks instead. He didn't really like Starbucks coffee and they had nothing that compared to the blueberry muffins at his coffee shop. But he would make that sacrifice, however brutal it might be.

Everyone inside Starbucks was either on their iPhones or their iPads. No one was actually speaking to another human. Noah had risen early and there weren't any tourists on the street for him to look at, so he sat at the window seat and mindlessly searched his own phone for something to hold his attention. Kai was walking down the street to start her day at the coffee shop when she looked in the window at Starbucks and saw him sitting there staring at his phone.

She turned around and went inside and walked up to his table and said, "What's wrong? Our coffee not good enough for you any longer?" Noah was so shocked that at first, he could only stare at her, saying nothing in reply. So she spoke again, "I guess I'll tell Luray that her muffins weren't up to your standards."

He recovered and answered, "No, it's not that, I love her muffins."

"Oh, it's just our coffee that you hate."

"No . . . I love your coffee, too. You know that."

Kai stared down at him at replied, "Well, if you like our muffins and our coffee, why in the world are you at this dump?"

Noah thought, *Why is she calling this place a dump? It's nice in here.* Then he answered, "I thought you and Luray might need a few days without me bothering you."

Kai leaned her head a little closer to him and said, "Pour that crap out and come on down to the shop and get you some good stuff." With that said, she turned and walked out the door. Noah then rose, dumped his coffee in the trash can, and followed her. She didn't wait for him. When he walked in the door, he saw Luray's face turn from smile to frown. Then he saw Kai talking to her and was hoping things would return to normal soon. He didn't want to have to worry about someone spitting in his coffee each morning when they delivered it to him.

Kai and Luray walked back into the kitchen and Kai came out with a tray, which she brought over to Noah with his blueberry muffin and coffee on it. He wanted to look closely into the coffee to see if he could tell if someone had spit in it, but Kai was watching him. He poured a little milk in and sipped it, then said, "Umm, much better than Starbucks."

Kai smiled, then went back to the counter. It was still fairly early and the tourists were still asleep, so Noah ate his muffin, drank his coffee, got a refill, paid his bill, and by the time he left, both Kai and Luray were smiling at him again. It was a good day. He went back home and decided to answer a few emails from work, his mood had definitely brightened.

"Noah: My wife and I just celebrated our 50th wedding anniversary. We're in great health for our age, but sometimes our memory fades a little. After the anniversary party that night, my wife told me she couldn't remember the first time we had sex. I could never forget it! Do you remember the first time you had sex? Signed, Donald."

"Donald: First, congratulations! Fifty years is really special. And to answer your question, yes, I do remember the first time I had sex. I kept the receipt."

"Noah: I'm trying to figure you out and I can't. Just when you make a little sense, you go and say something stupid. Why do you do that? Signed, Christine."

"Christine: I write because I don't know what I think until I read what I say. Hope that clears it up for you."

"Noah: I have a small legal thing I need to get taken care of. The yellow pages are slammed with all sorts of lawyers. How can you tell a good one from a bad one? Any ideas? Signed, Ed."

"Ed: In my opinion, a lawyer is a man who knows a hundred ways of making love but doesn't know any women."

"Noah: I have something to admit; anonymously, of course. I'm not who people think I am. I'm a manager at a large company here in town and I have to be the man in charge. People look to me to make major decisions and lead them into profitability and success. They expect me to be invulnerable and invincible! They are wrong. In fact, most of the time I'm scared to death I'm making a bad decision that could hurt my employees. What do you think of that? Signed, Bulletproof."

"Bulletproof: Most of us go through life thinking we're invincible, but the truth is, we're totally vincible."

Noah

"Noah: Our book club sometimes reads your columns at our meetings—for fun. However, no one seems to know anything about you, the person. We know you're single but we don't know what type of woman you're attracted to. Can you tell us? We're very interested. Signed, Heather."

"Heather: My, oh my, what an interesting question. I'll try to be as truthful as I can and hope I don't hurt anyone's feelings. But, honestly, I like women who are so thin that buzzards follow them to their car. Mmmm."

Noah felt like his old self again. His entire perspective on life had changed. His job was going great. Ana was coming to visit him. Kai and Luray were smiling at him again. Why, then why, was he still holding the arrowhead from Dorothy in his hand every spare minute?

22.

AS GOOD AS NOAH WAS FEELING, Dorothy was feeling that much worse. Dread was creeping in over the looming meeting with Noah. She had again convinced herself that it would be a total disaster and that she would cause the man that she loved to be as disappointed as anyone could ever be when he saw who she truly was. She needed a friend. She needed to talk to someone, but not someone from work; they could never find out how despicable she had become. She found Shirley Hudgins' card and stared at it for several minutes before finally deciding to call her.

The first three phone calls went unanswered. Dorothy didn't leave a message, deciding to have dinner and wait a couple of hours. The problem with that plan was that she was so despondent and excited at the prospect of talking to someone that she couldn't eat anything. So she kept calling every fifteen minutes. Finally . . .

"Hello?"

"Shirley, it's me, Dorothy. I had an appointment with you a few weeks ago . . . do you remember me?"

"Of course I do, Dorothy. How are you?"

"I'm not good, Shirley. Not good at all. I'm supposed to visit Noah in a few days and I'm completely dreading it and I think it'll be a disaster."

Noah

"No, honey, you're doing the right thing. You have to let him know who you are. How will you ever be able to live with yourself if you don't?"

"But, Shirley, he thinks I'm this goddess, Ana. When he sees who I am, just some hick girl from North Carolina, he'll probably cuss me out or punch me in the nose for the way I've been deceiving him. And I wouldn't blame him!"

The conversation continued that way for forty-five minutes, but Shirley eventually proved she was good at her job. Dorothy, once again, committed to following through on her visit to see Noah, but this time with one condition: Shirley would come with her for support. Not actually meeting Noah, but driving to Moab with her the day before, getting a hotel room together, and giving her moral support up until the time she left to meet him. Shirley agreed to everything. What Shirley didn't tell Dorothy was that this was the most excitement she'd had in her life in years! She felt a connection with Dorothy, like the daughter she never had. She wouldn't let Dorothy miss her chance at love and happiness, as she had done many years ago—she would not let that happen.

Shirley had been consumed with work and advancement her entire life and had always let personal relationships take a back seat to professional priorities. She'd let several interested men fade from her life because her work was more important. Now she was regretting those choices and there was no way in the world she was going to let Dorothy make the same mistake she'd made over and over. No way!

Meanwhile, with each passing day, Noah found it harder and harder to contain his excitement. As soon as he finished his work duties and his house cleaning duties, he was bouncing off the walls with anticipation of Ana's visit. He washed a few clothes and ate a sandwich, then waited for darkness to fall so he could visit the Moab Brewery and spend some time around people rather than with his thoughts and excitement. He had to park in the lot next door to the brewery because of the big crowd. He figured he'd go in to see if he could find a seat at the bar and either spot an old friend or just watch the tourists, which was usually a good night's entertainment in itself.

If there wasn't a seat available, he could always try the Fiddlin' Fish again, but he'd rather give Kai a few days to get back to normal, before talking to her again.

As soon as he walked in the brewery, he saw a young man guzzling the last drops from his bottle and then fist bump an older man seated next to him. He then got up and left the bar. Noah quickly went over to the empty barstool and asked the older man if this seat was free and the older guy told him it was all his. He sat and the older man said, "My name's Mike. You from around here?"

Noah ordered his usual Black Raven Stout, then answered, "Yes, sir, I am. Moab's a nice little place if you don't mind all the tourists. And even if you do, the scenery makes up for it all."

The older man smiled, then turned on his stool to face Noah, and said, "I'm a tourist."

Noah grinned and said, "I know you are. I was just messing with you, Mike. Nice to meet you."

Mike slapped Noah on the back and said, "I like you, son. What sort of work do you do around here? Cowboy? Miner? Tour guide? Professional lady's man?"

Noah smiled back and said, "All of the above, Mike. We locals have to be well-rounded." He never liked to tell people he was a columnist; he liked to keep that part of his life private. Then he asked Mike, "What do you do when you're not out here visiting God's country?"

"I taught philosophy until last year when I retired. Now, I just travel around, mostly out west, and try to see what I've missed all these years."

"Where'd you teach?"

"Northern Arizona University, in Flagstaff. It's a nice little school. I had a great time there. And before you ask, no, I'm not married, just on my own. You married?"

Noah

"No, sir, I'm not. But you know what? That might change soon. I'm meeting a young lady in a few days who is very special, and if I ever do get married, she just might be the one."

Mike smiled and replied, "That's great! I wish you great luck with that. What's her name?"

Noah smiled broadly and said, "Ana."

"Ana . . . that just sounds like a pretty woman. Tell me about her."

Noah took a long drink of his stout, then answered, "She is just someone that I look forward to talking to every day. I can't stop thinking about her and we just seem to be on the same wavelength. You know what I mean, Mike?"

Mike laughed and said, "Yeah, I think I do. What's she look like, if you don't mind me asking?"

Uh, oh . . . Noah didn't want to fall into this trap again. So, he hedged: "Mike, she's the type of woman that you think about when you're lying in bed at night and lonely as all get out. That's my Ana. Does that make sense?"

Mike paused, then patted him on the shoulder again, and replied, "Not really but I wish it did. I really, truly wish it did. You know, friend, sometimes you have to stop thinking so much and just go where your heart takes you."

Both men sat back and thought about that statement. Then, out of the blue, the unexpected happened. Vicki, Noah's old sex-friend, stepped right between Noah and Mike, wearing a very low-cut blouse, which made thinking rationally very difficult.

She looked at Mike and said, "Good evening, sir, I hope you're doing well. A word of advice, however." She then pointed at Noah and said, "Don't believe anything this low-down lying slut tells you. He can't be trusted." She smiled at Mike and continued, "Have a nice night, sir." Then she turned and walked away as every man in the bar watched--with pleasure.

After they recovered, Noah said, "Sorry about that, Mike. I just didn't want to get in an argument with her."

Mike nodded, took a small sip of his drink, then answered, "I totally understand. There are two theories to arguing with a woman. Neither works."

Noah then explained a little about his history with Vicki, leaving out some of the more lurid details, and finished by saying, "It's just that Ana has always been my dream girl. I don't know what else to say, Mike."

Mike looked directly in Noah's eyes and said, "Son, dream until your dream comes true."

Noah liked that. He liked it a lot. He said, "I can see why you taught philosophy at a university, Mike. You're a smart guy!"

He raised his glass to toast with Mike, then Mike added, "Be careful thinking like that, son. The thing about smart people is that they seem like crazy people to dumb people."

Noah wasn't sure if Mike was complimenting him or making fun of him; either way, they both toasted again as each guy watched Vicki from afar . . . thinking the same types of things that every guy in the bar was thinking. Noah finished his drink and decided he'd go home and email Ana. He enjoyed his short visit with the tourist, Mike. As he rose to leave and shake Mike's hand, he said, "Sir, it's the little things like our short conversation here that makes life fun. Thanks."

Mike nodded and smiled as he shook Noah's hand, but didn't let go until he added, "Enjoy the little things, son, for one day you may look back and realize that they were the big things. And then, ask yourself this question: How long can a man nourish himself on reminiscence alone?"

●●●

When Noah got back home, he opened his computer and wrote Ana a long email. Then, he thought, "I'm going to send her a picture of me just so she won't be surprised when she gets here." He got his cell phone and took six selfies of himself, trying to figure out which one was the most flattering. He really didn't like any of them but picked the one that looked the least annoying. He attached it to the email and sent the message to Ana. She would be here soon. He tried reading a little but couldn't concentrate. He started to work on his column from work but the same thing: he couldn't concentrate. He finally just laid in bed, while unconsciously picking up the arrowhead from Dorothy, and turned the light off while letting his mind roam wherever it might go. It didn't go far.

He thought about Ana coming and wondered what it would be like. He was both excited and apprehensive . . . he couldn't help it. He also couldn't help clutching the arrowhead tightly in his hand while visualizing the image of Dorothy in his mind. Thinking of Ana, yet visualizing Dorothy. Why did his mind have to be so cruel?

Dorothy opened the email from Noah and noticed there was an attachment. She opened it and saw the picture he had sent. She stared at the picture for so long that she lost track of time; she had yet to even read the message. After reading the message from Noah four times, she then emailed the attachment to her new friend Shirley, so she could see what Noah looked like. Less than three minutes after sending the picture, Dorothy got a reply from Shirley: "Dorothy, I received the picture and WOW! What a stud! Does he have any older brothers you could introduce me to? Or, maybe even his father! Seriously, he looks great. I can't wait to meet him. Your friend, Shirley."

It was hard for Dorothy to go to sleep after all that. The exhilaration of seeing Noah's picture, along with the dread of meeting him, and seeing the disappointment on his face, which she was convinced of, were almost too much for her to cope with. It would be a long, hard day's night.

●●●

The following morning when Noah woke, all he could think about was: *Two more days! Two more days and Ana will be here.* He jumped in his Jeep and drove downtown to the coffee shop, mulling over whether he should mention Ana's coming to Kai. He decided not to. When he walked in, he saw two people sitting at his favorite table.

He was strange about his table--he felt like it was HIS table, not some tourists from Wakulla. As he was standing there, deciding his options, Kai came from the kitchen carrying a tray over to the table with the two tourists. She had two blueberry muffins and two cups of coffee--HIS BREAKFAST!

When Kai set everything down, she started to turn away from the table and one of the tourists said, "Thanks, Kali. You were right, this looks great." Kai smiled and walked right past Noah, never making eye contact with him. Noah turned again to look at the tourists and noticed one of them had on a t-shirt with Dubrovnik printed on it.

He wondered to himself, *Why are these tourists sitting at my table, eating my breakfast, calling Kai by the name Kali, and wearing a Dubrovnik t-shirt . . . wherever in the world that is?* As he was trying to assimilate all this information, the older lady, Luray, called over to tell him there was a table open at the back wall. Noah frowned, then glared at the tourists, before slowly making his way to the back table. He wasn't happy. After a few minutes, Kai, Margaret, Lulu, Kali, or whatever her name is, came to his table and looked down at him before saying, "Can I help you?"

Noah looked up at her at asked, "Can you help me?"

"Yes, what can I bring you?"

He tapped his fingers on the table, then picked up a packet of sugar, and answered, "Five years, three or four times a week, fifty-two weeks a year--the same order every time and now you're asking me, 'Can I help you?'"

Kai's expression never changed as she asked, "Well?"

He took a deep breath, then said very slowly, "A cup of coffee with a blueberry muffin. The same thing THEY got!" He was pointing to the two tourists.

Kai took her note pad out and, very slowly, wrote Noah's order in the book. "Cup of coffee and blueberry bagel, right?"

"Right. NO!! Wait, not a blueberry bagel, a blueberry muffin! You know that, Kai!"

Kai nodded, then said, "Who?"

Before Noah could explode, she turned and went to the kitchen. He looked over at the tourists again and they were looking towards him, obviously hearing the commotion he had created. Without thinking, he quickly rose and walked over to them and said, "I'm sorry to bother you at your breakfast, but do you happen to know the name of the waitress who brought your food out?"

Before the one tourist could speak, the other one grabbed his arm and said, "I don't think we should be giving out any privileged information to people we don't know. Sorry."

"I'm just asking if you know what her name is. That's all."

The tourist replied, "I think you should ask her, sir. If she wants to tell you, that's her decision."

Before Noah could lose his cool, Luray stepped over and asked, "Is everything okay here?" No one spoke, so Noah turned and went back to his table. When he got there, his blueberry muffin and coffee were already there and Kai was nowhere in sight. He ate the muffin and drank the coffee, but he didn't enjoy it . . . not at all.

He went back home and tried to cool down. Maybe answering a few questions from work would help.

"Noah: My wife started buying decaffeinated coffee for us because she likes to drink coffee at night when she's watching TV and this decaffeinated stuff won't keep her awake. I hate it! She told me to stop whining and that I'd learn to like it. I doubt that will ever happen. What's your opinion of decaf? Signed, Lance."

"Lance: To me, decaffeinated coffee is like a hooker who only wants to cuddle."

● ● ●

"Noah: I've been divorced for about seven years now. A few months ago I ran into my ex at a party and, incredibly enough, we hit it off again, just like old times. These last months have been great; I really think he's a changed man. It's almost like divine intervention has brought us back together. Some of my friends are happy but some of them are leery—they knew my ex in the past. Do you have any advice or thoughts? Signed, Diane."

"Diane: Sometimes God sends an ex back into your life to see if you're still stupid. Only you can answer that question."

This last question from Diane and the events from the coffee shop earlier in the morning made Noah think. He decided not to answer any more questions for his column until later . . . when his brain had settled down. It was a good decision.

23.

SHIRLEY ARRIVED EARLY IN THE MORNING at Dorothy's place to pick her up. She was very excited and couldn't wait to get on the road for their trip over to Moab to meet Noah. Dorothy was so nervous that she hadn't slept all night. Shirley programmed Noah's address in her GPS and they were off. Shirley was talking up a storm, while Dorothy was still wondering if she should just jump out of the car at the next stop. The trip from Death Valley, where Dorothy lived, to Moab, where Noah lived, is just over 600 miles, which should take about nine hours if they didn't stop too often. However, before they'd even driven thirty minutes, Dorothy had to stop for a bathroom break--nerves.

Shirley tried to get Dorothy to talk about her childhood, her college years, anything at all, but Dorothy was too preoccupied to think about anything except the impending doom and despair she was certain would come her way when she met Noah. Shirley was one of the many people who had never traveled through southern Utah before-- she knew nothing about life outside California. Finally, she now found a topic that brought Dorothy out of her malaise. She started, "I remember that you used to work at a place in Utah, didn't you?"

This question immediately brought a smile to Dorothy's face. "Yes, Canyonlands National Park. I loved it."

Without thinking, Shirley asked, "Why'd you leave?" She had forgotten that Canyonlands was where Dorothy first met Noah. She looked over at Dorothy for an answer but Dorothy only stared at her. After about ten seconds, Shirley realized her mistake. She quickly came up with another question, "What kind of a place is Canyonlands? Do you think I'd like it?"

Dorothy now smiled and answered, "Only if you enjoy unbridled natural beauty that can't be rivaled anywhere else." For the next forty-five minutes, Dorothy told Shirley stories and vivid descriptions of the park she missed so much.

At one point, Shirley asked, "So, you like Canyonlands better than where you are now in Death Valley?"

Dorothy thought a few seconds and then answered, "It's like when you open a Christmas present and it's a nice toaster that you've been wanting. Then you open the next present and it's the keys to a new car out in the driveway. You like your toaster, but there's no way it can compare to a new car."

Shirley smiled but didn't respond. It was enough to see the joy on Dorothy's face as she remembered Canyonlands. They stopped for gas and bathroom breaks on the outskirts of a small town. Then they opted for drive-through burgers and fries before resuming the trip. Dorothy napped some, because she hadn't slept the night before, and Shirley ate the leftover fries Dorothy didn't want. She was content to look all around her at the desert scenery in southern Utah. When they were about thirty miles from Moab, Dorothy woke and was surprised to see how close they were. Both of them needed a bathroom, but in this remote area, unless you wanted to go behind a rock or a cactus, you just had to hold it for a while.

As they crossed over the Colorado River into the Moab city limits, they stopped at a gas station to fill up the car and empty their bladders. Just across the street was a parking lot where people gathered for river rafting trips, like the one she went on with Noah way back when. As she waited for Shirley to come back from the restroom, she had quick visions of that rafting trip: talking with Noah in the raft, sitting around the campfire with him, seeing each other nude as the entire rafting party went skinny dipping the final night on the river, and final and most agonizing memory of all, listening to Noah talk about his *Ana* and how much he missed her. Describing how *Ana* was like no one he'd ever met before. This really hurt, since he'd been with her, Dorothy, for a week now on the river. Did he want her? No! All he cared about was some phantom figure of his imagination--*Ana*. Dorothy hated Ana.

Dorothy had reserved them rooms at a place on the outskirts of town, just down the street from a new place called the Fiddlin' Fish. Dorothy had never been there since it wasn't open when she lived in Moab. They were both tired from the long drive, but after they stored their things in their rooms, Shirley wanted Dorothy to show her Moab. It was the least she could do after Shirley drove them all the way here. She only hoped that she didn't accidentally run into Noah--Moab was a small town, after all.

Her meeting with Noah was scheduled for tomorrow. She told Noah she would email him when she got there. She didn't want him to know she was already here; she needed time to prepare, time to get her courage up, and time to figure out an exit plan when disaster struck. Dorothy drove Shirley around Moab and showed her where she used to live, where the Moab Brewery was, and several shops on Main Street she liked. Shirley could easily tell that Dorothy loved the little town and missed it terribly.

They stopped and had a salad and a glass of wine before heading back to the motel. Dorothy had called her old boss at Canyonlands National Park and he invited her over to his house for a visit. Dorothy wanted to bring Shirley along but Shirley declined; she knew it would be better if Dorothy went alone. Dorothy took the car and went to see her old boss while Shirley took a shower and relaxed. After her shower, Shirley looked out the front window and saw the Fiddlin' Fish just down the street. She liked a glass of wine in the evenings and decided to take her laptop over there and catch up on all her emails with a nice glass of Utah's best wine. The Fish wasn't too busy but Shirley didn't want to occupy a table all to herself, so she just sat at the bar and opened up her laptop.

She decided on a nice pinot grigio from Castle Creek Winery, outside of Moab. The work emails never stop, even when you're on vacation. She dutifully answered them all and then eased her mind while she thought about her friend and what might happen at her meeting tomorrow with Noah. She wished she could be there to help . . . but, she knew she couldn't. Dorothy was all alone with this one.

●●●

Noah had slept like a log. When he woke, his first thoughts were about Ana's arrival the next day. No coffee shop this morning to ruin his mood. He needed to vacuum, clean, and polish up his condo because Ana would be here tomorrow. He spent most of the day cleaning, a little of the day answering questions for his column, and the rest of the day sitting on the back patio staring off towards the La Sal Mountains. He thought, *I should take Ana up there camping. As cold as it gets, she'll have no choice but to cuddle up close to me in the sleeping bag. Great idea! Then, I'll take her hiking in Arches National Park and warn her to look out for rattlesnakes; that way she'll stay close to me for protection. Then, we'll go rafting on the Colorado River and I'll get one of those small rafts that only holds two people and she'll have to sit close to me, with her legs touching mine.*

His mind was buzzing with all sorts of thoughts like these when he then heard an actual buzzing sound, like the sound that night when a snake bit his toe. He quickly looked around his patio, then eased inside and shut the door. No reason to take chances when Ana is on the way. The sun had started to set and he ate a quick sandwich then thought he would go down to Fiddlin' Fish for a drink and see if Kai was singing that night. He changed into his millennial clothes and hopped into the Jeep. A few minutes later, he was there.

Shirley had ordered a second glass of pinot grigio and started scrolling through old emails. She stopped at the message she had received from Dorothy that had the picture of Noah. She enlarged Noah's picture so that it took up her entire screen--she wanted to study his face for a few minutes. Noah entered the bar but heard no music playing. That was okay; he'd just have a beer or two then go back home. He decided to visit the restroom first and headed that way, which was on the other side of the bar. As he walking behind the row of bar stools towards the bathroom, something caught his eye. An older woman was sitting there with her laptop open and HIS picture was on her screen!

HIS PICTURE!! The picture he had taken and sent to Ana! He hadn't sent that picture to anyone else-- no one! He was so flabbergasted by this turn of events that he completely forgot about the bathroom; instead, he turned and walked to the back of the bar. He stared at the older lady, then thought, *I must've seen that wrong. That couldn't have been my picture. No one has that picture except Ana.* He walked back toward the bar and stopped directly behind the woman so he could see clearly--it was his picture, no doubt about it.

He quickly walked back to the rear and sat by himself at a table. He was in a complete and utter daze. He wondered why this older woman had his picture on her computer? He had only sent that picture to Ana. Then it dawned on him: *Is this Ana? I've never seen her before. She's never really told me how old she is. Is this why she never sent me a picture of herself? Because she's twenty years older than me.* He kept staring at the older woman. He saw her turn and look left, then right. She was an attractive older woman, but at least twenty years older than him. How could this be?

A waitress stopped by but he was too flummoxed to order anything. His main priority now was to somehow exit the bar without Ana seeing him. If he could do this, then he'd go home and figure out what to do, what options he had. He made it to the parking lot and his Jeep but couldn't get the key to open the door. He was scared to death Ana was going to come out of the bar and see him before he could get in. *Why won't my door open? Is God punishing me?* Then he realized it wasn't his Jeep at all; not even the same color as his. He looked around, found his Jeep, and quickly drove away. All the way home he kept muttering to himself, *Oh, my God. Oh, my God. Oh, my God.*

The older woman was attractive, but . . . twenty years?!? His mind was whirling as if it was in a tornado. What does he do? He quickly reached under his sink, behind the dishwashing liquid, and pulled out an old bottle of Maker's Mark whiskey. It had been left there years ago from a housewarming party. He unscrewed the cap and poured some into a glass with a few ice cubes. It was terrible! He poured it out and looked for something else. He didn't have anything except some Diet Mtn Dews, as he thought, *why?* Not, why did he only have Diet Mtn Dews, but why was Ana twenty years older than he thought she was?

He paced, he swore, he ate cookies, and he drank Diet Mtn Dews. And still . . . he didn't know what to do. The only thing that settled his mind was to sit down at the computer and answer a few questions for his column.

"Noah: Sometimes when I read your column I think you're really a good guy. Other times I think you're just a jerk on some kind of power trip. Which is it? Signed, Randy."

"Randy: Most of the time I think that I'm a good person, but the way I react when people drive slowly in the left lane would suggest otherwise."

"Noah: I'm a thirty-seven-year-old woman who has never been married, never been out of Utah, and never even been in love. I work hard, try to be a good person, and save money; however, I'm sad and lonely. Any advice my friend? Signed, Forlorned."

"Forlorned: Deep within your soul is a door that opens into a world of wonder. Open the door and let the magic in."

"Noah: I'm a junior in college and even though I'm young, I'm a huge Beatles fan. A lot of my friends here at school are as well. The other night we were listening to one of their albums and one of my friends said that there's one song that, if you play it backward, says, 'Paul is dead.' We tried it and it sort of does sound like that, but we're not sure. What do you think? Did Paul really die back in the sixties? Signed, The Lusker."

"The Lusker?: Okay. It is certainly possible that Paul did die; just as it is certainly possible that President Kennedy, MLK, Jr., and Curt Cobain didn't die and are all living in a commune in Myrtle Beach with Jimi Hendrix. It's ALL possible, The Lusker. It's all insanely possible."

Noah

These questions eased his mind a little; now he had to figure out how to answer the question of Ana.

24.

HE CONTINUED TO SIT THERE AND STARE at the computer screen. It offered no help at all. His mind was spinning; was he a bad person for letting the twenty-year age gap affect him so? Heck, from what he could tell, she may have been thirty years older than him—she was probably older than his mother! He could be dating his mother! This is how his mind was working.

Then he thought to himself: *No, this is my Ana. The woman I've bonded with, the woman who shares the same goals and thoughts that I do. The woman I've been dreaming about all this time. The woman I've wanted to talk with, spend time with, and yes, lay in bed with and hold and kiss and . . .*

He couldn't go any further with those thoughts. Yes, Ana was all those things, and more. But the woman he'd just seen sitting at the bar was not that woman. Noah wanted to cry. It wasn't her fault. She never lied to him, she never admitted her age, and she never led him down an uncertain path. She was always his Ana, his dream, the woman he had always hoped for. And now?

He thought of a thousand different scenarios of how to continue. None of them made any sense. He could wait and meet her tomorrow and somehow explain to her in person how he felt. No, he knew he could never do that. The only thing that made sense to him now was to do what all men seem to do in times of ultimate despair and trouble: lie.

He knew she was supposed to email him in the morning when she was ready to meet him. He would head that off now and email her tonight. He typed "Ana," then he sat there for over twenty minutes waiting for his brain to tell him what to type next. He had never lied to Ana before and he found it excruciatingly difficult to lie to her now. He put his fingers on the keypad but they wouldn't work. He sat there so long that the screen went blank and he had to log on again.

Once more, he tried to convince himself that, yes, he could overlook the age thing. That, yes, he could still want her as intimately as before. That, yes, he could . . . but he knew he couldn't. He was simply a sorry excuse for a human being by letting this age gap affect him so.

He got up from the computer and went into the kitchen and grabbed the bottle of Maker's Mark whiskey from underneath the sink and took a big swallow of that nasty blend. It went straight down his throat into his stomach, burning every single centimeter of the way down. His stomach had other plans. His stomach showed who was in charge. It threw the Maker's Mark back up Noah's throat, into his mouth, and then into the sink. Apparently, he had no control over anything in his life anymore. He was hopeless.

He paced in front of the computer, imploring it to somehow give him some guidance and wisdom. The computer completely ignored him. He finally put on his flip-flops and walked out his back door, past his patio, into the desert scrubland. Were there snakes out there? Yes, but he didn't care. He urged every snake out there to bite him, feast off his sorry self, and leave his carcass for the hyenas to lick his bones dry.

His luck was so bad that he couldn't get a single bite. He sloughed back in, kicked his flip-flops off in the direction of his couch, and sat once more in front of the silent, sorry, useless computer. He started typing:

"Ana, I have some terrible news. I cannot meet you tomorrow or any other day. I have been misleading you for some time now. I am not a good person. In fact, I'm a terrible person for what I've done to you. I had an old girlfriend, Vicki, which I haven't seen in over two years. She just came back into my life and we have connected and I am now with her full time. I'm sorry for everything. I know you can never forgive me and I don't blame you. Please forget about me and have a

wonderful life of your own. You're much better off without someone like me. I'm so sorry,
Noah"

He went out to his Jeep and drove down to the local convenience store and bought two twelve packs of Corona, hoping it would make him sick. It did.

●●●

After her second glass of wine, Shirley closed her computer and walked back to the hotel. About thirty minutes later, Dorothy returned from her meeting with her old friend from the park. They reviewed the day and Dorothy told of her meeting and how much she missed Canyonlands. Then she admitted to Shirley that she finally felt good about meeting Noah tomorrow. She was excited and Shirley was happy for her. They each went to bed that evening thinking tomorrow would be one of the best days in Dorothy's life.

Dorothy was up before dawn, the excitement of the day not letting her rest. She would soon know if Noah would accept her for who she was or kick her out of Moab for misleading him all this time. As she showered she was thinking of what time she should tell Noah she would be available to meet him. She decided on 10:00 that morning; there was no way she could wait any longer. She'd get it over with early and end the suspension, one way or the other.

After she toweled off and dried her hair, she sat down at the small desk in the room and opened her laptop to email Noah. She immediately smiled upon seeing that she had an email from Noah waiting on her. Wasn't that sweet of him to surprise her like that. Of course, that's exactly the type of thing her Noah would do . . . isn't it?

She opened the email and read it, not twice or three times like she did most of his emails. Once was enough. The next thing she remembered was Shirley leaning over her and tapping her face gently, asking, "Are you okay?"

Dorothy focused on Shirley and wondered what had happened. She asked Shirley what was going on. "I heard a loud shriek, then a thump. I tried calling your phone but there was no answer. That's when I went to the office and had them open your door, honey. What's wrong? Are you okay?"

"No, Shirley, I'm not okay. I'll never be okay."

"What's wrong, honey?"

Dorothy then sat up and pointed to her computer and told Shirley to go read the email. Shirley did and her face immediately turned a bright shade of red. She kept looking at the screen and started saying, "I'll kill him. He's dead! I'll kill him, Dorothy. I swear it, he's dead!"

"No, Shirley, hush. Just please delete that message and never mention it again, okay?"

Shirley wanted to hit something, and she wanted that something to be Noah's face. However, she did as Dorothy asked and deleted the worst message she'd ever seen in her life.

Dorothy told her she was fine. She asked Shirley to go back to her room and finish getting ready for the trip home. "Are you sure, honey? This is a small town. We can find him and confront him and beat the crap out of him!"

"No, Shirley. I'll be fine. Go get all your stuff ready and give me about an hour to gather my things. It's okay." So Shirley did go back to her room and packed up everything, then sat on the edge of her bed and wondered how one human being could be so cruel to another human being. She had no answer.

After the hour had passed, she knocked on Dorothy's door but there was no response. Surprisingly, the door wasn't locked and Shirley opened it and found the room vacant. She first thought that Dorothy might be waiting for her at the car or in the office, but then she noticed the sheet of paper lying on the bed. She picked it up and started reading:

"My dear friend, Shirley. I need you to honor my wishes. Please! I'm so sorry to abandon you but I need to be alone. Go back home and please forgive me for leaving you like this. Don't worry about me; I used to live here and I'll be fine. I know plenty of people and I have

two weeks of vacation to flitter away. I'll be fine. I'll call you when I get back home. Again, I'm sorry,
  Your friend, Dorothy"

Shirley sat on the bed and read the note once again. Then she looked out in the parking lot and up and down the street. She finally packed the car, then rode up and down the main street of Moab looking for her friend. She almost started crying, then composed herself and headed out of town with a long nine-hour drive ahead of her, while all the time thinking of her friend and knowing there was nothing in the world she can do to help.

Dorothy had called the car rental place in town and they came and picked her up and took her back to the rental lot. She rented a cheap two-door Japanese something or other—she didn't care what it was. Then she stopped at a grocery store and bought enough food to last her eight to ten days. She started driving to her old stomping grounds, Canyonlands National Park, about an hour south of Moab.

When she arrived at the park offices, all her old friends wanted to chat and hug and talk. It was the hardest thing Dorothy ever did-- pretending to be happy and sociable. She went into the office of her old friend, the park superintendent, and asked him if she could borrow some camping equipment for about a week. No problem there. Everybody loved Dorothy. Everybody, it seems, except the only person in the world that she wanted to love her.

She got her backpack filled with the food she would need, along with her sleeping bag, small tent, and water purifier. She hugged everyone again and drove out to the most remote section of the park, The Maze. No one actually hiked into The Maze; people would walk along the edges and think about it, but not hike into it. There was nothing there but wilderness. It was too remote, too dangerous, too rocky, too everything. Exactly what Dorothy wanted. To have no chance on earth of seeing another human being. Was that asking too much?

25.

SHE PARKED HER CAR AND LEFT HER PARK SERVICE identification on the window letting officials know the driver was okay when they saw it parked there for eight or ten days. Otherwise, they may have thought it was a tourist who had lost his or her way in the vast wilderness.

Dorothy's pack was pretty heavy but she didn't care. She bent over a little and adjusted it so that it didn't hurt so much, then she started walking. There are no trails in The Maze; you're on your own. She did carry a compass with her to help find the way back to her car, in case she wanted to come back to her car. She wasn't sure of that yet.

Dorothy rounded a bend, climbed some rocks, slid down an incline, went over some hills, crossed some unidentifiable terrain, and continued to repeat that scenario until she couldn't walk any longer. Then she stopped; exhausted, thirsty, hungry, and brokenhearted. She pitched her little tent just at nightfall, laid on top of her sleeping bag, and went to sleep without eating anything—only a few sips of water.

Her first morning, she ate some food while sitting on the ground, leaning against a rock, and staring off into the wilderness. Except for a few bathroom breaks, that's all she did. Mid-afternoon, she moved around a little and found a small creek where she got some water to run through her purifier. But that was all. She only wanted to be alone. She didn't want to explore, or hike, or anything, except to be alone.

She thought of everything she shouldn't be thinking of. She couldn't help it. She wondered if it would have been worse if she'd actually met Noah and he found out she wasn't his dream girl, Ana. But then she thought, *how could it be worse?*

The second day in the wilderness, she started moving around. She went off on day hikes but kept her base camp so she wouldn't have to carry that heavy load everywhere. The first day she went north, the second day south, the third day east, and the fourth day she went west. It all looked the same to her, not because it actually did look the same, but because she didn't care.

Her fifth day out, she rested again and didn't leave her camp. She began watching some buzzards floating overhead at one thousand, maybe two thousand feet up . . . who knows? She saw a few lizards and one rabbit but nothing else. Her mind slowly began to ease; she soon started thinking of things other than the things she shouldn't be thinking of. She hoped Shirley made it back home okay. She thought of her friends at the park office. She even thought of her mother and father for a while, and her time growing up in Lumberton, North Carolina.

But as hard as she tried not to, her mind kept coming back to the email from Noah. Like the bad dream that keeps you up at night and will not fade away.

The sixth and seventh days she spent roaming in no distinct direction—just roaming. She started to return to her car on the eighth day but changed her mind and stayed. She went back to the small creek, which couldn't have been more than a foot deep, and took off all her clothes and laid down in the water. She stared up at the buzzards, stark naked, and thought of . . . nothing. She may have dozed off a little, she wasn't sure. But she was sure of one thing: it was time to return to civilization. Get back to work, to her friends, to her life . . . to nothing.

On the ninth day, she packed up and trudged out. Probably a few pounds lighter, definitely a shade or two darker, but not less troubled.

●●●

Noah woke up the following day around noon. His self-induced Corona hangover did everything he hoped it would: made him sick, made his head throb, made him throw-up, and made him hate himself more than he thought possible. He took a handful of some type of pill from the kitchen cabinet. He didn't read the label and didn't count the number of pills he spilled into his hand. He just gulped them down by turning the faucet on and leaning over to drink directly from the source—he wouldn't waste a perfectly good glass on his sorry self.

He went back to bed but couldn't rest. He tossed and turned and pulled at his hair hoping the pain would stop. But there was no way his hair could stop the pain he was feeling . . . the feeling of infinitely hurting someone he cared about. He dozed and woke, and dozed and woke until it was nightfall. He started to get up and take a shower but didn't. He did sip a little of the last Diet Mtn Dew he had. He was a little hungry but refused to eat, as self-inflicted punishment. He deserved worse.

He finally sat at his computer and clicked on his work emails. Should he even try to answer any of these questions in the state of mind he was in? Why not?

"Noah: I'm currently dating a very beautiful woman and we're having a great time with each other. I'm thinking of going to the next level with her because we have such a good time together. We usually go out twice a week, during the week, not on weekends, because she spends that time with her family. It seems a little strange, but it makes her happy. Is this 'no weekends' rule of hers a little weird or does it seem normal to you? Signed, Ricky."

"Ricky: Buddy, either you deal with what is the reality, or you can be sure that the reality is going to deal with you."

●●●

"Noah: My grandfather died recently and I took it hard. He was a great man. He died in his sleep so at least he didn't suffer. This has led me to think about my life and the eventuality of my death someday. Do you ever think about death and how hard it will be? Signed, Mary"

"Mary: Dying is easy; it's living that's difficult."

That was all he could do. Not because he felt bad about his answers, but because he felt bad about what he'd done and what he didn't do, and what he should've done, and what he knew was right, and what he knew was wrong. He went to the kitchen and took another handful of pills, turned off all the lights, sat in his lazy boy, and stared at the blank television screen.

Dorothy drove back to Death Valley National Park, only stopping for fuel, food, and bathroom breaks. She didn't turn on the radio, she didn't notice any of the spectacular scenery on the way; in fact, she almost missed the turn-off to her destination. Not that she was concentrating so much on the drive; rather, she was only concentrating on the one thing she shouldn't have been concentrating on.

She resumed her work as the dependable, thoughtful, efficient employee that she was; however, something was missing from her now. She didn't know if she would ever find it again.

Noah went back to work and answered emails every day from the good people of Salt Lake City. If anything, he had become a little less cynical, a little more understanding, and a lot more boring. After several weeks, his editor called him on the phone and immediately asked, "What's wrong with you?"

"Nothing's wrong. What are you talking about?"

"Noah, what's going on? The readers are starting to complain. Your column is too predictable, too plain, and too . . . I don't know what. Heck, I could've written most of that stuff and you know how boring I am."

Noah didn't respond. He didn't know what to say. Finally, the editor said, "Look, whatever is bothering you will pass. We need the old Noah back. We need that sarcasm and wit and nonsense that people look forward to every day. Can you do that?"

Noah

"Yes, sir. Don't worry, everything will be fine." Noah ended the phone call and stared out the window. *I'm such a liar,* he thought. *Nothing will ever be fine again. Ever.*

TWO YEARS LATER

26.

NOAH WALKED INTO THE COFFEE SHOP and sat at his favorite table. He needed caffeine in the worst way. Vicki had kept him up most of the night trying to satisfy her apparent neverending sexual appetite. He wasn't complaining, mind you, but he was tired. Because of her biking duties, he was only seeing Vicki about four nights a month, and that was probably at Noah's limit of what he could physically handle. He'd only been sitting at the table a couple of minutes when Luray, the older waitress/cashier, brought his cinnamon raisin bagel and coffee out to him. He'd been a regular customer for so long that he didn't have to order; everyone knew what he wanted.

The only change, ever, in Noah's breakfast order came about two years ago when he suddenly changed from a blueberry muffin each morning, to now wanting the cinnamon raisin bagel. He never explained why he changed his order and they never asked. Usually, Grace brought his food over to him but he hadn't seen her this morning. When Luray came to refill his coffee, Noah asked her where Grace was. She answered, "Babysitting problems again. That poor girl has the worst luck with babysitters. She should be in later."

Grace had delivered a baby girl about a year and a half ago and named the baby Kai. Noah originally thought Grace's name was Kai, or Margaret, or Lulu--she would never tell him the truth about her name because she didn't like the name Grace. Grace's parents named her after one of their favorite singers, Grace Slick. However, Grace thought the name sounded like an old woman's name, so she started calling herself Kai, at least until her baby was born. She did like Kai, so that's what she named her baby.

Noah

Noah asked Luray, "Is she playing tonight at the Fish?"

"If she can find a babysitter."

Noah nodded and took a bite of his bagel. He enjoyed watching Grace perform; she was a talented singer and guitar player. Plus, Vicki had left town this morning and he really needed a break. After breakfast, he went back home and worked on his column for a bit, then sat outside and stared off into the La Sal Mountains . . . dreaming. Or rather, trying not to dream. For the past two years, aside from his sexual forays with Vicki, Noah had not had any other female companionship except some long and interesting conversations with Grace.

Usually, after her musical set at the Fish, she would come to his table and they'd discuss everything from how useless men were, to the state of the affairs in the European Union. Grace was intelligent, inquisitive, and at times very opinionated. She reminded Noah of a younger version of himself.

He bummed around his house all day. Almost washed some dishes, then thought better of it. He did go for a walk in the desert scrubland behind his house--with hiking boots on. He saw two ravens fly from juniper tree to juniper tree as they kept an eye on him, either hoping he'd spill some food on the ground or fall over dead so they could peck his eyes out—ravens are like that.

After a suitable period of wasting time, he dressed down and headed out for the Fiddlin' Fish to see Grace perform. It was a little over half full, but Noah always liked to sit at the back, so it didn't matter to him how many people were there. Grace was singing some type of cowboy song when he walked in but she noticed him and they made eye contact. Noah ordered a beer and sat down just as she started singing an old Eagles' song while looking directly at him:

> I wish you peace when the cold winds blow
> Warmed by the fire's glow
> I wish you comfort in the lonely time
> And arms to hold you when you ache inside
>
> I wish you hope when things are going bad

Kind words when times are sad
I wish you shelter from the raging wind
Cooling waters at the fever's end

I wish you peace when times are hard
The light to guide you through the dark
And when storms are high and your dreams are low

I wish you the strength to let love grow,
I wish you the strength to let love flow.

After the song ended, Grace set her guitar down and came over to sit with him. She asked, "Did you order me anything yet?"

"And just why would I order you anything?"

Grace looked closely at him and replied, "Because I'm your hero and you love my singing?"

Noah set his glass down and leaned in close to her and said, "I know you sang that last song for me. You can quit feeling sorry for me . . . I'm fine."

"You're fine?"

"Yes . . . fine!"

Grace picked up Noah's glass and took a drink from it, then replied, "Fine, says the man who has ignored all women now for two years, all except the same old slut he keeps hidden in his harem."

He tried to act upset and mad but he couldn't pull it off. Instead, he said, "I haven't been ignoring women for two years, and Vicki is a nice girl. You just have to get to know her."

"A nice girl? She comes into town once a month for four or five days and does nothing but drink at the bar and then screw your eyes out! And that's nice? I bet you wanna take her home and meet your mama, don't you, Noah?"

Noah

He wanted to say, *Shut up!* Or, *Leave me alone.* Or, even, *You just don't know her well enough.* But he wisely kept his mouth shut; he seldom won arguments with Grace. Instead, he reached for his glass that Grace was holding and took a long drink from it—just so he wouldn't have to say anything to her.

She said, "I've got to get back on stage. Try not to cry in your beer, okay?" Before he could think of a witty comeback, she was gone.

He sat there and thought, *Had it been two years? Dang, it felt like twenty.*

He left the Fiddlin' Fish and started driving home, down Main Street, past the Moab Brewery, and just after the city limits sign, the road where he was supposed to turn . . . except he didn't turn left. He kept going straight out of town, straight south out toward Canyonlands National Park where he'd met Dorothy almost three years ago. It was pitch black out here at night: no street lights, no businesses, no homes . . . nothing but desert and more desert. And this late at night, there were no other cars either. No reason for anyone to be out here.

Noah slowly started increasing his speed: 70 mph, then 80 mph, 95, 100 . . . The Jeep started to shimmy a little but he kept pushing. 110 mph, 115, and then, BOOM! The motor stopped and the Jeep started coasting. Fortunately, it was a straight stretch of highway, because when the engine stopped, there was no power steering and the brakes barely worked. He just coasted along until the Jeep was almost stopped, then he pulled over off the road and turned the lights off.

Fortunately, he had Triple-A, so he gave them a call. It took nearly two and a half hours for them to send someone out, so he just sat there in the dark, in the desert, in his broken-down Jeep, thinking about his broken-down life. Grace was right; he had to change. How?

●●●

Bad news from the garage: the engine in his Jeep was blown. They asked him what had happened and he said, "I don't know, it just blew up." Apparently, lying was now a life habit of his. He got some insurance money and went to the used car lot to pick out a new used Jeep and found a fairly new one with only thirty-seven thousand

133

miles on it. The exterior was a deep blue color and looked good, at least until the next dust storm came rolling through town—which was a regular occurrence.

He started most days with a trip to the coffee shop and talking with Luray and Grace. Then he'd work on his column for the paper, then . . . nothing. He had nothing. Oh, sure, every three or four weeks Vicki would pop in and make things exciting, but was this living? No, it wasn't. Just as thinking about Ana and what could have been was not living either. Could he ever forgive himself for what he'd done to her? He doubted it. Certainly not as long as he sat on his patio every afternoon and thought about it. He had to change.

The next morning, as he was slowly eating his bagel and sipping his coffee, staring out the window at two college-aged girls walking down the street, Grace tapped him on the shoulder and said, "Whatcha doing?"

He thought she was questioning why he was staring and the two college girls and implying they were way too young for him.

So he stammered a little as she then continued, "Next weekend, what are you doing? Anything?"

She knew he wasn't doing anything, because, well . . . he never did anything. So he answered, "I don't know, maybe clean the house a little and hike in the desert. I don't know. Why?"

"Because I just got an offer to play at a little club in Vegas, off the strip, next Friday and Saturday nights. You wanna go?"

Noah was stunned. "They want you to play Vegas?"

Grace acted upset. "You don't think I'm good enough to play Vegas?"

"No, not that, umm . . . "

"Oh, hush, Noah. I'm just messing with you. It's only a little club way off the strip, but still . . . it's Vegas and it could lead to something bigger."

Noah

Noah sighed a breath of relief and said, "That sounds great. Yeah, you should definitely go."

Grace then pulled the chair out next to Noah and sat down. She had a serious look on her face and said, "That's the problem, Noah. How do I get there? My old broken-down pickup truck will never make it all the way to Vegas, and even if it did, who would watch Kai for me?" This really wasn't a question Grace was asking; it was a hint. The problem was that poor, old Noah didn't get the hint.

He said, "Well, there are buses that run up that way every day, and I'm sure they would have babysitting available, wouldn't they?"

Grace slowly shook her head and sighed, "Noah . . . "

"What?"

"To be so smart, sometimes you're just dumb as a rock."

Now he was very confused and once again said, "What? What do you mean?"

She was both frustrated at his inability to read her intentions and fearful of asking him to do something for her this monumental. So, she just got up from the table and left. When he looked back outside the window, the college girls were gone. He still didn't understand what Grace was talking about until Luray came over to refill his coffee cup. She asked him, "Well, are you going to take Grace up to Vegas?"

He was so stunned he couldn't answer her. All he could do was repeat that sentence in his mind: *Take Grace up to Vegas? What?* When he obviously wasn't going to answer her question, Luray walked away. Noah's mind was spinning as he thought, *Take Grace to Vegas? Me and Grace going to Vegas? Babysitting? Grace and me going to Vegas?* He let his coffee get cold as he kept repeating these thoughts in his head.

Finally, he rose from the table and walked over to the counter where both Luray and Grace were working, then looked directly at Grace and said, "Yes, of course, I'm taking you to Vegas." Then he turned and walked out the door, as excited as he's been in nearly two years.

27.

NOAH DROVE STRAIGHT HOME, very excited about the prospect of the upcoming Vegas trip. Of course, he'd do all the driving, and probably do a lot of babysitting while Grace performed, but still, it's Vegas . . . right? He decided to answer a few emails while he ruminated on this subject.

"Noah: I've been on a diet since we came back from a cruise. I thought boot camp in the Army was hard, but this dieting crap is much worse than that. I hate it! Any thoughts on food that might help me? Signed, Donnie."

"Donnie: Food is like sex: When you abstain, even the worst stuff begins to look good."

●●●

"Noah: I've read your comments about golf before. Why is it that you hate golf so much? It's a great sport! Signed, Mikey"

"Mikey: I don't hate golf. In fact, golf is fascinating to me. An interesting thing about golf is that no matter how badly you play, it is always possible to get worse. Fascinating!"

●●●

"Noah: Quit beating around the bush and tell us who you're voting for in the election. Don't you want the best man to win? Signed, Roger."

136

Noah

"Roger: I always want the best man to win the election. Unfortunately, he never runs."

28.

THE DAYS LEADING UP TO THE TRIP to Las Vegas were excruciating for Noah; he was excited and ready to go now. He assured Grace everything would be okay with Kai and the babysitting would be no problem. Even though he'd never cared for a baby before or even been around babies before, he was certain he could handle it. Grace didn't believe a word of what he said, but she trusted that he would try hard and she knew that Kai would be safe with him.

They left Moab on Thursday morning for the drive over to Las Vegas. They could have taken a bit longer route and driven over to the interstate, but since Noah was driving, he wanted to drive through the back-country and enjoy God's beauty. Before they'd driven the first hour, Noah was questioning himself and wondering how he could endure four days of a baby continuously crying like Kai had been since they left Moab.

Grace said Kai probably had an ear infection. Noah definitely had an ear infection—the worst kind! Eventually, Kai calmed down and they made it to the hotel just after dark. Grace had a room booked through the club she was performing at, which was a small but nice place off The Strip. Noah booked a room of his own at Bally's, his favorite hotel in Vegas, right in the middle of everything. He helped Grace check in and get something to eat for her and Kai, then he went over to Bally's to check in his room.

He unpacked his suitcase and flopped down on the bed to relax after the long drive, while trying to decide what he wanted to do the rest of the night: slots, blackjack, roulette, maybe a show, or just get a drink

Noah

at the bar and people watch. While he was enjoying thinking of all the possibilities Vegas had to offer, his cell phone rang. It was Grace.

"Noah?"

"Yes, everything okay, Grace?"

A few moments of silence, then she said, "I can't stay here."

"What do you mean, exactly?"

"I mean, I can't stay here, Noah. They're having some sort of fraternity party or something and there are young guys running up and down the halls drinking and yelling and trying to get hookers to come over to their rooms."

"Okay, calm down. We'll find you something else. Let me check around and see what's available."

Before he finished that thought, Grace said, "I can't afford anything else, Noah. The club people paid for this place, and I can't afford a hotel room in Vegas on my own. Can I stay with you?"

Beads of sweat immediately popped up on Noah's forehead. *Stay with me? Is that what she just asked? She wants to stay with me?*

As he was still thinking about those questions, Grace asked, "Noah, you still there?"

"Yeah, I'm here, I'm umm . . . "

"Well, if you don't want me to stay there, Noah, just say so!" And she clicked off the call.

Noah thought, *Holy cow! Women!* He called her right back and said, "It's okay, Grace, I was just thinking about where the baby would sleep. My room's not real big."

Immediately, Grace answered, "It's all taken care of. I called the desk at Bally's and they have a small crib they can bring to your room. Everything will be fine."

Noah replied, "Wait a minute, it was only about ten seconds before I called you back. You didn't have time to call the desk here and ask about a crib."

"I called them first, before I ever called you, Noah. Don't worry, they'll be bringing it up in a few minutes."

Noah didn't say anything. But he knew he'd just been played. Then, he said, "Okay, but there's only one bed here."

Grace answered, "I like the left-hand side if you don't mind. When can you get back over here to pick us up?"

●●●

Noah picked them up, the crib was delivered, and his dream of a wild few days in Vegas came to a screeching halt. Fortunately, Kai slept through the night, but Grace tossed and turned. Worst of all, she snored. If Noah slept any at all, he was unaware of it.

Grace was in her early twenties and a very pretty girl, but Noah, who was at least a dozen years older, never thought of her in a sexual way. She was Grace . . . that's all. More like his long-lost sister and someone he needed to take care of. Sleeping together in the same bed was nothing more than an inconvenience to both of them. He was inconvenienced by Grace's snoring and rolling around all night, and Grace was used to sleeping in the nude. Her constant tossing and turning at night made wearing pajamas quite uncomfortable because they kept getting knotted up. But, for Noah, she settled on a tee shirt and shorts. So, they each compromised in their own ways and tried to get through the evenings as best they could.

The next morning, Friday, Kai and Grace slept in while he went exploring. He walked through the hotel and casino, played a few quarter slots, then went to sit out by the pool, drinking a mimosa while watching all the girls sunbathing. Vegas had its perks. He had almost dozed off when his cellphone woke him. It was Grace again, "Whatcha doing?"

Noah

Noah knew what she really meant: *When are you coming back over here to get us and take us to breakfast?* So, he did. As much as he liked to berate himself, especially after Ana, he was a good guy—he couldn't help it. During breakfast, Grace asked him what his plans were for the day, but before he could think of an answer, she said, "I need to be at the club by 3:00 to do sound checks and review my set with them. You can sit with Kai then, right?"

3:00? Really?? What about Vegas? Slots? Blackjack? Girl watching? Sipping gin & tonics?
But, he said, "Sure." He drove her to the little club, which was named Opie's, just before 3:00. Then, as she was getting out of his Jeep, he said, "We'll see you at the show tonight. Good luck with everything."

Grace stopped immediately before shutting the door, then leaned back in and replied, "No, Noah, they don't let little kids in places like this. You and Kai will have to find something else to do. I'll call you when I finish and you can come back and pick me up." And with that, she closed the door and walked into the club.

Noah thought to himself, *You'll LET me come back and pick you up!* Then he looked back at Kai, who was in the child seat sucking on a pacifier, and thought to himself: *The first show starts at 7:00, the second show starts at 10:00; she probably won't call me until after midnight.* He looked at Kai again and said, "Well, here we are, all alone in Las Vegas, sin capital of the world, whatcha wanna do?"

Grace had a nice stroller for Kai and a well-stocked baby bag as well. Enough milk and snacks and diapers to last for a couple of days if needed. Well, Noah couldn't play slots or blackjack or anything else where people generally donate their money to Las Vegas. He also couldn't go to any shows or bars with an infant to tow, but he could walk and he could visit some of the high-end hotels on the strip and take in the sights. So, he and Kai strolled down the infamous Strip to see what kind of trouble they could get into.

Caesar's Palace, Luxor, MGM Grand, The Flamingo, The Mirage, etc., etc., etc. After touring the sixth hotel, Noah was tired. He just wanted to sit and rest, have something to eat, and people-watch. Kai seemed to be having a ball. She seemingly loved all the attention she was getting from strangers along the halls of all the hotels and casinos.

Pretty soon, however, she fell asleep after Noah fed her and changed her diaper.

They were in the New York, New York hotel/casino and it had a common area where guests and tourists could sit and relax, while having a drink, if they so desired. It wasn't a bar; it was more of a common, open area. Noah was tired and thirsty and he still probably had at least three hours until Grace would finish her shows. He found a seat out of the main traffic area and looked for a waiter to come and take his order. He found that he could also order sandwiches and snacks as well as drinks. Perfect!

He ordered a ham and cheese sandwich, some potato chips, and a cold beer. There were people everywhere. Vegas is the convention capital of the world and Noah loved watching the constant stream of people pass by. Old, young, male, female, handsome, beautiful, and not-so-beautiful, he saw it all pass before him. Just past midnight, his cell phone rang and Grace said she was ready to go home. Noah and Kai went to the car--Kai never woke up--and drove off The Strip to the night club.

Noah spotted Grace standing at the curb talking to a man. He stopped the car and she hopped in, leaned into the back seat to check on Kai, and then talked non-stop all the way back to their hotel room. Her performance went very well and she even received a bonus for the two shows. She told him that tomorrow's show, on Saturday night, was only one performance at 8:00, so at least he wouldn't have to babysit so long.

They both took showers and then Noah listened again as Grace reviewed the night and showed him the cash bonus she received. He was impressed; it was more money than Grace would make for an entire week at the coffee shop. Grace finally drifted off to sleep, Kai slept like a log, as Noah listened to a constant roar of snoring from the left-hand side of the bed. But . . . he didn't mind at all.

29.

IN DEATH VALLEY NATIONAL PARK, life continued for Dorothy. She was promoted to Assistant Park Manager and received a well-deserved pay raise. She moved into a larger condo and was thinking of buying a new pickup truck. She made a few minor friends in the area and continued her close, intimate friendship with Shirley. Even though Shirley lived in California, the two communicated daily by text, email, and phone. They also visited each other at least once a month. Dorothy did more of the visiting because, really, who wants to visit Death Valley?

Dorothy's job description had changed with the promotion. Except to go to meetings and conferences, she didn't get out of the office as she did before. The Park Superintendent hated going to conferences, so he usually assigned Dorothy to attend all these gatherings--unless one of the meetings was in San Francisco or New York, then he'd go.

Dorothy shuffled papers, did reports, filled out requests, and did everything she was supposed to do and more. Everyone loved Dorothy! Everyone except Dorothy. At work, she smiled and was very congenial to everyone she met. She answered every crazy question from every tourist who stopped by, always with a pleasant tone and a smile. Dorothy was good.

Her natural beauty drew the attention of every other park ranger in the system and she was asked out on dates every single week. It got to the point where rumors started circulating that Dorothy might not be attracted to men at all; however, she set the record straight after the second time she was asked out by non-male park rangers. So, to all those around her, Dorothy was a conundrum: beautiful, smart, successful, charming, and yet, lonely by choice. No one could understand her; no one except Shirley.

If not for Shirley and her total understanding of Dorothy and her past, and providing a shoulder to cry on, and a companion to trust, Dorothy would have probably sunk into the abyss of life months ago. Shirley kept her going, provided her with hope and care, gave her purpose in life, and kept on encouraging her that life could, and would, still be all she wanted it to be. She kept Dorothy afloat in a time when it would have been easy to drown.

Usually, Dorothy had to attend conferences every few months. If Shirley was free, and she was free most of the time, she would go with Dorothy for a "girls' weekend." Even though Shirley was more than twenty years older than Dorothy, they had a special connection that transcended age. Everything they did was more fun with each other. They could talk about anything and everything with each other . . . except for the one thing that drew them together in the first place: Noah.

The first week Dorothy returned from Moab after the failed meeting with Noah, she made it clear to Shirley that she never wanted that subject to come up again. Even though Shirley knew that Noah was on Dorothy's mind every waking hour, every day, every month, she kept her promise and never broached that subject but she wanted to. She knew Dorothy was suffering and hurt and lonesome: She just didn't know how to help her except to always be there for her. And she loved doing it. She was lonely too. A couple of failed marriages had left her a little cynical and despondent along the way. Plus, she wasn't twenty-five years old anymore and there weren't that many men left who were available. Truthfully, they needed each other.

Even though Dorothy and Shirley never discussed Noah, that didn't mean Dorothy's mind could blot out all those memories. Oh, sure, she'd love to forget that last day and the last email where Noah told her he was involved with another woman—Vicki. How could she ever forget that name? But she also remembered the good times, the hikes they went on, the river trip, and more than anything, she remembered all the emails between the two of them when Noah thought she was his imaginary friend, Ana.

Noah

It's not like Dorothy tried that hard to forget, however. She never deleted any of his emails (except that last one) and she would occasionally read one or two before bedtime. She knew she shouldn't be doing that, but those emails made her feel so good. She longed for that feeling again.

She'd changed a little over the last two years: She had joined a gym and become a bit more toned and had lost a few pounds. There was not a single man in the gym, of any age, who wasn't aware of Dorothy. A few had tried to take her out. None were successful; she just wasn't interested. She wondered how long this would last. Was she going to go through her entire life being in love with someone who doesn't even know who she is?

So, she went to work every day, she went to the gym every day, she emailed, texted, or called Shirley every day, she was lonely every day, and she was miserable every day. What a life!

●●●

Dorothy was busy working on next year's budget when her boss came in and said, "I need you to attend the annual Western Parks Association meeting next week in Las Vegas . . . okay?"

Dorothy thought: *Are you kidding me? Another conference?* Then she thought: *Well, okay, Vegas might be alright.* So, she dutifully replied, "Yes, sir, anything else?"

He smiled, secretly thinking: *That girl wants me.* But instead, he said, "No, I'll forward you the information. You'll be staying at Bally's on The Strip . . . don't get in any trouble!"

Dorothy immediately emailed Shirley telling her of the trip and asking if she could come with her. Free room and a food allowance which they could both eat from . . . she was pretty sure Shirley would jump at the chance to visit Vegas. Shirley loved playing nickel slots and had once won over eighty dollars in a single pot--she never forgot that. Dorothy hit "send" and less than forty seconds later got a reply from Shirley: "YESSSSS!"

She still had to get through this boring weekend before she and Shirley left for Sin City. Usually, she did nothing on her weekends except shop, work-out at the gym, and talk to Shirley on the phone. Sometimes she would drive up into the mountains and hike in the wilderness areas--never on trails where she might see other people. All the hiking and gym workouts gave Dorothy a body and legs all the other women were extremely jealous over. And for the last two years, she had not cut her hair either; it was long, voluminous, and extremely sexy-looking. She kept it tied up or under a hat at work, but all the men in the entire park service knew: Dorothy was HOT!

The weekend before the Vegas trip, Dorothy was sitting home on a Saturday afternoon thinking, which was usually a bad idea. She was thinking of the upcoming trip, among other things, and she decided to look in her closet and see what sort of clothes she might want to take with her. She had a dress in there that she had never worn. She bought it with the hopes of wearing it to meet someone that she never met. Now, it was time to wear it.

It was all black, very short, with a very low-cut front. She tried it on and almost embarrassed herself by seeing how sexy she looked. She took it off and laid it on the bed, staring at it, thinking about it, wondering: *Why not?* The low-desert country, where she lived, didn't have many places worthy of this dress, but there was this one bar she'd heard of that wasn't as redneck as most of the others. It was time to put the past in the past and see what can be available in the future. Right?

About 8:00 that night, she laid the dress on the bed and looked at it again, then she went to the refrigerator and poured herself a glass of wine. A little encouragement never hurt. She brought the wine back into the bedroom and slowly sipped it while staring at the dress and trying her best to forget why she bought that dress in the first place. Unfortunately, her memory was much better than she wanted it to be.

About 8:45, she finally got dressed and stared at herself in the mirror. She kept trying to pull the front up a little to hide some cleavage, while at the same time trying to pull it down to show less of her thighs. She gave up and then put on her high-heeled shoes. "*Oh, no . . . this will never work! I can't go out like this. First, I can't even walk in* these *ridiculous shoes, and second, I look like a slut!"* She started to unzip the dress but stopped, then thought: *Girl . . . you have to start living.*

Her first challenge was to figure out how she was supposed to climb into her pickup truck in that dress. Then, how was she to climb out of the truck without everyone in the county seeing everything? Her next problem was to figure out how she would carry her wallet, keys and essentials. She didn't own a cute little purse; all she had was her park-issued backpack, which probably wouldn't accessorize properly with her slinky, slutty attire. Hmm, this was going to be a tough one.

She finally decided not to take anything with her. She would take a twenty-dollar bill and stuff it down into her tiny bra and hide the keys to the pickup truck on top of the front wheel—no one would ever see it there. Great! She was ready. She repeated these words to herself: *You're ready.* And, once more: *You're ready.* And, the third time: *Aren't you?* She walked out to the pickup and almost turned her ankle as she stepped on a rock in those ridiculous shoes, then she had to pull the dress all the way up to her waist to actually climb in the truck. She quickly looked around to make sure no neighbors saw her do that. And, she was off.

She wished the drive was more than six minutes so she could build up her courage, but it wasn't. She was there. She sat and waited several minutes until there was no one around her so she could exit the pickup. The parking lot of the bar was pretty full, which led to unnecessary anxiety, but, the decision was made. She started walking. Inside, it was fairly dark, very loud, and extremely full of people. Fortunately, she spotted an open bar stool and quickly went over to it, only to realize that it would be impossible for her to sit on that barstool without everyone in the place seeing her underwear. So she stood behind it and waited for the bartender to come over.

Dorothy thought: *Why is he pointing at my boobs?* Then she looked down at herself and saw that the twenty-dollar bill had worked itself out of her bra and was nearly falling completely out. She quickly grabbed it and said, "Thanks. I'll have a glass of white wine."

The bartender nodded and said, "ID."

"Huh?"

"I need to see some ID . . . state law."

Dorothy didn't bring her license with her: she had nowhere to put it. She stood there holding the twenty-dollar bill and not knowing what to do with that either. She had no purse, no pockets, and no idea of what to do; then, someone behind her said, "Allow me." A guy dressed in a leisure suit looked at the bartender and said, "'A glass of wine for the lady, Jay, I'm buying." Jay nodded because he knew the guy and went to pour the wine. He looked at Dorothy and said, "I'm Ryan. Nice to meet you."

Dorothy started to shake his hand but realized she was still holding the twenty-dollar bill. She quickly changed hands and greeted Ryan, "Thanks, Ryan, that's very nice of you."

Ryan took a half step back and looked at Dorothy very closely, then said, "I'm sure I've never seen you in here before. I definitely would have remembered a lovely lady like yourself." Dorothy smiled but didn't say anything, so Ryan continued, "What's your name?"

Dorothy's mind was spinning as she held a wine glass in her right hand and a twenty-dollar bill in her left hand. Ryan arched his eyebrows slightly, so Dorothy answered, "Shirley, my name's Shirley."

"Well, nice to meet you, Shirley. Do you live around here?"

"Just moved here, but not sure how long I'll be staying."

Ryan was trying not to let Dorothy know that he was doing his best not to look at her cleavage, but he was unsuccessful in those attempts. He said, "I've been here all my life. I'm an assistant manager at Walmart. Five years now."

Dorothy suddenly had an epiphany and said, "Can you hold this for me, Ryan? I need to visit the ladies' room." She handed Ryan her glass and walked toward the restrooms, which were near the entrance, but instead of going in the restroom, she veered quickly out the exit door and went directly to her truck. She found her keys on top of the tire, the only thing that went as planned, and she immediately drove home.

Noah

She pulled in her driveway, turned the motor off, and sat there stunned at how pitiful, pathetic, and dismal her life had become.

The next week, before the Vegas trip, was menial and uneventful. The requisite daily forms she had to fill out were mostly concerning the crazy things that tourists do while visiting the park. It's almost a full-time job doing the paperwork needed to prevent lawsuits from people who get themselves in trouble.

On Monday, an older man intentionally walked into the women's bathroom, to "throw away some trash." When asked why he didn't use the men's room to throw away his trash, he said, "The women's bathroom was closer."

Tuesday, a middle-aged man had to be restrained before he physically assaulted an older man who had questioned how many drinks he had in the park restaurant.

Wednesday, a college-aged guy was taken into custody after he took his pants off to wade into a small stream in the park. He left his Wake Forest University shirt on and thought that would be enough. He didn't want to get his pants wet.

Thursday, a man and his rather hefty girlfriend, who happened to be an Indian, were caught in the act of love-making behind some rocks on one of the trails.

It was Dorothy's job to document all these occurrences and ensure the proper authorities were notified. It was never boring but it was tiresome. By Friday, she was ready to go to Vegas. She packed her pickup and left before sunrise. Shirley was flying in and Dorothy would pick her up at the airport in Las Vegas. Dorothy's mind was so packed with memories and thoughts of things she couldn't release, that she hardly remembered the drive at all. In fact, she almost ran out of gas on the way because she never noticed her fuel gauge.

30.

WHEN DOROTHY ARRIVED AT THE AIRPORT, Shirley was standing outside the terminal waiting on her. They made the short trip over to Bally's and checked in their room. Friday nights were usually busy and tonight was no exception. First, they went to the buffet before anything else. The food choices were amazing. Over dinner, they reviewed their plans for the weekend. Tonight would be slots for both ladies. Saturday, Dorothy was busy with conferences all day, then Saturday night they had tickets to see Bill Medley in concert. Shirley loved Bill Medley! Sunday, they would sleep in and Dorothy would start her drive back around noon, while Shirley's flight wasn't until five o'clock.

After dinner, they went to the casino, Shirley to the nickel slots and Dorothy to the quarter slots. Each lady had her own specific way of losing her money. Dorothy sat at a machine and played that one machine until her forty dollars were gone. Shirley had a more scientific approach: She would play five coins on one machine and if it didn't pay off, she'd move to the next machine. She was in constant motion all night long.

It took Dorothy about an hour and a half to lose her allotted Vegas money. After an hour and a half, Shirley was just getting started. She'd hit a five-dollar jackpot, then a ten-dollar pot. She'd lose most of that and then hit another five-dollar pot . . . waiting, hoping, and dreaming of that big eighty-dollar jackpot again. Dorothy found Shirley as she had just moved to a different machine. She watched her for a few minutes but soon grew bored of the constant jingling and moving around. Dorothy said, "I'm going up to the room, Shirley. See you later."

Noah

Shirley never moved her eyes off the spinning spaces of the slot machine as she answered, "Huh?"

"I said I'm going up to the room. Have fun."

Shirley was mesmerized by the allure of an easy eighty-dollars as she replied, "No, I'm fine, I'll get something to drink later."

Dorothy smiled and said, "Goodnight," wondering if Shirley would even make it up to the room at all. There were people, people, and more people. Dorothy was fascinated by all the faces but she was also tired from the long drive. She went to the room and took a long, hot bubble bath before bed.

Shirley was in constant motion, machine to machine; win three dollars, lose four dollars—back and forth all evening—she loved it! There are no clocks in casinos, and no windows either. At times, you wouldn't know if it's 3:00 AM or 3:00 PM. This was Shirley: She was completely transfixed and had lost all concept of time, but she could tell when she had to go to the bathroom. She gathered up her plastic cup of nickels and her phone and started for the restroom. Just as she left the casino area and started walking into the main concourse, she saw him. Noah. Plain as day, pushing a baby carriage. "Pushing a baby carriage?" She had to say that out loud to herself to make sure it registered.

She knew Noah from the picture he had sent Dorothy a couple of years ago. Even though she didn't think Noah had any clue who she was, she hid anyway. She jumped behind a fountain as he approached, rolling the carriage without a care in the world. She instantly thought, I've got to find Dorothy. Where is she? She started to walk back into the casino but then remembered something about Dorothy maybe going up to the room. During this mental confusion, she lost Noah in the crowd; couldn't find him anywhere. She quickly grabbed her phone and started to call Dorothy, then . . . she thought, Wait a minute. Do I really want to do that? Do I want to ruin Dorothy's night, and weekend, and life?

She put her phone up and started to sit on a bench and think before she remembered she had to go to the bathroom. When she came out, she couldn't decide what she should do. Noah had a baby! He doesn't want Dorothy anymore; he proved that a couple of years ago. She decided to go back to the casino and resume her quest for the eighty dollars. The problem with that plan was that she couldn't concentrate now. She couldn't remember if she had put in four or five or six nickels. She was all flustered.

Her plan was now blown, she had to quit. She had two nickels left in her hand, so she dropped them in the machine and BOOM! Bells started ringing and lights started flashing. Shirley had won a $500 pot! Under normal circumstances, she would probably have passed out. But now, all she could think of was, *How can I not tell Dorothy who I just saw?*

●●●

Shirley collected her winnings and decided to go up to the room and tell Dorothy about seeing Noah. She almost made it. There was one last "Super Jackpot" slot machine just at the exit of the casino. She thought, *What's five more dollars?* Turns out that five more dollars were really nothing compared to the one hundred fifty dollars she ended up losing. However, she reasoned, three hundred fifty ain't bad, so she was still happy. But it was nearly 3:00 AM now.

Dorothy had left the bathroom light on for her. She came into the room quietly, sat on the edge of her bed facing Dorothy's bed, and wondered what she should do. Certainly, Dorothy would want to know RIGHT now about any news regarding Noah, wouldn't she? Would Dorothy be mad if she didn't wake her with the news? She couldn't decide . . . not until Dorothy suddenly said, "What's wrong?" Dorothy's sudden comment startled Shirley so she didn't initially respond, then Dorothy again asked, "Shirley, what's wrong?"

"I saw Noah."

With that comment, Dorothy jumped out of bed and turned on the lamp between the two beds. She then sat on her bed facing Shirley and asked very slowly, "You saw Noah? My Noah? Tonight? Here, in this hotel?"

Noah

Shirley was nodding and answered, "Yes, yes, yes, and yes."

Dorothy couldn't sit any longer, she jumped to her feet and starting walking towards the window, muttering, "Oh, my God. Oh, my God. Oh, my God." Then she turned and came back to Shirley and sat on the bed and said, "I can't do it, Shirley. I can't see him again. I just can't do it. Not after everything that's happened. There's no way! Where was he? What was he doing? Do you think he's still there? No ... I can't, Shirley; I just can't. Can I?"

Dorothy expected Shirley to be happy and smiling but she wasn't. She reached over and took hold of Dorothy's hand and said, "He was rolling a baby carriage with a little baby in it."

Dorothy was stunned. She didn't know how to respond. She sat there two or three minutes in complete silence. She finally looked up at Shirley and asked, "Noah has a baby?" Shirley nodded and they both sat there looking at the floor. Then without another word, Dorothy turned off the light and laid back in her bed and turned away from Shirley, facing the wall. Shirley went into the bathroom and took her shower, then went to bed as well. Neither of them slept the rest of the night: Shirley was too worried about her friend and Dorothy realized her last and faintest dream was now irrevocably broken.

31.

FOR NOAH AND GRACE, SATURDAY WAS A REST DAY. She didn't have to be at the club until about 6:00 that evening, so she and Kai spent most of the day at the pool. Noah wanted to get away, so he ventured over to The Mirage to enjoy his day of solitude. While he was sitting in the casino there, at a quarter slot machine, he got a text from Vicki.

"Noah, I'm at your house. Where are you?"

He answered, "I didn't know you were in town. I had some business up in Salt Lake, won't be back till late Sunday night." He really had no reason to lie to her, but he had no reason to tell her the truth either. When she didn't answer him back, he thought, *Good.* He kept putting quarters in the slots, hoping it would take him most of the afternoon to lose the forty dollars he allotted himself. It took fifty-five minutes.

He walked by the blackjack tables and thought about trying his luck but wisely kept on walking. He had a couple of drinks while he watched all the people file by, nearly all of them wondering how they lost their money so quickly. Vegas can do that to you. Basically, he just enjoyed his time alone. He didn't count the thousands of other tourists milling around—in his mind, he was alone. He thought of Vicki, only in the way men think lustful thoughts, that's all. Then he thought of Ana and what might have been, what he wished would've been, and how sorry he was that it never was.

Noah

He was staring at the crowds passing by, but never really seeing anyone. His mind was in the "feeling sorry for myself" mode. He remembered Dorothy, the park ranger up at Canyonlands National Park, and how much he enjoyed their hikes, and rafting trip together, and how pretty she was, with those great legs of hers. He remembered the feelings he had for her, the feelings that he could never dismiss, no matter how hard he tried. Then, he unconsciously put his hand in his pocket and held the arrowhead that Dorothy had given him. The arrowhead that he always kept with him. Why? He didn't know. Dorothy was long gone. He'd never see her again. Yes, but why couldn't he throw away the arrowhead? Or at least put in a drawer somewhere and forget about it. Why?

●●●

Dorothy and Shirley finally drifted off to sleep around sunrise, but Dorothy's wake-up call woke them up very rudely. Dorothy had to get up and go to the conference all day—that was going to be torture. But, being the good girl that she was, she got up, showered, dressed, drank a cup of bland coffee, and trudged down to the conference center. Shirley slept.

Dorothy sat through slide shows, boring speakers, and interminable park business sessions. All the while, repeating and reliving the events of last night in her mind: Noah has a baby. Those four words would not leave her head: Noah has a baby. Noah has a baby.

Finally, after three hundred years, the conference ended. She was numb. She shook hands with everyone, especially all the other rangers who knew her boss, then she called Shirley and got no answer. She figured Shirley was, once again, testing her luck with the nickel slots.

Shirley was indeed at the slots but she hadn't been there long. She slept till nearly noon, then after she dressed, she walked around Bally's looking for Noah again. She looked in all restaurants, the bars, she checked out every corner of the casino, then the swimming pool and tennis courts. No Noah. She took a quick break for a late lunch, then she started her search once more, never finding him. Only then did she settle that itch for the slots.

Dorothy went upstairs and changed into something more comfortable, then went to the casino herself. No use calling Shirley; it was impossible to hear a phone ring in all that noise and commotion. She found Shirley exactly where she thought she would be: feeding nickels as fast she could into the ravenous machines. Shirley stopped the feeding frenzy long enough for them to go to the nearest bar for a drink.

Shirley told her she had searched for Noah all afternoon, never seeing him. Dorothy said, "That's okay, Shirley. What would've been the point, anyway? He has a baby, which means he has a wife, which means he never wants to see me again. I understand that. Just let it go."

Shirley knew Dorothy was right, but she couldn't help it. She hated seeing her friend suffering. Dorothy knew Shirley wanted to get back to the slots, so she let her go. They had tickets to a show later that night to see Bill Medley. It was the second show of the evening and it didn't start until 10:00, so Dorothy had plenty of time to kill. She told Shirley she'd come back and pick her up about 9:30.

Noah and Kai dropped Grace off at the club for her show that night, then they went back to the hotel. Poor little Kai was so tired from her playtime at the pool that afternoon she was sound asleep in the car. Back at the hotel, Noah strapped her in the baby carriage and began his quest to fill in the time until he could pick up Grace later tonight. He figured he would get something to eat at one of the many restaurants at the hotel, then walk around and visit some shops, and probably end up back in the large common area and enjoy a drink while he people-watched.

Noah

Shirley was immersed in the business of winning nickels, Noah had finished his dinner and was cruising the hotel's shopping areas, and Dorothy was aimlessly wasting time while letting her mind punish her, as only your mind can do. She was on the upper level of the two-level mall area, looking at nothing, feeling nothing, and expecting nothing, when . . . Boom!

She just happened to look down at the lower level and there he was— Noah, pushing a baby carriage. All her feelings over the last two years suddenly came rushing out and her brain quit functioning rationally. She turned and started following Noah's course, staying a few yards behind him, on the upper level, looking down at him. When he would stop and do some window shopping, she would get a good look at his face.

During one stop, Dorothy happened to be standing next to a store that sold beachwear and they had some of these big, floppy hats near the entrance. She rushed in and bought the widest-brimmed hat available. She tore the price tag off and then put it on and pulled it down tightly over her face, just in case Noah happened to look up.

She noticed how attentive he was to his baby, always stopping to check on it and constantly looking down at it. She wondered if it was a boy or girl--she couldn't tell from so far away. The baby looked as though it was fast asleep, but even so, Noah kept a vigilant watch over it. He was a good dad. Her heart broke even further if that was possible.

She followed them the entire length of the shopping area and then when Noah turned and came back the other direction, she changed sides and followed him still. She was totally and ultimately consumed by her quest. She never once thought, *What's next?* Or, *What should I do?* Or, anything else. She had followed him like a shadow while her mind was a total blank.

Eventually, after stopping to gaze into the casino for a few minutes, Noah went to the common area and sat near the far wall and ordered a drink. Dorothy couldn't tell what it was, alcoholic or not, but she was sure Noah would never drink an alcoholic beverage while taking care of his baby.

Noah sat at his little table and pulled the baby carriage over next to the wall, right beside his leg, and ordered an Iron Maiden. Kai was asleep, he was tired and bored, and he still had a couple of hours before he was to pick up Grace. Sipping and people-watching seemed to be an excellent combination for him.

When Dorothy was certain he would be sitting there for a while, she made her way over to the steps and carefully walked down to the level Noah was on. She was still probably forty or fifty feet away from him with her hat pulled down over her face. She went into the same common area where Noah was but stayed at the other end from him, and when she sat down, she didn't sit facing him. Her subterfuge was admirable; she could've been a spy during the Cold War. But during a war, there is a purpose for spying. Dorothy had no purpose, no plan, no reasoning whatsoever; she just couldn't help herself.

Noah sipped his Iron Maiden very slowly, keeping one eye on Kai while watching the constant movement of people. He played a game with himself: count the next ten women that walk by. He had to choose one of the ten to spend the night with. However; if he chose, say the third woman who walked by, then the remaining seven were off-limits. Or, if he didn't choose any of the first nine, he automatically HAD to take the tenth woman back to his room that night.

The first group of ten was very good to him. A young, blonde with great legs came by as the second woman of the group. He chose her! Great choice. The second group of ten women started strolling by and they were mostly older, out-of-shape ladies, with their pot-bellied husbands. Noah was stuck with the tenth woman; he had no alternatives.

Noah

Okay, one more group of ten. In his mind, this was for the championship of the world: the woman he'd have to spend his entire life with. He started to take the first woman who walked by; she was okay, but he let her pass. The next four were bad and he was starting to get worried. Then numbers six, seven, and eight passed by and were uglier than all the others. Finally, number nine was a very pretty middle-aged woman and Noah was relieved as he looked up to the sky and said, "Yes!"

When he said, "Yes," and looked upward, his gaze came back down toward the lady he chose as she was walking away--that's when he saw her. Dorothy, sitting at a table by herself. In his excitement, he must've bumped the baby carriage with his knee because Kai awoke and started crying very loudly. All the people around him started looking at him and his crying baby. He quickly got a bottle out and gave it to Kai, which instantly stopped the crying. He quickly looked back in the direction where he saw Dorothy . . . but she was gone.

Even though Dorothy had the best of spying intentions, she could not keep herself from staring at Noah. When he looked in her direction, she was staring directly at him. Their eyes met only for a second, maybe a half-second; but it was enough. It embarrassed her. As soon as Noah looked down at his baby, she immediately got up and left with the crowd. When Noah looked back, she was gone and he couldn't even tell which direction she took.

They were both in shock. They were both excited, and they were both troubled at the same time. They both asked themselves: How did this happen? What does it mean? What do I do now? Is this really happening? Neither of them had an answer to any of those questions.

32.

AS NOAH SAT THERE STUNNED, an elderly lady stepped directly in front of him and pointed down at Kai. A brown liquid was streaming out of the diaper at a pretty good rate. Noah must not have applied the last diaper change to the correct specifications. He hurried into the restroom and cleaned up everything as best as he could, then went back out looking all around him—but he knew she was gone.

He started asking himself questions: *Was that really her?* And also answering his own questions: *Of course it was, stupid!* Then: *What was she doing here? I have no idea.* And the craziest of all: *Was she here looking for me? Idiot! If she was looking for me, why did she leave when she saw me?* Many other questions as well, none of them making any sense whatsoever. He wanted to start walking and looking for her; however, it was time to go pick up Grace at the nightclub.

He craned his neck in every direction as he walked out of the hotel, hoping for a miracle. None would occur. He strapped Kai in the seat and started for the club to pick up Grace, but he forgot where to turn and ended up way out near the Stratosphere Hotel and Casino before he realized his error. As he was turning around, his cellphone rang. It was Grace, "Noah, are you on the way?"

"Yeah, you know, traffic is always bad on Saturday nights. I'll be there in about five minutes." It was actually twelve minutes before he arrived but Grace wasn't mad . . . she was beaming.

She said, "Noah, they loved me. They want me to come back. They want me to sing next weekend and think about becoming a regular. They offered me a great deal, Noah! What do you think?"

Noah never looked over at her and said, "Yeah, we're fine. Kai had a little accident but I cleaned it all up and we had a great night. Thanks for asking."

"Noah! I know Kai is always alright with you . . . I'm never worried about that. Did you hear what I just said?" Noah didn't respond quickly enough, so she continued. "I'll make more in two weekends than I could make in a whole month at the coffee shop! And, I'd be doing something I love, not making old, ornery men blueberry muffins and coffee."

Noah then looked over at her, because they were at a stoplight, and replied, "I have changed to cinnamon/raisin bagels, thank you."

She then slapped Noah's arm and said, "I thought you'd be happy for me."

"I am, Grace, but you have to really think about this whole thing. Sure, you'll make more money, but it'll also cost you a bunch more to live in Vegas than it does in Moab. The cost of living is probably double what you're used to. And, did they offer you any sort of contract that guarantees you a job for any length of time?"

It was obvious Grace had never thought of any of those things. She reached into the back seat and adjusted the baby bottle that Kai was holding, then said, "You understand me, don't you baby?" Kai burped, then smiled, and Grace said, "See, she agrees with me."

Dorothy walked away as fast as she could. She pulled the big floppy hat down tightly over her face and went straight for the elevators. She tried in vain to call Shirley, but that was pointless. In the room, she threw the hat on the bed and changed clothes. She put on blue jeans, an old floppy sweatshirt, then put on a baseball cap and stuffed her hair underneath the cap as best she could. Then, she put on a pair of over-sized sunglasses she used for driving and left the room. She had to have a second look. Why? She just had to. She'd never forgive herself if she didn't.

She had no intention of confronting Noah. She didn't want to talk to him or come between him and his new family . . . she just wanted to see him. As primal as that sounds, that's all it was; she just wanted to see his face again one more time. She hurried to the open area and walked around. She walked all through the casino, past every bar and restaurant. She checked out every shop and nook and cranny of the hotel . . . nothing. Then, she went back to the large open area and sat near the same table she was sitting at when Noah saw her. She took off her hat and shook her hair free; she took off the sunglasses and ordered a martini. She'd never actually had a martini before, but it felt like the thing to do.

Shortly after 2:00 AM, things started to slow down a little in the hotel and casino. Some of the shops closed, the casino closed a few of the tables, and the restaurants began turning their lights off. Dorothy just sat there. Around 3:00 AM, one of the waiters told her he was leaving and asked if she wanted anything else. What she wanted, he could not deliver. She rose and shuffled off to the elevators. Only when she was inside the elevator and reached to punch her floor number did she remember Bill Medley!

Oh my, God. How could I forget that? Shirley is going to kill me. She went to the room and opened the door expecting the worst. What she found was Shirley in the shower singing, "Iiiiii, had the time of my liiiiffe and I owe it all to you, the time of my liiiiiffffe." Shirley was singing that refrain over and over. It didn't matter that the words were wrong, it was the pure joy that mattered. When Shirley came out of the shower, she told Dorothy that she had looked all over for her and tried calling her repeatedly. Then, when the show was over, she had looked again and couldn't find her, so she played some more nickel slots, then came to the room. Bill Medley had her so excited that sleep seemed nearly impossible.

●●●

After Grace showered and put Kai to bed, she quickly went to sleep, snoring like a freight train. For Noah, sleep was hopeless. He couldn't stop thinking about seeing Dorothy. Just that one-second sighting had turned his world upside down. He went to the small desk in the room and opened his laptop; might as well answer a few questions for his column as long as he was awake.

Noah

"Noah: I'm a young, single lady here in town and I wanted you and your readers to understand how hard it is to find a nice guy in the local bar scene. I'm giving up. I'd rather sit home and watch TV than keep going to the bars expecting to meet a decent man. Aren't there any good ones? Signed, Casey"

"Casey: The worst thing about trying to meet a good man in a bar is that when they are not drunk, they are sober."

"Noah: I gave my grandson some advice years ago that I think might help you as well. He didn't fit in with his fellow high school students and he was socially awkward like you seem to be. I told him to start going to dances and join some clubs so that he can get socially acclimated. I think this advice is good for you as well. I hope it helps. Signed, Lois."

"Lois: Thanks for the advice. I really appreciate it; however, I must admit I have absolutely no desire to fit in . . . at all."

"Noah: I just moved to Utah from Vancouver, Canada. So far, I love it here. Any advice you can give me as a new arrival in your country? Signed, Colin."

"Colin: I will give you some advice from a great American patriot: Resist much, obey little."

"Noah: From what I can tell, you like to have a drink occasionally. My question is this: Are you sure that sometimes your drinks aren't doing the talking for you? What do you say, Noah? Signed, Phillip."

"Phillip: I thought about your question very hard. And I think if drinks COULD talk, here is what they'd say:
Coffee--You can do this!
Wine--You don't have to do this!

Tequila--Holy crap! Did you really just do that?

Work got his mind off Dorothy for a few minutes, but as soon as he turned the light off, the memory of that one-second sighting returned. Between Grace's snoring and Dorothy's memory, any chance of sleep would be fleeting. Tomorrow's long drive back home to Moab was going to be very cruel.

SIX MONTHS LATER

33.

NOAH WAS ON HIS DRIVE OVER TO LAS VEGAS to help babysit Kai and hopefully see Grace perform at the club that signed her to a contract. She moved there and found a one-bedroom apartment on the edge of town that suited her needs—meaning cheap. She usually performed two shows on Friday night, one longer show on Saturday night, and a regular show on Sunday night. She also found a nanny she could trust with Kai during the showtimes. After paying a higher rent than she did in Moab, and paying the nanny, then adding the higher cost of everything else in Las Vegas as opposed to a small Utah town, she was struggling financially. That's why Noah came over to help her whenever he could.

He couldn't come every month, but he did try to get there every five or six weeks for a three-day weekend, where he could babysit and save Grace the cost of a nanny for those three days. In the six months that Grace had been performing at the small club, Noah had only seen her in person twice. And just as he thought, she was very good. Whether or not she had a long-term future as a performer was yet to be seen. Usually, in cases like the one with Grace, you had to "know" someone in the business. Performers in Vegas are literally a dime a dozen.

However, Grace wouldn't change a thing. She loved it. She was doing something she truly enjoyed and it also gave her much more free time to raise her daughter, whom she adored. It didn't take much convincing to get Noah to come and help out when he could. He was looking for an easy excuse to come to Las Vegas in the hope of somehow, some magical way, running into Dorothy again. He had already decided that if he saw her again, no matter what, he would drop everything (except Kai) and run to her without question. He also knew the chances of that happening were slim and none . . . and slim just left the building.

But he was persistent; he and Kai would drop Grace off at her club, then they'd go to Bally's Hotel and Casino, where he last saw Dorothy. And he would push the stroller up and down the hallways, all over the shopping areas, the casino, the restaurant areas, the mall areas, and the swimming pool outside. He didn't leave anything to chance. Kai loved all the jingling, jangling excitement of the large hotel and seemed mesmerized by it all.

Six months ago, when Noah was back in Moab after seeing Dorothy in Las Vegas, he tormented himself about whether he should try calling her at Death Valley National Park. He knew she worked there because he had tried to call her over two years ago. She wouldn't take his call then and some official told him if he tried to call her again, they would notify the authorities for harassment. He did not need that publicity. But now . . . after nearly two-and-half years? He had to take the chance. So one day, after his third cup of regular coffee, and a cup of Irish coffee, he called. He was going to tell her how he felt and let the chips fall where they may.

And . . . she didn't work there any longer. Dorothy had transferred to another national park and, as policy, they don't divulge any personal information about the park rangers. He had no clue where she went. Now, he only hoped that she enjoyed going to Las Vegas occasionally and that he could somehow, magically, run into her again.

●●●

When Dorothy returned from Las Vegas, after seeing Noah that one fateful night, she immediately took a leave of absence. The park service called it a furlough, which meant she was still an employee, just not working. She did nothing the first week she was home . . . nothing. Shirley tried calling her but Dorothy simply didn't want any conversations--she wasn't up to it. Being a counselor, Shirley understood a little of what Dorothy was feeling, but she was still worried about her friend.

The second week, Dorothy decided she'd had enough of Death Valley. She applied for several jobs in other national parks, all out west, and told herself she'd take the first opportunity that came available. With Dorothy's experience and work record, it didn't take long for the job offers to come. The second day after she applied, she received an offer to interview at Zion National Park, in Utah. She accepted and drove over to Zion, which is in southern Utah, two days later.

The park superintendent at Zion knew of Dorothy because he was friends with her boss at Death Valley. When he saw her application, he called Dorothy's old boss and knew then he would hire her immediately. The interview was more of a meeting to see if she liked them. She did. She told them she would need three weeks to work out her notice and be available, which was fine. However, she didn't need three weeks at all to work out a notice. Her boss would've let her go with one day's notice. She needed extra time to get over the events of Las Vegas and to visit Shirley in California.

When Shirley knew Dorothy was coming, she took a week off from work so she could be with her friend. Dorothy needed that. She needed all the consoling, soothing, and encouraging solace that Shirley could offer. After a week, she was ready to go back to work: at a new place, with new people and new duties, and hopefully with a new mindset.

●●●

For Noah, life kept going. He kept answering questions from the good people of Salt Lake City and every four or five weeks he would "entertain" Vicki. However, he was growing less and less enamored of his role and actions in that so-called relationship. Lately, he had taken to hiding from her. When she called him, he wouldn't answer; instead, he'd get in his Jeep and go hiking in the desert where there was no cell phone service--a convenient excuse. And, for some reason now, the desert seemed to satisfy him more than Vicki ever did. Even his responses to his readers had changed:

"Noah: I feel useless and worthless. I don't know what to do. Any suggestions? Signed, Kay."

"Kay: Trust me. You are here for a purpose. There is no duplicate of you in the whole wide world. There never has been, there never will be. You were brought here now to fill a certain need. Take time to think that over."

"Noah: I think I'm in middle age now, I'm not sure. I might be old, or middle-aged, I'm confused. How old is old now? How do you know when you're old, Noah? Signed, Shelley."

"Shelley: Do not grow old, no matter how long you live. Never cease to stand like a curious child before the great mystery into which you were born."

"Noah: I keep waiting for that magical moment to hit me when I'm dating someone. I have yet to find it. Is that all a fairy tale? Is life just boring and predictable? I'm getting depressed. Signed, Jan."

"Jan: The really magical things are the ones that happen right in front of you. A lot of the time you keep looking for beauty, but it is already there. And if you look with a bit more intention, you'll see it."

Noah's editor was under pressure to bring him back into the office and find out what was wrong with him. His readers liked wit, humor, sarcasm, and Noah's eccentric way of seeing the world; not this psychological mumbo-jumbo. They wanted to be entertained. They enjoyed seeing Noah's humorous insight with people. They wanted the old Noah back. The editor was under pressure. But, so was Noah. He had lost the joy in his life. His hope was fading. He hadn't even picked up his arrowhead in weeks now. He was taking on the persona of the desert itself: dry, barren, desolate, bleak, and lonesome.

Noah had been doing most of his hiking in Canyonlands National Park, where Dorothy used to work, because . . . well, it's where Dorothy used to work. Each time he went there now was a history lesson in how to lose a girl. Every trail reminded him of her. He had to abandon this magical place; he couldn't keep tormenting himself. And, he had to get rid of the ever-present arrowhead that Dorothy had given him. He planned to hike there one last time and take the arrowhead to the most remote corner of the vast park and leave it as a symbol of their lost love. It seemed fitting, if not just a bit melodramatic, but at least it was a good hiding place in case Vicki called again.

When he arrived at the park, he drove to the most remote region and parked his car in the dirt lot at the trailhead to the Confluence, which was the point where the mighty Green River and the powerful Colorado River merge on their way through Utah, Arizona, and California. From the trailhead to the actual overlook, where you see the two rivers merge, was a long, tiring, dusty, primitive, loosely-marked trail. Very few tourists ever attempted this day-long hike. Sometimes, some locals would give it a try, and there were always a few die-hard knuckleheads who kept remembering the unforgettable; but they were dying off as time crept by.

He knew that, most likely, he would not see another human being all day. Just a rabbit, maybe, or a few buzzards and probably not much of anything else. The only problem with this scenario was that if something happened to him--health problem, accident, anything at all--there was no cell phone service out there in the back of beyond and no one to come along and help him. So, Noah was careful. He packed plenty of water and food for the all-day hike, along with the arrowhead, which he was going to place at the tip of the overlook to the confluence itself. He was going to leave it there as a reminder; no, not as a reminder, but as a way to get rid of a memory. No, not that either . . . in fact, he didn't really know why he was going to leave it there. He just knew that, somehow, it made sense to leave it. Just don't ask him to explain it.

It was a little overcast as he started, but soon, the clouds fled and left him alone with the burning sun and no shade whatsoever. He hoped he had packed enough water. As the temperatures rose and the dust chocked his throat, he soon began the art of rationalization and deception. He reminded himself that a gallon of water weighed eight pounds, which was a heavy load in his backpack. But it wouldn't be nearly as heavy in his stomach. *Yeah, that makes perfect sense! I'll drink it up quickly, so it'll be easier on my back.*

Noah

By the time he arrived at the confluence, he only had a little of his precious water left. But his back felt great! He sat down and leaned against a rock and looked closely at the actual confluence itself. The Green River was a bit lighter in color and clearer than the dark foreboding waters of the Colorado. When they met and converged, they didn't blend; the Green River stayed on one side and the Colorado stayed on the other side as they flowed side-by-side down the canyon, one side lighter and the other side darker, as if the two rivers were hesitant to mix with each other.

Noah sat there and held the arrowhead in his hand, the same arrowhead that Dorothy had placed in his hand years ago. The same arrowhead that he held nearly every night since then. The one object that always brought back memories that he couldn't or wouldn't abandon. He finally went over to the edge of the overlook area and built himself a rock cairn about two feet high and placed the arrowhead in the middle of that rock monument. Buried, forgotten, and hidden, never to be seen again—just like his memories and hopes of Dorothy. When that was done, he picked up his waterless pack and headed back down the trail. He had snacks of almonds, crackers, and granola bars, all of which made his empty water container seem even more cruel--but his back felt great.

On his drive out of the park and back home, he stopped at the only gas station/convenience store between Canyonlands and Moab to buy three bottles of water, which he hoped would last him on the hour drive back home. He drank the first bottle before ever leaving the parking lot, then went back in the store and bought two more bottles, just in case. By the time he arrived in Moab, all five bottles were emptied and he still had no desire to pee. He was very tired but didn't want to go home, just in case Vicki was driving by looking for his car. He stopped at the Moab Brewery, which had thinned out a little since earlier in the evening because most of the tourists were back in their hotels at this hour.

He ordered his usual Black Raven Stout, plus a bacon-burger and fries. He needed calories but not conversation, which is why he wasn't thrilled when his old friend Sandy came and sat next to him. He never stopped eating as Sandy began, "Noah, dude, how ya doing?"

Very hesitantly, with his mouth full, he answered, "Good, Sandy."

"Whatcha been up to? I haven't seen you lately."

"Nothing. You?"

Sandy was looking around the pub, as if searching for someone, and replied, "Well, you know how it is." Noah had absolutely no idea how it was with Sandy and truthfully, did not care, so he didn't answer. She continued, "I'm actually kinda bored. Don't have another river trip lined up till next week and I'm sorta in-between things, if you know what I mean." As before, he had no idea what she meant, and he still didn't care. So, she went on, "I was wondering what you're doing later?"

He had just taken a drink and could barely swallow when he heard this comment. All he could think to say was, "Huh?"

She lightly elbowed him and said, "You know, if you're not busy, maybe we could hook-up and help pass the time. What do you think?"

Noah set his drink down, then picked up one fry and ate half of it, and said, "No, Sandy. I'm really not interested. Sorry."

"Well, I thought we were friends, Noah."

"We are friends, just not THAT kind of friend."

Sandy looked really hurt. She pouted and said, "Well, you kissed me that night on the raft trip. Remember?"

He remembered alright. Everyone was drinking shots and pretty much wasted when they all decided to skinny-dip in the river after it was dark. Sandy had come up behind him, in waist-deep water, and suddenly splashed in front of him, then kissed him before he knew who she was, then she immediately puked in the river and passed out. It took four guys to drag her out of the river and lay her on the bank while she slept it off. Noah had no idea Sandy could have ever remembered that happening. She had never brought it up before. He didn't know what to say to her. Before he could think of anything, she said, "Remember the river, Noah? Remember? The river??"

Noah

He took one last, long drink of his stout, then thoughtfully replied, "Sandy, rivers never go in reverse. So, try to live like a river. Forget your past and focus on your future. Always be positive, Sandy." With that, he got up and walked out of the pub, greatly hoping Sandy wasn't following him. She wasn't. She was far too confused by Noah's statement to even think of following him. She sat there, ate the last of his fries, and started looking around the pub for someone else she had kissed in the past. It wouldn't take her long.

Noah drove home but stopped at the corner first just to make sure he didn't see Vicki's car anywhere. When he started to put his key in the lock, he noticed a piece of paper taped to the door. When inside, with the door securely locked, he read the note,

"Okay, Noah, I get it. You don't have to keep hiding from me. Don't worry, you'll never see me again.
Oh, and one other thing, Noah . . . F#@k you!

Sincerely, Vicki."

34.

DOROTHY'S MOVE TO ZION NATIONAL PARK was a whirlwind of
activity. It surprised her how much "junk" she had in her old place.
She took this opportunity to relieve herself of sentimental items and
things she didn't need anymore. This would truly be a new beginning
for her in every sense. Everything was different in Zion. Going from
Death Valley (aptly named) to Zion was like going from Dante's
inferno to the Sistine Chapel. Glorious mountains, waterfalls, a
beautiful river, stunning canyons . . . Zion had it all and Dorothy was
in love with it.

She found a small house for rent in the little town of Springdale,
which was as close to the park as she could get without being inside
the boundary. It was literally on the western edge of Zion as you drive
out of the park. Zion had more employees than Death Valley, more
male employees who took a keen interest in the beautiful Dorothy and
noticed right away that she wore no ring on her wedding finger.

Her job at Zion was an administrative one but it also involved a first-
hand visual review of the park's roads and campgrounds each week.
Dorothy loved this. Zion's vistas and scenery were breathtaking. The
only problem was that Zion is in a remote region of southwestern
Utah that is far off the usual tourist paths. It's not an easy place to get
to, that's why it's not as famous as many as the other parks in the
country.

Shirley came and visited Dorothy when she was settled in, but
Shirley's idea of a grand vacation was sitting in front of a nickel slot
machine all day and night. Hiking trails and climbing up mountain
slopes were not on Shirley's agenda of a memorable experience.

Dorothy drove her through the park, then they spent their evenings in Springdale, which offered several eclectic restaurants and pubs to choose from. They talked about everything except the one thing that brought them together in the first place. That subject was strictly off-limits. Noah's name was never mentioned . . . but it was never forgotten either.

Within the first three weeks of Dorothy's employment, she had turned down seven offers of "getting some coffee," or "having a drink," or "catching a movie," and even, "would you like to have some fun tonight?" It was a combination of Dorothy being very attractive and the dearth of attractive women in and around Zion and Springdale that made her particularly conspicuous and significant to the male population. She almost accepted an offer of "coffee" from an older park employee named Kevin, but before she could give him an answer, he added, "My apartment is just down the street from the coffee shop."

When Shirley had visited earlier, one of the park employees had seen Dorothy and Shirley out at a local restaurant. Then, with Dorothy not accepting any of the date invitations from the male employees, the rumors began circulating that maybe Dorothy's interest level was a bit different. That would explain why she had turned down all the exciting offers of male companionship. Dorothy heard all the rumors and she was fine with it. If it kept her from getting hit on nearly every day, she was in no hurry to change anyone's opinion.

She impressed everyone with her work enthusiasm and her dedication; she was the perfect employee. She fixed up her little house and kept in touch with Shirley and with some friends from Death Valley. She joined a small gym in Springdale and kept herself in great shape. She hiked the vast canyons and mountains of Zion on her off-days. And, she was so lonely that she could cry. She never said it out loud, but the thought was always in her mind: Noah is married.

The problem with that logic was that Noah wasn't married. In fact, he was as lonely as she was. His problem was that he had no idea where Dorothy was, and even if he did, what difference would it make. She obviously didn't want to see him anymore. She had her chance that night in Las Vegas, but instead of coming over to him, she walked away. Case settled. Well, the case might be settled, but his heart was another thing altogether. As Woody Allen so cleverly stated it once-upon-a-time: "The heart wants what the heart wants."

There are approximately 210 miles, as the crow flies, between Moab and Zion National Park. 340 miles if you have to drive it in a car. But it's all irrelevant if you don't even know that the love of your life resides in one of these places. They might as well be on the moon, or Texas, or some other God-forsaken place. So, they each spent their time hiking--Dorothy in the vast wilderness and beauty of Zion and Noah in the red-rock, unsurpassed beauty of Arches and Canyon-lands--each engulfed in their own aloneness, in their own lonesome-ness, in their own solitude, desolation, and heartache.

Noah's life had reverted to its quieter and lonelier days. Grace was in Las Vegas, Ana was an illusion that faded away, and Dorothy was a ghost of his imagination now. And, his column had gotten back to its regular tone.

"Noah: I know this might make some people mad but I feel like I should be heard, like a voice crying in the wilderness. Our country is dying and something has to be done! We need to stop immigration, stop all welfare payments, stop unemployment payments, and give everyone a gun! There! It needed to be said and I said it. Well, Noah? Signed, Bob."

"Bob: You make me wish that birth control was retroactive."

"Noah: I know you don't go to a gym or workout, you've said that for years now. Aren't you worried about your health and especially your cholesterol? Signed, Amy."

"Amy: I drive way too fast to worry about cholesterol."

"Noah: Last year you listed some of your favorite country songs. Do you have any new ones you like? Signed, Roscoe."

"Roscoe: Yes, I do. My favorite country song right now is '*I Can't Get Over You Till You Get Out From Under Him.*'"

"Noah: I hate my job. I mean I really hate it. What should I do? Signed, Gwyn."

"Gwyn: You hate your job? There's a support group for that. It's called EVERYBODY, and they meet at the bar each week."

"Noah: Okay, we get it. You don't like to exercise, you don't like golf, you don't like this or that . . . what DO you like, Noah? Signed, Tiphany."

"Tiphany: Are you sure your name is spelled right? In answer to your question, all the things I really like to do are either immoral, illegal, or fattening."

"Noah: My son is about to enter college and we're trying to decide what he should major in to be successful. We want him to either be a doctor or a lawyer. Which do you think is best? Signed, Barclay."

"Barclay: Doctors are just the same as lawyers. The only difference is that lawyers merely rob you, whereas doctors rob you and kill you."

And so it went for Noah: working on his column, hiking in the desert, visiting the Moab Brewery and Fiddlin' Fish occasionally, and dreaming of what could've been. Plus, he was having a hard time going to sleep at night. In the past, he'd lie in bed and hold his arrowhead and think. It made him feel good. It was a reminder of one of the best times in his life. And, what did he do? Left it under a pile of rocks at the confluence. He wanted his arrowhead back. Why? Have we already forgotten what Woody Allen said?

He went to his coffee shop in the morning; however, it wasn't the same since Grace had left for Las Vegas. Luray, of course, was still there and she'd hired her niece to replace Grace. The niece, Andra, was not on Noah's list of most favorite people. She routinely confused his order, as simple as it was. She even brought him tea one day instead of coffee! He never said anything about her lapses because Luray was Grace's friend, and really his friend as well, in a weird sort of way.

However, all that changed one day when Andra brought Noah's order to his table, and just as she started to set it down, she sneezed right on his bagel. He could see all the phlegm, mucus, and germs exiting Andra's uncovered mouth landing directly on his food. Andra said, "Whew, excuse me." Then she sat the bagel down in front of him and walked away. Noah looked over at the cash register at Luray, who quickly looked down and avoided his stare. He got up from the table and started walking for the door when he heard Andra yell out, "Hey, sir, you haven't paid your bill yet." He kept walking. It was the last time he visited his coffee shop. HIS coffee shop . . . where HE was the man, where things were always the way HE wanted them done.

Dang! He walked down the block to Starbucks and started to walk in, then changed his mind and went to an appliance store and bought himself a Keurig. He took his coffee maker home, changed his clothes, and drove off towards Canyonlands National Park. He had to get his arrowhead back . . . now! Why? Because he had to, that's why. Because it's all he had left of Dorothy. Because even though he knew he'd never see her again, she gave him the arrowhead. She gave it to him. It transferred from her hand to his hand. That's why!

As usual, the small, dirt parking lot at the trailhead to the confluence was empty except for an old dilapidated Volkswagen beetle from about 1968. Noah filled his pack with water, nuts, crackers, and candy—for energy! Not a cloud in the sky, nothing except the sun and several vultures either looking for dinner or asleep; it was hard to tell. After the first incline, which made him lose his breath, he stopped thinking so much and just concentrated on the day, no . . . the hour, no . . . the minute that Dorothy had handed him the arrowhead.

Noah

He had found the arrowhead earlier in the day while on a hike with Dorothy. It was very unusual to find one in the wild like that. As soon as he picked it up, he showed it to Dorothy and then put it in his pocket. Dorothy immediately chided him, saying, "You can't keep that, Noah." She was, of course, a park ranger and she knew the rules. Any artifact found in a national park must be replaced; you cannot keep them—that's the rule! You are expected to put it back right where you found it. Noah had never heard of that rule, and like most (meaning ALL) people who have found artifacts in the past, he was going to keep it.

If it had been anyone besides Dorothy, he would've told them to stick that rule where the sun don't shine—that arrowhead was his! But this was Dorothy, and she was a park ranger, and it was her job to enforce the rules. Noah took the arrowhead out of his pocket, rolled it around in his hand for a few seconds, then he looked once again at Dorothy's beautiful face. She looked back at him and said, "No."

He nodded, then placed the arrowhead back on the ground, several feet off the trail, so no one else would find it, and then he tried to act mad. It was a poor act. He started back down the trail and Dorothy quickly caught up with him. After a few minutes, his "mad" act was over. They made the rest of the trip as if in a dream. When they arrived at the trail end and the car, it surprised them both, and disappointed them both—they didn't want the hike to end.

Noah drove them back to Moab and they each were silently begging the clock to slow down and the miles to lengthen. But no matter how slowly he drove, they eventually arrived back in town at Dorothy's car. He stopped beside her car and wanted to reach over and take her hand, and kiss her, and touch her . . . but he didn't. She sat there silently but wishing Noah would touch her hand, would kiss her, would do something . . . but he didn't. After a few futile moments, Dorothy opened the door slightly but stopped and then reached in her pocket and pulled out the arrowhead that Noah had found earlier in the day. When he had huffed away, trying to act mad, she quickly retrieved the artifact and put it in her pocket.

She reached her hand over to him, with the arrowhead in her palm, and started to give it to him, then pulled back slightly and said, "If you ever tell anyone I gave this to you, I'll kill you." She smiled and

Noah almost fainted. Not because he was given the arrowhead, but because Dorothy smiled at him. She broke the law, her law, the national park law, for him. And, she smiled at him.

This is what Noah thought about all the way to the confluence. This is all he thought about all the way to the confluence. He was almost shocked when he reached the end of the trail and saw the two mighty rivers converging right in front of him. He was so lost in thought that he hadn't even drunk any of his precious water. Then, something moved in front of him. Someone was sitting at the edge and leaning against a rock. The person turned when they heard him approaching; it was an older man, with white hair and a goatee. Then it hit Noah, he must be the person who was driving the old VW beetle at the trailhead.

35.

"HELLO, SIR. HOW ARE YOU DOING?" Noah asked this question just to be sure the older guy was okay.

"I'm great, I hope you are. Beautiful out here, isn't it?"

Noah nodded and walked over toward the man and sat on the ground several feet away from him. After he drank a little water, Noah introduced himself and the man answered, "Nice to meet you, Noah. My name is George. Don't usually see many hikers out this far in the desert. You surprised me a little."

Noah answered, "You surprised me too, George. I've been out here to the confluence several times and you might be the only person I've ever seen."

George smiled and said, "I've probably hiked out here a hundred times over the years. Used to do it with my wife but she died about a year and a half ago. Now it's just me."

"I'm sorry to hear that, George. You live around here?"

"Not too far away; I live in Monticello. You ever been there?" Not only had Noah never been there, he'd never even heard of Monticello. George could tell by the blank look on his face, so he continued, "It's a little town of about two thousand people. We're about seven thousand feet up in elevation though, which makes it nice in the summers but snowy and cold in the winters. Don't get many visitors in the wintertime."

They continued their introductions, with each guy wondering why the other guy was way out here by himself. George told Noah that his wife had taught school in Monticello, all the way from first grade to the eighth grade. He also worked at the school as a jack-of-all-trades. He would fix anything that broke, drive kids home, help grade papers, clean the bathrooms, or anything else that needed to be done. When his wife died, he retired.

Noah asked, "So, your wife used to hike out here with you?"

"Oh, yeah, she was a better hiker than me. She never got tired; I couldn't keep up with her. This is the first time I've been out here since she died. It might be the last. This was her favorite place and I ain't as young as I look." George smiled and Noah nodded and smiled back. Then George asked, "Why are you out here by yourself?"

Noah pointed to a pile of rocks over near the edge of the cliff, the little rock cairn he had made to hide his arrowhead in. "I came to get something out of that pile of rocks."

He knew George would never understand what that meant and he was wondering just how much he should explain, when George said, "Something about a girl, huh? Something she gave you and you want to get it back?"

Noah was dumbfounded. He didn't answer right away, and George continued to stare at him. Finally, he said, "Yeah, yeah . . . how did you know that?"

"What else could it be? A man doesn't come out here by himself with no good reason. Only a woman can make a man do crazy things, unless he's already crazy and you don't seem naturally crazy to me. So, it had to be a woman. What's under the rocks?"

"An arrowhead. She gave it to me."

"And why did you come way out here and leave it under those rocks?"

Noah spent the next twenty minutes explaining his history with Ana and Dorothy and the arrowhead. George listened intently and never interrupted. When Noah finished the story, George said, "Go get it. I want to see this famous arrowhead." So, Noah rose and went to the little rock cairn and carefully moved all the rocks until he found what he was looking for. When he picked up the arrowhead, he held it in his hand and was temporarily lost in thought. Then, he remembered George and brought the arrowhead over to him so he could see what would cause a man to hike way out here to the middle of nothingness.

George only held the arrowhead briefly, then handed it back to Noah and told him, "You know you'll never be happy till you go find this girl and tell her how you feel, don't you? How long can a man nourish himself on reminiscence alone?

"I don't where she is, George."

"Bull hockey! Go find her and quit using these lame excuses, son. Trust me, every day you lose now, you'll regret it later."

They both sat there a few minutes thinking about what George had said. Noah knew it was true. So did George. Noah was truly missing his girl. So was George. Finally, George rose and said, "Let's start back. Do you mind if I walk with you?"

Noah smiled and answered, "I'd love it."

They stood up, gathered their packs for the long hike back, and then they both turned to stare out at the amazing spectacle of the confluence one last time. Noah said, "George, just imagine how long it took God to create that scene, and then I almost spoiled it for myself by leaving my arrowhead here."

George turned to look at Noah, who was still eyeing the confluence of the two great rivers, and he said, "Son, God dwells in eternity but time dwells in God. He has already lived all our tomorrows as he has lived all our yesterdays. It's up to you now." Noah wanted to get out a pen and write that down so he could use it in his column but all he had in his pack were some empty candy wrappers and a water bottle. He'd try his best to remember it.

George told Noah a little about his wife; it was very evident she was the love of his life and that he missed her terribly. She had died suddenly. She hadn't seemed sick; she just didn't wake up one morning. The doctors said it was a heart attack. For George, it certainly was a heart attack. One his heart would never recover from. Then, the mood lightened as they tromped on down the path. George never seemed to tire or need a water break, unlike Noah, who was struggling a bit. It helped Noah to keep George talking so he could concentrate on the conversation rather than on how tired he was.

They were discussing people and friends they both had, then they started talking about celebrities and sports stars. Finally, Noah asked George, "What sort of people do you like best, George?"

Without hesitation, George answered, "I like people who make me laugh, make me think, and make me coffee. Not necessarily in that order."

"Are you on Facebook, George? I'd like to connect with you if you don't mind."

"Son, to be honest with you, Facebook sounds like a drag to me. In my day, seeing pictures of people's vacations and what they ate for dinner was considered to be a punishment."

Noah laughed and replied, "Sir, I think you're a lot smarter than your age. Now, if you don't mind, can we stop for a minute and let me catch my breath and have a drink of water?" George stopped and looked up at the sky for some reason. Noah didn't understand what he was looking at—there weren't even any clouds to see—only the sun. There was a small rock nearby and Noah sat down and got his water bottle for a long drink. George kept standing and continued to look at the sky.

When they started hiking again, both men were silent for a few minutes, then Noah asked, "I guess you think I'm a little crazy to hike all the way out here just to get my little arrowhead back, huh, George?"

"Son, sometimes the smallest things take up the most room in your heart. I understand completely."

They hiked in silence for quite some time, mostly because Noah was dead tired and didn't have the energy to talk. George sensed that he should stop for a bit and let Noah catch his breath again. Noah ate the last chunk of candy he had and even offered George a bite of it. George declined. Noah then asked him about getting older: "George, seems to me you're in great shape, aging doesn't seem to have bothered your stamina at all. I'm impressed."

George smiled at this compliment, or maybe he was smiling because Noah was not in great shape, it was a little unclear. Then he said, "Funny thing about getting older, your eyesight may weaken yet you can see through people much better." Again, he smiled at Noah, and Noah instantly wondered if George was pontificating or talking about him personally. Before he could decide which, George said, "You ready? Not much further."

They finally arrived at the end of the trail just before the sun started dropping below the horizon. They shook hands and exchanged thanks to each other for a fine afternoon. Noah started to ask George for his phone number, in case they might want to get together again, but . . . he didn't. He did walk over to George's old Volkswagen with him and watched him put his pack in the back seat. Noah looked a little sad to George, so George asked him, "You okay, son?"

Noah was holding the arrowhead in his hand and answered, "Yeah, I guess I am, George. I just hope I'm doing the right thing."

George looked directly in Noah's eyes, all the way into his soul, and replied, "Remember, if you're headed in the wrong direction, God allows U-turns!"

They shook hands again and Noah went over to his Jeep and started it up while he watched George pull out on the little road and head for the exit. Noah took a long drink of water, then decided to change his shirt, which was wet with sweat. When he was finished, he also started for the exit gate. When he arrived, the park ranger was waiting on him so he could close the gate for the night. Noah pulled up and asked the ranger, "That Volkswagen that just left here, with the older guy driving it, do you happen to know him?"

The park ranger stared back at Noah and asked, "What Volkswagen?"

"The one that just left here, right in front of me?"

"Sir, there hasn't been another car come through here for at least fifteen minutes and it was a big pickup truck. I haven't seen any Volkswagens."

Noah asked, "Are you sure?"

The park ranger didn't exactly appreciate this inquisition; he was ready to go home. He said, "Yes. I'm quite sure."

It was a long, lonely, thought-provoking drive back to Moab. One in which Noah's left hand never left the steering wheel and his right hand never let go of the arrowhead.

●●●

Noah wanted to think about what his options were with finding Dorothy but he was so tired when he got home that he went straight to bed. He woke in the morning with the arrowhead lying in the bed next to him. He closed his eyes, wishing the arrowhead would magically turn into Dorothy. It didn't. He got up and plugged in his new Keurig, only to realize that he hadn't bought any pods for it. So, he got dressed and went quickly to the grocery store for pods and a few other things. After returning from the store, he made his first cup of coffee with the Keurig. He sat down at the computer to answer a few emails from work. The first one was this:

"Noah: I'm lost and lonely and broken-hearted. The man I love has left me and married another woman. I don't know what to do. Is there anything that can ease my pain and make me forget? Please? Signed, Dorothy."

●●●

Noah knew this wasn't his Dorothy writing this email to him. He knew it was only one of his readers from Salt Lake City with the same name. Still . . . he didn't know how to answer it. He couldn't answer it. He stared at the question for so long that his first cup of coffee, from his new Keurig, got cold and was undrinkable. He turned the computer off and went to make another cup of coffee. One he'd sit out back on the patio with and stare off into the mountains, dreaming dreams he hoped would come true one day.

At her home in Springdale, Utah, Dorothy re-read the email she just sent Noah, wondering if he ever would figure out that it was her who sent it, and not some lonely girl up in Salt Lake City.

36.

"NOAH, I WAS WONDERING HOW YOU'RE DOING and if you're busy this weekend? We'd really love to see you. Kai misses you sooooo much! Let me know if you can make it. Love, Grace."

This email from Grace didn't surprise him. It had been four weeks since he'd been to Las Vegas to visit them (e.g., babysit) and he knew Grace was struggling a little, both financially and emotionally--she was lonely. He emailed her right back, "I'd love to come if you're sure it's not too much of an inconvenience." He was messing with her.

"No, come as soon as you can. I'll have your room all cleaned and ready for you. By the way, I might need to go to the grocery store when you get here. I just haven't had the time to stock up since I've been so busy lately."

Noah knew this was a hint that she needed food and supplies. He'd stop at the grocery store when he got in Vegas and purchase some stuff for her. He made it through the rest of the week with his column but it didn't seem natural to him. He felt like he was contriving answers and not feeling them like he usually did. Maybe a few days babysitting would help him ease the memories of Dorothy and clear his mind a little. He decided he'd leave a day early and do a day hike in Zion National Park. After Arches and Canyonlands, Zion was his favorite place in Utah, and it was on the way to Las Vegas anyway.

He left Moab early Thursday morning--well, it was actually 9:00, but that was early for Noah. He drove westward toward Capital Reef National Park and through the Grand Staircase of the Escalante, which was also one of his favorite places. It was a magical, mystical area that the tourist industry had yet to discover, probably because there were no other towns anywhere near this area--it was desolate and hidden. Onward through Bryce Canyon National Park and finally into Zion by mid-afternoon. He didn't want to do any long hikes, just a few short ventures off the road so he could take in the majesty of this area.

He pulled into the park headquarters so he could use the bathroom facilities and get a snack and something to drink. He had finished a bottle of water on the drive and really needed to hit the john quickly. He parked his Jeep and hustled inside, straight to the bathroom. If he'd only taken his time, just a little, he would have seen Dorothy talking to another ranger behind the counter, over to the side. But, he didn't. And she didn't either. She was too busy explaining to a fairly new ranger all the rules and regulations and when he was supposed to stop tourists and when not to. The visitor center at Zion was large and always had a lot of tourists milling around, buying souvenirs and snacks. The rangers on duty never really paid any attention to the people inside, unless they were asking questions.

Noah relieved himself, washed his hands, then bought a Diet Pepsi and some BBQ potato chips before leaving the building. As he left, he was only about twenty-five feet from Dorothy as she talked to the other ranger, but he was distracted by a small group of college girls, with short-shorts on, all standing next to souvenir rack and giggling at something. Dorothy never looked up and Noah never looked over in her direction. He got back in his Jeep and headed out for his first short venture into the majesty of Zion.

The small parking lot was nearly full, but he found a spot near the entrance where he parked his Jeep and put on his boots, then took off down the trail for a view of the valley, which was bordered by two massive mountain walls. He would only be gone about thirty minutes, then come back and go to the next short excursion before heading out of the park. Dorothy finished her meeting at the Visitor Center and got back into her official park SUV and started back to her office at the edge of the park. She always had the habit of driving through most of the parking lots, just to make sure she didn't see any crazy stuff going on. As she pulled into the second parking lot, she saw a Jeep that was the same color as Noah's Jeep. It brought back vivid memories of riding in the Jeep with him the day she gave him the arrowhead.

She stopped and looked at it and saw that it had Utah license plates; most of the vehicles here were from out of state. That was odd. She started to get out of her SUV and walk over to the Jeep and look inside, but another vehicle pulled in behind her and she had to keep going. If she had stopped and looked, she would have noticed the small sticker on the bumper that read Moab Motor Works, where Noah bought his Jeep. And she would have seen the small Dream Catcher ornament hanging from the rearview mirror--the one Noah always kept there. But, she didn't. She drove on out of the parking lot and went back to her office, like the good ranger that she is, and finished her daily duties.

Noah spent longer on the trail than he had planned. The grandeur of the entire area swooped him up and he lost track of time. When he got back to his Jeep, it was time to get back on the road towards Las Vegas. He pulled out of the little parking lot and turned right, towards the park exit, several miles down the road. As he left the park, he immediately entered the little town of Springdale, home to Dorothy, unbeknownst to him. He needed gas, so he stopped at the first station he saw in town. He filled up, then went into the store to get something else to drink and a little something to eat on the road. He still had a few hours of driving before arriving in Las Vegas.

The workday was over and Dorothy left her office, still thinking about that Jeep in the parking lot earlier. She left the park and drove into Springdale, on the way to her home, where she would pass the gas station, where a Jeep with a Moab Motor Works sticker on the bumper and a Dream Catcher token hanging on the rearview mirror, was gassing up. Just before she came to the gas station, her cell phone rang--it was her boss so she had to take it. She reached over to the passenger seat and grabbed her phone, then punched the button to receive the call. He phoned to tell her that she had forgotten to lock the door to her office. He wanted to make sure she had the key before he locked it for her. She thanked him and drove on home.

If he hadn't called, if she hadn't reached over and grabbed the phone at that precise moment in time, she would've seen Noah walking out of the gas station with a Diet Pepsi and a honey bun in his hand.

Noah

Funny how in one moment your entire life can change. How one inconspicuous phone call can have such an impact on your future. She turned at the corner two blocks down and Noah drove straight by that same corner about one minute later, on his way over to intersect with I-15 South toward Las Vegas, Nevada--the place where dreams come true.

Noah had a room booked at Bally's, his favorite place to stay in Las Vegas. Grace wasn't expecting him until Friday, which gave him all night tonight to be free with no babysitting chores. He checked in and then wandered around, taking it all in. He had an Iron Maiden at one of the bars, then tried his hand at blackjack, where he lost his allotted fifty dollars in less than half an hour. Next, he walked and looked and searched. Every restaurant, every shop, every nook and cranny of that magnificent hotel/casino. He knew it was a long shot, but still . . . it could happen, he could see her again. He saw her once, right?

So, what does a single, good-looking man, in the prime of his life do in Sin City, USA? He goes to his room at 10:30 and watches SportsCenter. That's what. He thought to himself, *How long is this going to last? What sort of idiot am I? I should buzz me up a call-girl and have some action! I'm in Las Vegas, by God!* Did he? No. Instead, he went to bed, opened up his laptop, and read that email he received from the woman up in Salt Lake City named Dorothy. Something about that email he just couldn't ignore.

He slept in and had coffee delivered to his room. Then he went downstairs for a late brunch before checking out at noon. He stopped by a large superstore and bought nearly $250 worth of groceries and supplies for Grace. When he pulled in the driveway and she ran out to hug his neck and Kai was hugging his leg, the $250 was nothing . . . he couldn't buy that feeling at any price. They sat around and talked and listened to Kai run through her expanding vocabulary, which only contained one cuss word. Grace wanted to know about Noah's love life, which took him about fifteen seconds to explain. He finished the fifteen-second summary, which ended with, "I'm not seeing Vicki anymore."

Grace stared at him and said, "You've got to get over this, Noah. That woman is going to be the death of you. How can you keep on hurting yourself like this? Tell me!"

He wanted to tell her his dream of Dorothy was over. He wanted to tell her he had other ladies lined up. He wanted to tell her anything, except the truth. Instead, he said, "Let's go get something to eat before you have to leave for your show." She nodded and went to change Kai's diaper while he sat there wishing that his heart didn't want what his heart wanted.

●●●

The babysitting went well; Kai was a good baby, she hardly ever cried. And Noah was getting pretty good at diaper-changing; the smells didn't even affect him anymore. Friday night, after dropping Grace off at her club, he and Kai came back home and they watched television until Kai fell asleep and it was time to pick up Grace after her show. They stopped at an all-night diner on the way back and had pancakes and bacon as a late-night feast. Grace slept in Saturday morning and Noah took Kai for a stroll around the neighborhood, wondering if he would ever be able to do this with a child of his own.

That night, Noah decided he and Kai would go over to Bally's once more and see, just to see, if magic would strike again. They dropped Grace off and made their way over to Bally's at a snail's pace--traffic in Vegas on a Saturday night was a nightmare. He strapped Kai in her stroller and off they went, searching everywhere for someone he knew he'd never see. Oh, well. When he got tired of walking, he found a large open area where a burly, bearded man was playing a guitar and singing cowboy songs for a small group of people. He ordered a drink (one drink was his limit when he was with Kai) and sat down to listen to the man sing.

The guy sang one song about driving a truck across from Mexico, then he sang a song that almost made Noah cry.

> *"There's a bottle on the dresser by your ring*
> *And it's empty so right now I don't feel a thing*
> *And I'll be hurting when I wake up on the floor*
> *But I'll be over it by noon*
> *That's the difference between whiskey and you*
> *Come tomorrow, I can walk in any store*
> *No problem, cause they'll always sell me more*

Noah

But your forgiveness
Well, that's something I can't buy
There ain't a thing that I can do
That's the difference between whiskey and you

I've got a problem but it ain't like what you think
I drink because I'm lonesome and I'm lonesome 'cause I drink
One's a liar that helps hide me from my pain
And one's the long gone bitter truth
That's the difference between whiskey and you"

The small crowd gave a rousing ovation to the bearded man, but he never looked up at them and Noah felt that the cowboy was trying not to cry. Just like he was. He got up and pushed Kai on down the walkway, leaving his half-empty drink on the small table, wishing he could have also left his emotions there as well.

Grace did another show late Sunday afternoon. After that, they all went out for dinner, then Noah took them home and started on his drive back to Moab. Grace wanted him to spend the night and leave early Monday morning, but he needed some time alone. He figured he'd drive about halfway back then stop at a motel, but he didn't. He drove all the way back, not arriving until the wee hours of Monday morning. He was very glad he had his new Keurig available when he walked in the door. Right now, that was his closest friend in the world. Even though he'd driven most of the night, he didn't feel that tired. He sat in front of his computer, with a cup of fresh, hot coffee, and decided to answer a few of his emails.

"Noah: I sit in my backyard at nights, and stare off into the stars, millions and billions of them. Surely, there must be intelligent life out there somewhere, don't you think? Signed, Michael."

"Michael: You bet. The surest sign that intelligent life exists elsewhere in the universe is that it has never tried to contact us."

"Noah: My friends and I are sitting around having a glass of wine trying to figure out why there are no good men left. You're a man, right? So, tell us why none of us can find a good man! Signed, Barbara, Mary, Tana, and Ruthie."

"Girls: There's a simple reason for that . . . men are like pumpkins. It seems like all the good ones are either taken or they've had everything scraped out of their heads with a spoon. There!"

Then, he came back to the email from the lonely girl up in Salt Lake City, named Dorothy, who wanted to know how she could continue to exist since the man she loved left her and married another woman. He read this email at least eleven times. Almost convincing himself that it was not from some lonely girl up in Salt Lake City, but that it was indeed from his girl, Dorothy. Which it was.

37.

HE FINISHED UP A BUNCH OF HOUSEHOLD CHORES, then sat out back staring at the mountains while holding his arrowhead tightly in one hand. His mind roamed. He thought about Grace and Kai in Las Vegas and wondered what sort of future they'd have. He even thought of Vicki, not in a sexual context, but rather, how she was and what her future would be like. Would she always be like she is now or would she hopefully find someone she truly loved? He thought about Luray and the cafe and whether he should still go there or just be happy with his Keurig. He thought about Ana and questioned himself deeply about that entire situation. He thought about his work . . . and his boss . . . and his professional future. Then, of course, he thought about Dorothy. Heck, he always thought about Dorothy. He bounced back and forth about what he should do: go all out and try to find her or let it go and try to get over her? He didn't know what to do.

It was starting to get near dusk and he was in his flip-flops, so he started inside and realized he hadn't checked the day's mail. He detoured out front and opened his mailbox to find only one letter. The odd thing about this letter was that it had an old stamp on the front as well as Noah's name and address. It had no postage meter telling where the letter was mailed from and no return address. The oddest thing was that the stamp in the upper right-hand corner was a $0.25 stamp. Stamps hadn't cost a quarter in probably forty years. But here it was, in his mailbox, and now in his hand. He walked inside so he could see better and then opened the envelope. It was a one-page letter on pure white, unlined paper, written in cursive with beautiful penmanship. It wasn't addressed to anyone:

195

Gary Hope

There are images around us, in everything we see
Some are real and some are fantasy
To the one who sees his vision,
To the child who lives his dreams
You're the one to decide what you're gonna be

So give it your best, and don't worry about what some may say
Follow your dreams, it's really all that you can do
Give it your best, and remember that life is what you choose
Follow your dreams, and do what you love to do

There are places you'll remember, and times you may recall
Faces that refresh your memory
May the thoughts that you will picture, help you come to see
That you're the one to decide what you're gonna be

Go on, Noah, follow your dreams and do it,
Follow your dreams, and do what you love to do

It wasn't signed. There was nothing else on the paper or in the letter. Nothing but a $0.25 stamp. He walked back outside to his mailbox and looked up and down the street . . . why? Because he didn't know what else to do.

●●●

Dorothy's friend, Shirley, came to visit her at her new home in Springdale. Shirley was no hiker or outdoorswoman but she was a good listener and friend—exactly what Dorothy needed at this point in her life. She arrived Friday night and they ordered a pizza and had white wine with it. Most of the night was spent catching up on Dorothy's move to Springdale, Shirley's personal life, and funny stories they each had from work.

Saturday morning, during coffee, was when the subject of Noah came up. Both women had told themselves that they would not, under any circumstances, bring him up—period! They both failed. They spent hours reliving all the events of Dorothy's past with him. The good and the bad. The relevant and non-relevant. The actual and the fantasy. Shirley understood how Dorothy felt; however, she still wanted to punch Noah in the face for the way he treated her in Moab. Dorothy didn't know what she wanted.

Saturday night, after a dinner out at Springdale's best restaurant, they went back to Dorothy's apartment and drank gin & tonics until it was time for bed. Dorothy needed to laugh and giggle at Shirley's nonsense and terrible jokes. She needed to be able to experience fun again, to laugh again, and to forget . . . for a while. She needed that. Shirley left Sunday morning after croissants and coffee and aspirin. Dorothy decided to go hiking in Zion, down the Virgin River, beneath the waterfalls and the cascading, colorful images of the canyon walls.

It was during this hike in the river, in water just below her knees, that she decided to be happy again. It was a conscious decision, one that came upon her suddenly, and one in which she was fully committed to: She would start emailing Noah once again.

She thought back to the happiest time of her life: when she was emailing Noah every day. Why couldn't she do that again? She could resume her emails as the fictional Dorothy that lived in Salt Lake City. She could be happy again. One thing, however, she would under no circumstances let this emailing evolve into anything other than friendly messages between long-distance friends. She knew Noah was married and she would not do anything to jeopardize his marriage or happiness. She only wanted some contact. Some communication. Some connection. Anything . . . she wanted something . . . she wanted anything.

It took her three days to get up the courage to write Noah. Three days to figure out exactly what she wanted to say and how to say it. Three days to convince herself that this was okay, that she was not trying to win his love or break up his marriage. Three days to leave the tomb and be alive again. She stared at the computer screen for nearly an hour before she started. She knew it had to be something simple, straightforward, transparent, and clean. There could be no hint whatsoever that Noah would ever suspect the writer was her. He had to be convinced it was indeed from a lonely woman in Salt Lake City with her same name--Dorothy. She failed:

"Noah: I live in the northern part of Salt Lake City and I often go out in the desert hiking by myself. I once found a pottery shard and an arrowhead out in the middle of nowhere. Is it okay for me to keep them or should I donate them to some museum somewhere? What's the protocol for this? Signed, Dorothy"

When Noah first read this email and saw the name of the writer, Dorothy, he paused slightly. Then he intently re-read it . . . then read it twice more before he got up from the computer and went into his kitchen to get a beer from the refrigerator. He opened the beer and took a healthy drink, then walked back to the computer to realize he already had a glass of Diet Pepsi sitting on a coaster there. That's okay; the desert makes a man thirsty. He read the email from Dorothy again, then reached in his pocket and took out his arrowhead, the one that never leaves his possession. His mind started swirling. Her name is Dorothy, she has an arrowhead . . . no, stop it, you stupid fool. Then, his inner voice reminded him, *It's okay to dream.* His reality voice countered, *Idiot!*

Noah finally answered the email:

"Dorothy: I had a similar experience one time, long ago. I, too, found an arrowhead and wanted to keep it but was told that I must replace it where it was found. So, I did--reluctantly I might add. However, it all turned out well for me. Now, in your case, Dorothy, if anyone asks you where you got the arrowhead, you must decide whether integrity, in telling yourself the truth, is more important than honesty is, in telling the truth to other people. Good luck."

● ● ●

He usually sent in eight or ten of these questions from his readers, with his answers, to the paper each day. Then it would take the paper at least three or four days to publish them. Those four days, waiting on Noah's response, were the longest four days of Dorothy's life. When she finally saw her question in the paper, with his reply, she was very excited, until she read what he wrote. She didn't truly understand what he meant . . . but that didn't really matter, did it? It was from Noah. Noah had communicated with her. He had actually written to her! Now what? Does she send him another question and then wait another four days for his answer? Oh, my. She had to think about this.

Noah

Immediately upon arriving at work the next morning, Dorothy was met by several police cars and other official park vehicles. That was never good news. She met everyone and learned that a tourist's car was found abandoned at Angel's Point, which is a scenic overlook with a thousand-foot drop-off. The car was registered to a man from El Monte, California, whose relatives told police was on his way to Reno, Nevada to visit his girlfriend.

The girlfriend had received several selfies from her boyfriend yesterday, then they suddenly stopped late yesterday afternoon. It was assumed by the authorities that the young man was attempting a selfie at Angel's Point and accidentally fell over the thousand-foot drop-off. Dorothy was now in charge of trying to find his body and coordinating the events. She knew that whatever she found at the bottom would not be pretty. There was nothing but rocks and boulders at the bottom of the canyon.

It was late afternoon before they finally found the man's body, and just as Dorothy knew, it was not good. His body was bloodied and nearly broken in half by his fall on a large boulder. Most of his internal organs were missing, presumed to have been scavenged by predators, and identification was only possible by his wallet and driver's license. Dorothy handled all the aspects of the day like the true professional she was until she opened up the man's wallet. His name was Adam Noah Gabriel. When she read his middle name, she froze.

This could have been her Noah. If he had died and she never got the chance to connect with him again, she would never forgive herself. It took her several minutes to return to reality and begin the process of recovering the body. But she knew for sure that she could not waste any more time following her dream. She knew she could never have Noah because he was married to someone else, but she could have his friendship through emails. As far as she was concerned, that was enough. That's what she convinced herself of anyway.

It took all evening to complete the paperwork on the accident. Dorothy didn't leave her office until after 9:30 that evening. She drove home and took a long, hot shower to wash away the events of the day—it was hard to do. Then she poured herself a glass of pinot grigio and sat in front of her computer. She wrote:

"Noah, this is Dorothy from Salt Lake City. I wrote to you a few days ago about finding an arrowhead in the desert and you answered me in your column. Thanks for the advice. I'm writing you now to ask if I could email you personally and not through the newspaper? I like your personality and your openness and I need a friend like you to connect with. Just an email friend to communicate with and share thoughts with. Would you be interested?
Please think about it and let me know,
Dorothy"

Noah received the email from Dorothy, along with the other dozen or so he received every day, and immediately stopped his work and sat staring at the computer screen. Why? Why was this email, asking for a friendship from some woman up in Salt Lake City affecting him so? Was it only because her name was Dorothy? Was it because she was a woman and he was lonely? He didn't know. But he did know he would accept her offer of friendship. But he would not let it evolve into something like he had with Ana. He would not allow himself to be hurt like that again. Or so he told himself.

38.

"DOROTHY, THANKS FOR THE EMAIL. It would be perfectly fine for you to email me as a friend. Anything I write to you and you to me will only be between us, none of it will ever go into the newspaper. So, that being said, tell me a little about yourself or as much as you're willing to divulge. I'm a good listener.

Your friend, Noah."

When Dorothy read this email, she couldn't stop smiling. She now had what she'd always wanted: a relationship with Noah, albeit a false one with unrealistic expectations and a desperate attempt at something that was built on false hopes, dreams, and lies. But, hey . . . life ain't perfect. She went to the bathroom to wash her face, then came back and typed a reply:

"Noah, thanks for accepting my offer of friendship. As you know, I live in the northern part of Salt Lake City and work as a secretary for a non-profit agency. I am a college graduate and love the outdoors. My favorite hobby is hiking in the desert and wilderness areas. I've never been married and have no children. I'm 5'5" and not fat--you know how women are about divulging their weight. I'm in good shape and have short, light brown hair--almost blonde. I hope this information helps you get a picture of who I am. Now, how about you? What can you, or what will you, tell me about your personal life? Your new friend, Dorothy"

Noah read this email from Dorothy about 7:30 that evening but consciously decided not to answer right away. He wanted to think overnight about his answer and where this was going. Instead, he changed into his millennial clothes and decided to drive over to the Fiddlin' Fish for some entertainment and a cold drink. Since Grace left for Las Vegas, the Fish had used a revolving door of singers and musicians, some pretty good, others pretty bad. Tonight, there were two guys playing guitars and from what Noah could tell, they were singing old songs from the Everly Brothers and Elvis era. They weren't bad, but the music was unrecognizable to the mostly young crowd.

Noah took a seat at the bar, which was at the opposite end from the stage area, and he ordered a Brookstown Brown Ale. He turned around in his seat so he could see the stage and before he could even take his first sip of the ale, a woman a few years younger than him walked up to him, pointed at the open seat next to him and asked, "Is this seat taken?"

"No, ma'am. Help yourself."

She sat down and crossed her legs, exposing a generous portion of her upper thighs to anyone who cared to look. She wore a short denim skirt with cowgirl boots and a plaid western button-up shirt with several buttons left open. She wasn't what you would call a pretty girl, but she wasn't ugly either. She struck Noah as a lonely girl who was trying too hard. He understood. Life can be lonely and hard . . . he knew. She had a glass of something that wasn't beer and wasn't water, Noah wasn't sure. They listened to the next song in silence, then the girl looked at him and said, "My name's Glenda, what's yours?"

He smiled at her and answered, "Noah. Nice to meet you, Glenda." She smiled back and her smile seemed to greatly enhance her appearance; it gave her a completely different presence. Glenda took a small sip of whatever it was she was drinking and Noah took a healthy drink of his ale and they listened to the singers start in on their next song. Glenda crossed her legs halfway through the song and he was certain all the young men in front of her appreciated that gesture.

When the song ended, there was a light splattering of applause, then Glenda leaned a little closer to Noah and asked, "You want to go back to my place?"

202

Noah

He was stunned at this question. He didn't know how to answer. He finally muttered, "What?"

"You know, go back to my place. I live alone."

Noah's mind quickly ascertained that there was no reply possible that would end this conversation in a civil manner, so he just got up from the stool, sat his glass down, and started walking towards the door.

When Glenda realized he was walking out on her, she yelled at him: "And don't ever come back here either! There's no way on earth I'd go home with you. Pervert!"

The music was between songs and everyone within twenty-five feet heard Glenda yelling at him. He started to stop and face her but quickly realized that would only make it worse. He went to his Jeep, thanked it for starting up immediately, then drove home to sit out back on the patio and stare at the moon and the stars while wondering what in the world was wrong with people.

Noah had a restless night's sleep. It was becoming increasingly hard for him to try and figure out life. Vicki wanted him for her personal reasons, Glenda seemed to want him for nefarious reasons, Grace wanted him for all sorts of reasons, Ana wanted him for anonymous reasons, and the only one he wanted didn't want him at all . . . Dorothy.

After coffee from his new Keurig, while he wished he'd also bought some bagels and a toaster, he sat down to do some work on his column:

"Noah: I'm sick of reading how you don't exercise and you basically eat anything you want, like it's not going to affect you. Don't you care about your body? Have you ever heard of a diet? Signed, Tammy."

"Tammy: Diet?? I'll have you know that in the last fifteen years I've lost 789 pounds. There!"

That was all he could do. Why? Dorothy was on his mind. Both of them. The one he missed and wanted and didn't know where she was, and the one in Salt Lake City that he was aimlessly curious about. He couldn't concentrate on work emails. First, he had to respond to Dorothy's email:

"Dorothy, thanks for the email, I enjoyed reading it. I'll try to be as honest as you were without boring you too much. I live in Moab and also enjoy hiking in the deserts and national parks around here--the most beautiful places in the world, I might add. We seem to have a lot in common, don't we?"

He paused momentarily and wondered exactly how much personal information he should be giving to a stranger-- he really didn't know this Dorothy woman at all. He continued:

"I would say that I'm just an average guy, certainly not anyone special, just a guy who tries to take care of himself and probably needs a haircut. I did go to college and got a degree in Geography. Why Geography? I have no earthly idea. It hasn't helped me in the least, but I do know a lot of state capitals. I hope this information helps you know me a bit better.
Looking forward to your next email, Noah."

Dorothy read the email and was both excited and disappointed. He didn't really tell her anything she didn't already know. She desperately wanted to know about his wife and how he met her, and about his baby. At least, she thought she wanted to know. She was also afraid that learning this information might also break her heart a little more than she could stand. Plus, she didn't want to seem pushy and drive him away by asking too much of a personal nature. She needed to think.

The first emails between Dorothy and Noah were fairly innocuous, just some bantering and joking and not much at all of a personal nature. However, Noah's mind was creating a fusion of sorts that he wasn't entirely aware of. Each time he read an email from the fake Dorothy in Salt Lake City and each time he wrote the Dorothy in Salt Lake City he unconsciously held and caressed the arrowhead that the real Dorothy had given him.

Noah

Sunday afternoon, as he was making himself a peanut butter and bacon sandwich, his phone rang. It was Grace. He answered, "Hello, is everything okay, Grace?" She had only called him twice in two years; they always communicated by emails and texts.

"Calm down, everything's fine. Well, sort of. I might need your help again. This other club here in town has offered me a tryout, to see if they like me and if I like them. It's bigger and the money would be better . . . a lot better."

"Okay, so what's the problem?"

"They want me to work three nights this week, during the week, Tuesday, Wednesday, and Thursday as a sort of audition. I don't have anyone to watch Kai during the week. Could you . . . "

Before she could finish, he said, "I'll be there Tuesday."

"Really?"

"Grace, you know I'm always here for you, don't you?" Grace couldn't answer because she started crying. She knew he would come. She knew he loved her and Kai, just as they loved him. It was hard to describe their love for Noah. It wasn't either a romantic type or familial type of love. She couldn't categorize it; she only knew they had a special bond and that he would always be there for her. It was comforting.

●●●

He left Moab before sunrise on Tuesday morning for the long drive down to Las Vegas. He only planned one stop because he didn't want Grace worrying that he would be late. His route took him through the scenic desert country of southern Utah, through the little town of Springdale, where Dorothy's home was. His plan was to stop in Springdale for gas, a snack, and a bathroom break before hitting the interstate towards Vegas. As he came into town, he was stopped by one of the three stoplights in Springdale. He used this opportunity to change CDs and was fumbling through his collection looking for the new Adrian Rogers CD he recently bought.

Coming from the other direction, stopped at the same light, was Dorothy, on her way to work. Unfortunately, she was facing east into the morning sun, which was low in the sky and glaringly difficult to look towards. She pulled the visor down and squinted towards the light to see when it changed. If she'd only been able to look straight ahead, on the other side of the light, she'd have seen the man of her dreams fumbling with a CD as he tried to insert it properly in his CD player. Noah popped it in just as the light changed to green. He looked at the park service vehicle coming towards him from the other direction but could only see the visor pulled down low against the sun's glare.

Dorothy could barely see anything facing the early morning glare. She only started moving when she noticed the vehicle on the other side of the light moving forward. As they passed each other, going about fifteen miles per hour, Noah glanced over at the other driver only to notice that whoever it was had long, dark hair like Dorothy used to have. It brought back a fond memory for him . . . he smiled. Dorothy couldn't see anything except to notice that the car that just passed her was a Jeep, the same color as the one she saw in the parking lot that day, and the same color as the Jeep that Noah had. She then stared in the rearview mirror a quick second to see that it also had Utah license plates--like Noah's Jeep had.

She started to pull over in the drug store parking lot and turn around . . . but she didn't. She quickly thought, *There's probably a million Jeeps that color in Utah.* So, she kept going. If she had turned around in the drug store parking lot, she would have seen Noah's Jeep pull over into the gas station, which he had just done, to gas up, get a snack, and use the restroom. Sometimes incredible coincidences happen that change your life and sometimes they don't.

39.

WHEN NOAH ARRIVED IN LAS VEGAS Grace was outside sitting on the door steps. As he got out of the car, she hurried over to him and gave him a big hug. He said, "No need to worry, I'm here."

"I wasn't worried about you getting here, I'm worried about tonight! This is a big opportunity for me, Noah. It could change everything!" She began to tell him about the new club, the much higher salary she could get, and the chance at maybe opening for a name act at one of the big casinos in town. She kept rambling and running on and on; obviously, she was so excited she couldn't concentrate or make sense.

Finally, Noah said, "Whoa! One question?"

Grace had a worried look on her face as she said, "What?"

"How's Kai?"

"Oh, she's fine. She's asleep inside. Let's go wake her up and you can change her diaper and feed her." Noah thought Grace was kidding with him. She wasn't. They went inside and she brought a sleepy-eyed Kai out to Noah and he dutifully changed her diaper, then fed her while Grace was looking in her closet trying to decide what she should wear to the show that night. She modeled several ensembles for him to get his opinion, and toward the end of all the changing clothes, she was running in and out of the bedroom in nothing but her panties and bra. She didn't think anything about it; after all, it was only Noah.

He was worried about how in the world she could play her guitar as nervous as she was, but he knew when she got onstage that she would be okay. Playing and singing always seemed to be the one thing that calmed Grace, as though she was in her own world. He knew she'd be fine. She drove herself to the club and Noah thought about taking Kai over to Bally's once again and walking around--looking for a ghost-- but he didn't. They stayed home and Kai played until she fell asleep. He then took out his laptop and checked for emails. He had one from Dorothy, which was the only one he really cared about.

"Noah, I remember in my first email to you that I mentioned I wasn't married. But you never told me if you were or not. I sorta think you are. If so, I'd love to hear about your wife and what her interests are and how you two got together. Can you share that?
Your friend, Dorothy."

When Noah read that, he wondered why in the world she would think he was married. He never mentioned a wife to her. He never mentioned anything to her about women or relationships. He thought this was a little weird. He started to write back, then thought better of it. Maybe he should wait until tomorrow, give himself a little time to think about the appropriate response. Kai was sound asleep, Grace wasn't due back from the club anytime soon, so he grabbed a beer out of the refrigerator and tried to watch a ballgame on TV. He did watch the game; however, he couldn't have told anyone what the score was . . . all he was capable of doing right now was holding his arrowhead and thinking about Dorothy--both of them.

 The next two nights went great for Grace. She performed well and the new club loved her. Thursday night, after her performance, they offered her a job at nearly double what she was making at her old job. She would be performing four nights a week rather than three, but that was fine with her. She signed a contract to start full-time work there in two weeks. She could work out a notice with her old club and start then. She went in to see her old boss on Friday morning to tell him she was changing jobs and to give him a two-week notice, but he blew up, cursed her, and told her she was fired. He seemed to have forgotten that she had already resigned.

Noah

Grace was free for two weeks now and tried to talk Noah into staying in Vegas with her so they could lounge around together. He had no intention of staying in Vegas for two more weeks. Rather, he convinced Grace to come with him back to Moab and visit some of her old friends, most of all Luray, who had always taken care of Grace at the coffee shop. He told her to come for the two weeks and he would bring her back to Vegas after that. She accepted. Noah took Kai for a stroll around the neighborhood while Grace packed up everything and prepared for the trip. If they left now, they would have enough time to ride through Zion National Park, which Grace had never visited. They wouldn't be able to stay long, but he wanted her to get her first glimpse of this majestic place with him. He loaded up the Jeep, they strapped Kai's baby seat in the back, and they were ready . . . as soon as Grace ran back in the house to use the bathroom.

Dorothy was happy: She had made contact with Noah, she loved her job at Zion, and everything in her world was copacetic. That afternoon, Dorothy got a call in her office from one of the new rangers at the visitor's check-in gate. He had become sick and was throwing up; he needed to go home. Dorothy would have to cover for him that afternoon. It was a pretty simple but boring job. The ranger checks in all visitors and takes the fee for each car, then opens the gate to allow that visitor into the park. Monotonously simple and repetitive. She wasn't looking forward to it but that was part of her job to ensure everything ran smoothly.

Noah and Grace made good time and took the turn-off for Zion as Noah was describing some of the sites and landscapes they would see. They pulled up to the entrance with only four cars in line ahead of them. Noah had a National Park Pass on his windshield, which allowed him access to all National Parks in the country for the one-time fee he paid for the pass. When the park rangers saw the pass on his windshield, they simply waved him through. They were next in line when Kai started crying in the backseat. Grace leaned into the back to give her a bottle and adjust her clothing just as Noah drove his Jeep to the entrance station--where Dorothy was standing at the window. He pulled up to the window but had his attention on Grace and Kai. He knew he didn't have to do anything except wait for the gate to be opened so he could drive through, so he didn't even roll his window down to acknowledge the ranger who would see the pass on his windshield . . . the ranger who just happened to be the one girl in the whole, entire world he'd been searching for, forever.

But she saw him. And, she saw Grace and Kai in the Jeep with him. His wife and daughter, or so she thought. She was so stunned that she forgot to open the gate so he could drive through. Instead, she turned and walked to the other side of the little outpost, leaving Noah stuck there with the gate down. After a minute or so, he honked the horn, and Dorothy backed over to the gate button and opened it. She wanted to go home and cry but she had two more hours of checking in tourists and opening the gate for them. Sometimes, life can be incredibly cruel.

He drove through Zion and showed Grace the highlights; however, Grace wasn't the outdoor enthusiast that Noah had hoped she would be. She was much more content to turn on some music and listen to Bob Dylan dribble on about some abstract imaginary figment of his imagination. He could quickly tell that Grace wasn't enamored with the park's beauty, so he quickly turned around and headed out a different exit and motored toward Moab.

Dorothy dutifully performed her tasks through the end of the day, then she went home and opened a bottle of red wine that Shirley had left in her refrigerator. She didn't even like red wine, but she didn't like the way she felt even worse. It seemed as though reality smacked her in the face and she realized that emailing Noah, knowing that he had a wife and a baby, was one of the most insane things she'd ever done. She decided right then that there would be no more emails. If her life was to be one unhappy, unfulfilled waste of human space, then so be it.

The following morning, Noah, Grace, and Kai went to the coffee shop to visit Luray and tell her of all the events in Las Vegas. Luray was excited and could not let go of Kai. She convinced Grace to come and stay with her for a few days. Grace looked over at Noah to make sure he was okay with it, which of course he was. So, Noah went back home and checked his emails for something from Dorothy, up in Salt Lake City. He didn't find anything.

During the entire two-week visit, Grace and Kai only spent one night with Noah, but that was okay . . . he understood. He did forego his daily Keurig and meet them all at the coffee shop each morning, which he truly enjoyed. The waitress that had sneezed on his bagel that fateful day didn't work out and Luray hired a young man with long hair to fill in. He seemed to be doing a fine job. Three nights, during Grace's stay, she and Noah went to the Fiddlin' Fish to listen to music and hang out. Grace truly loved that; Noah enjoyed it, but he was missing something . . . something he guessed he would always miss.

Since the emails from Dorothy had stopped and Vicki had been banished, the opportunities at female companionship were pretty slim in Moab. Grace's stay helped for a couple of weeks but Noah almost dreaded taking her back to Las Vegas and returning to nothing but an empty condo and an empty heart. Sometimes it wasn't very much fun being himself.

Grace's two-week visit had ended and Noah drove her back to Las Vegas. Grace was sad at first since she had to leave Moab and her best friend, Luray. Then she started thinking about her new life and her new job and the new salary she'd be making--she perked up quickly. Noah was quiet . . . too quiet. Eventually, Grace said, "What's wrong with you?"

"Nothing's wrong with me."

"Noah, you've hardly spoken. One of three things: You don't want me to go back to Vegas, you're going to be lonely without me, or it's something about a woman."

He looked over at her quickly and replied, "Wrong, maybe, and wrong."

She smiled that he answered "maybe" to being lonely without her, but she knew it had to be about a woman . . . it's always about a woman. She knew him too well and he knew that she knew him well. She finally coaxed it out of him that he was looking forward to having an email friendship with a woman from Salt Lake City, but that it had ended before it really ever started. That's as much as he would reveal; he wouldn't even say her name out loud. They arrived in Las Vegas with both Grace and Kai asleep. Noah didn't want to bother them, especially since tomorrow was Grace's first day on her new job, so he told them he was going to drive halfway back and spend the night somewhere. In reality, he'd made himself a reservation at Bally's in the faintest of hopes that magic would strike again.

Once more, he walked around Bally's for hours with all the other tourists, never seeing the only tourist he was looking for. He knew it was a dim hope, at best, but at least it was something. When he was tired of walking, he sat and played a few hands of blackjack and basically broke even—which was quite an accomplishment. He decided to have a drink and a sandwich at one of the many places inside the casino, then he went out to the pool, patio area, and sat under an umbrella and dozed. Vegas was so exciting.

He started to go to one of the shows at the hotel that night but decided not to. Instead, he walked around and around until he even bored himself with that, then thought, *Noah, you gotta stop watering dead plants.* So, he went to his room, took a shower, watched television, and fell asleep. He woke early in the morning and decided to start for home as soon as he had coffee and a bagel. He decided he'd once again ride through Zion National Park since it was on the way.

When he got to the turnoff for Zion, he hesitated, then kept going straight towards Moab. Such was his state of mind. If he'd only known that the gate attendant had called in sick again and the only woman in the entire world who he was looking for was sitting at the gate waiting for him to drive up so she could greet him. However, life is under no obligation to give us what we expect.

40.

IT FELT GOOD TO BE BACK IN HIS OWN PLACE and in his own bed. He slept late and made himself a hot cup of Keurig coffee—he still missed having a bagel. After he read the paper, he knew he had to catch up on some work emails. He turned on the computer, hoping against all despair that Dorothy may have written him . . . she did not. So, he read and responded to the work emails of the day:

"Noah: I must be doing something wrong. I can't seem to find a nice woman, I didn't get a good raise this year, and my dog recently died. Any advice? Signed, Cameron."

"Cameron: Life is hard. Not because we're doing it wrong. Just because it's hard."

● ● ●

"Noah: I just graduated from college and have an entry-level job as an accountant. How boring does that sound? My problem is that I'm not sure I have what it takes to change anything. What should I do? Help me? Signed, Linda."

"Linda: It's not who you are that holds you back, it's who you think you're not."

● ● ●

On it went throughout the morning as he caught up with the backlog of questions and comments from everyone in Salt Lake City, everyone except the one lonely girl he actually wanted to hear from.

213

The one girl who was sitting at the entry station at Zion National Park waiting on a certain Jeep to enter her kingdom once again.

The weeks passed with a monotonous regularity. He switched his morning routines from Keurig back to the coffee shop for two reasons: he missed the bagels and he missed the human contact. People need people. Even if they sometimes make you mad and piss you off, we still need each other. Luray's new waiter at the coffee shop did a fine job and Noah was happy with him. He seldom spoke, except to ask if everything was okay and if he wanted more coffee, which was all fine with Noah. Luray was friendly, in a motherly fashion, and between them, they kept each other informed of any news from Grace and Kai. Noah was friendly with the staff at the Moab Brewery and knew a few people at Fiddlin' Fish, but really had no other close personal friends. He missed having a close friend. In particular, he missed having a close girlfriend. He missed having someone to hang out with, someone to talk with--talk about nothing--just talk with. He missed having someone to think about, someone to dream about, someone to . . .

One day at the coffee shop, just after he'd added milk to his cup, Luray walked over to his table and said, "I've been talking to a friend of mine and she'd like to meet you. Is that okay?"

"What?" Noah looked up at her and didn't know what else to say.

"She's single, like you, and professional, and very nice looking. I think you'd like her."

He nodded and took a sip of coffee, then said, "Sure, that would be fine, Luray. Let me know when."

As he said that, he heard the door to the coffee shop open and Luray looked over at the door and smiled, saying, "How about now? Over here, Catherine." Luray waved and Noah turned in his seat to see a woman walking his way. He never had a chance to decline Luray's offer or to even wipe the bagel crumbs from the corner of his mouth before Luray's friend was standing right in front of him.

He quickly rose and said, "Hi, I'm Noah. Nice to meet you."

Noah

Luray quickly jumped in and said, "Sit down, Catherine. I'll bring you some coffee over and you two can get to know each other."

Catherine quickly answered, "Can you make that hot tea, please?" Then she looked at Noah and asked, "Do you mind?" He smiled and pulled out the chair for her, as Catherine added, "I'm as surprised as you seem to be. Luray asked me to come over this morning, but she didn't tell me she was going to introduce me to anyone. I'm sorry."

He smiled again as they both sat down, and added, "No, it's fine. I'm glad to have the company, but don't feel you have to stay. It's fine if you need to go." They both smiled and tried to ease the tension and awkwardness with each other. Luray brought her a cup of tea and Noah didn't know if he should continue eating his bagel or not. He wanted to . . . he was hungry.

Then Catherine said, "Don't let your bagel get cold. It looks good; is that cinnamon and raisin?"

"Yep, the only kind that us rugged, he-men of the desert ever eat." That broke the tension as they both laughed and eased into a less-than-strenuous conversation. Noah could see that she was maybe a year or two younger than him . . . maybe, maybe not. And that she was well-spoken, obviously educated beyond the norm for this remote desert town. She also had her dark hair tied in some sort of knot behind her head, making it unclear exactly how long it would be if it was free. He wasn't very good with colors but it seemed her eyes weren't exactly blue, and not really gray, but somewhere in between. She also had a pair of glasses hanging from a strap, like a necklace, in front of her. He also noticed her holding a book in her lap. He asked, "What are you reading?"

"Anna Karenina. Are you familiar with it?"

Noah quickly thought to himself, *Does she know my history with my Ana? Does she not think us desert rats know who Tolstoy is?* So, he answered, "Yeah, isn't that the story of a rafting trip down the Colorado where they all got lost and were never found again?" Then, he also thought to himself, *Boy, she really does have a beautiful smile.*

215

It took Catherine about three seconds to realize that Noah was pulling her leg, figuratively that is. Those comments eased the conversation and led to a thirty-minute talk about everything. Eventually, Catherine said, "Noah, I hate to say it, but I have to leave. I have an appointment that I really need to make. I hope we can do this again."

Not being one to let an opportunity pass, Noah quickly asked, "How about tomorrow morning? Coffee, tea, and bagels. Same place, same time."

Catherine quickly smiled and said, "Love to." She picked up her book and stood next to Noah, extending her hand towards him. As he took her hand, she continued, "It's been great. Thanks for letting me share in your breakfast." It seemed to him that she held his hand a little longer than the normal handshake would probably take . . . but that could just be his imagination.

When she left, he sat back down, a little tingly from this experience, when Luray appeared next to him and asked, "Well?"

He looked up at her and said, "Ah, she was alright." Luray laughed at him, shook her head, and walked back to the counter. Noah continued to sit there, staring out the window, and thinking.

Noah and Catherine met each morning at the coffee shop for five consecutive days. He always ordered coffee, with cream, and a cinnamon/raisin bagel. Catherine always ordered hot tea, also with cream, but she varied between bagels, muffins, croissants, toast, and some days, nothing but tea. Noah figured that's what educated women of the desert did for breakfast. Catherine told him she had graduated from the University of California at Santa Cruz, with a degree in Native American History and Culture. She was the Director of the Southwestern Native Cultural Center, which was located in Moab. She was originally from Monterey, California, and had only been in the desert for about eight months. It was a tough transition, coming from a coastal environment to one like Moab--105 degrees in the summer and 25 degrees in the winter.

Noah

The second day she and Noah met for breakfast, as they were leaving, Noah reached in his pocket to leave some change on the table for a tip. He reached in and grabbed several coins and his arrowhead by mistake. He was still looking at Catherine's beautiful smile as he dropped the handful, of what he thought were only coins, on the table. Catherine looked down at the table and asked, "What's that?"

"The tip; should be enough for us both." He never looked down at the table as he said this.

"No . . . what's that?" She said as she pointed at the arrowhead.

His face instantly turned red as he quickly reached down and grabbed the only thing he'd ever had that was a memory of Dorothy--the real Dorothy. He stuffed the arrowhead back in his pocket and lied, "It's just a souvenir I bought at a gift shop up at Arches. I thought it looked pretty authentic."

Catherine wondered why his face suddenly turned red and asked, "Can I take a look at it?"

Noah's mind was swirling! Her degree was in Native American History and Culture; certainly, she would know this wasn't some trinket bought in a gift shop. But what can he do? He slowly brought his precious arrowhead from his pocket and handed it to her. She studied it, turned it over and over in her hands, then said, "Very authentic. Nice edges.9788 Interesting grooving . . . almost as though it was done several hundred years ago." She looked up at him to get his response.

"Thanks, I thought so, too." He said as he quickly grabbed his precious piece of stone and stuffed it back in his pocket. He immediately changed the subject and added, "Tomorrow, I want to bring you a book to read, one of my favorites, and see if you'll like it."

Catherine's look of concern suddenly changed into a smile as she asked, "Oh, how nice. What book is it?"

He had no clue what book it was since he just made up the entire story to change the subject. He quickly added, "Well, it's a surprise, young lady. You'll just have to wait." They each left the coffee shop after agreeing to meet the following morning, Noah thinking, *Whew, I lucked out there.*

And, Catherine thinking, *He's trying to hide something!*

41.

DOROTHY'S LIFE WAS A MONOTONOUS BORE. If she didn't have the beauty of Zion National Park all around her, she may have gone off the deep end. She did paperwork, helped tourists, filled out reports, and went to meetings, like the good, responsible employee she was. About once a month, she would drive over to California and visit her friend, Shirley. She loved these visits; they helped her get through life. Shirley used to love these visits, but recently, with Dorothy's depressed and despondent attitudes, she had been no fun whatsoever. Shirley liked to laugh and cut-up and have a glass or two, or three, of wine as the night progressed. But lately, Dorothy was content to sit and let her mind roam back into nothingness. Shirley would pour her a glass of wine and it might sit untouched for an hour or more. This was unacceptable. Shirley had to do something.

Dorothy arrived Friday evening and they sat around, both experiencing the morose and utter lack of any social graces on Dorothy's part. Shirley put up with it only because she knew Saturday night would be different. She had a plan. She had made dinner reservations at Dorothy's favorite restaurant and had, unbeknownst to Dorothy, invited a young man to dinner as well. This handsome young man was a year older than Dorothy and was the Assistant Director of the YMCA where Shirley was a member. She'd met him one evening, on her once-a-month visit to the Y, when she lost her car keys and asked for his help in finding them. Since that day, she always looked him up and they chatted for several minutes while becoming socially acquainted.

She had described Dorothy to him in glowing terms, not that Dorothy needed any added superlatives, but that was just Shirley being Shirley. They agreed to meet at Michael's Restaurant at 7:30 Saturday night.

Shirley was very excited the entire day and could barely conceal her surprise, which she was certain Dorothy would not approve of. That's why it had to be a surprise. When it was time to leave for dinner, Dorothy came from her bedroom dressed in shorts, a Zion park tee-shirt, and sandals, with no makeup whatsoever. Shirley was shocked! She had to think fast, "Umm, Honey, I forgot to tell you. Tonight is a special night at the restaurant; they're celebrating their anniversary and have asked everyone to dress appropriately. Do you mind?"

Dorothy was very surprised. She'd been to Michael's Restaurant before and nobody ever dressed up going there. She asked, "What do you mean?"

"Well, you know, maybe wear a dress and some regular shoes and maybe a little mascara and lipstick?"

Dorothy was totally confused. She never wore a dress when visiting Shirley, and she only brought sandals with her, and no makeup whatsoever. She could only utter, "But . . . "

And, Shirley continued, "Come back here with me, I'll find something, it'll be fine." They went back to Shirley's room and found a nice blouse and a pair of slacks that Dorothy could wear if she tightened the belt up enough notches. But she still had to wear her sandals; Shirley had no shoes that would fit. Then Shirley took her into her bathroom and applied a little makeup and lipstick, over Dorothy's objections. But Shirley was Shirley. When finished, Shirley stood back thinking, *Oh, my. It's a good thing she's naturally pretty or this wouldn't work at all.*

Dorothy looked at herself in the mirror, thinking, *You've got to be kidding!* But, for Shirley, she kept her mouth shut and they left for the restaurant.

When they pulled in the parking lot at the restaurant, Shirley saw her friend, Michael, standing out front waiting for them. She had a plan, so she kept quiet. She and Dorothy started walking toward the entrance and when they arrived, Shirley acted surprised to see Michael and said, "Michael, so nice to see you. How are you? This is my friend, Dorothy."

Michael thought this greeting was rather strange since Shirley had orchestrated this meeting and invited him to be here, but he answered, "Good evening ladies. I'm fine, I hope you are. So nice to finally meet you, Dorothy."

When he said that last sentence, "So nice to finally meet you, Dorothy," she knew she'd been set up. She looked over at Shirley, who seemed to be occupied with a piece of paint peeling off the lamp post, but she replied, "Very nice to meet you as well, Michael. I guess we should all go in." Michael opened the door for them as they entered, with Dorothy "accidentally" bumping into Shirley as they walked through the door. A young lady at the desk greeted them and led them back to a booth where Shirley sat on one side but did not slide over enough for Dorothy to sit next to her. Instead, she motioned for Dorothy to sit across from her. Then, she also motioned for Michael to sit across from her, next to Dorothy.

Awkward conversations soon led to a familiarity that was, at least cordial, if not, rather entertaining. Michael had a way about him and told some interesting stories from his job at the Y. Plus, he seemed very interested in Dorothy's job at Zion and wanted to hear all about it, much to Shirley's delight. Shirley ordered them all glasses of white wine, hoping that it would help ease Dorothy's mind and feelings so that she wouldn't be too upset with things. Shirley ordered the spaghetti with meat sauce, Michael ordered the veal parmigiana, and Dorothy ordered a salad. She drank her first glass of wine before the salad arrived. Michael didn't seem to notice her empty glass, but Shirley noticed and thought, *Uh, oh. Don't do it, girl.* But it was too late.

When the waiter brought the salad, Dorothy lifted her empty glass so he could easily see it, as he asked, "Another glass, ma'am?"

Dorothy glanced over at Shirley and answered, "Oh, yes. Thank you." Michael seemed oblivious to the interplay between the two women, but Shirley knew. She wished she didn't, but she knew

By Dorothy's third glass of wine during dinner, Michael was beginning to wonder a little, Shirley was wondering a lot, and Dorothy was feeling no pain and a little frisky. Shirley tried to head things off as she turned down the request for dessert from the waiter, as did Michael, but Dorothy said, "Yes, I'll have the banana pudding and another glass of wine."

"I'm sorry ma'am, but we don't have banana pudding."

"Then, just give me another glass of wine."

Shirley was beginning to think that her grand idea might not be so grand, but all that changed when Dorothy had almost finished her fourth glass of wine and leaned over and kissed Michael on the lips when he had turned to ask her a question. At that point, Shirley was certain her grand idea was not grand at all. Michael seemed a little flustered by the kiss but Dorothy just smiled and held up her empty wine glass. Shirley quickly motioned for the check and tried to head off any further displays from her friend. As the waiter brought the check over and Shirley reached for it, Michael suddenly jumped in his seat and looked quickly at Dorothy, whose smile only became wider and a little wicked as well. Shirley did not want to know what Dorothy had just done beneath the table.

Michael walked them to their car, as it took all of Shirley's strength to keep Dorothy from stumbling in the parking lot. He smiled and thanked them for a "lovely" evening, then quickly made his getaway. Shirley was almost home when she first heard Dorothy snoring from the passenger seat. At least she knew the formula now: A half-eaten salad and four glasses of wine would put Dorothy to sleep. She didn't bother trying to undress her, as she flopped her on to the bed. She just covered her up and left a trash can next to the bed, just in case.

In the morning, Dorothy needed coffee and Excedrin, lots of Excedrin. They both sat in silence for a bit, then Shirley finally said, "I'm sorry. I shouldn't have done that without telling you. But I thought you needed to meet someone. Honey, you've got to get over this whole Noah-thing."

Dorothy never looked up from her coffee cup and replied, "Right, you shouldn't have done that. And, I am over this whole Noah-thing. Why do you think I am like I am?"

●●●

Noah

Noah arrived at the coffee shop for his daily ritual with Catherine only to find Luray at the door waiting on him. He thought that maybe Catherine was going to be late or had to cancel their morning coffee together. Luray greeted him, "You need to call Grace, she's having a hard time."

"What do you mean, 'Having a hard time?' I just saw her a couple of weeks ago and she was fine."

"She's not fine, Noah! Well, professionally she is. She likes her new job but she's lonely and doesn't have any friends in Vegas."

Noah said, "Okay, I'll call her and find out what's going on. Don't worry, she'll be okay." After saying that, he started over to his window table to wait on Catherine for their morning coffee and bagels.

"Well, are you going to call her or not?" He looked back over his shoulder to see Luray staring at him with her hands on her hips. When a woman is staring at you with her hands on her hips, it's always best to say "yes, ma'am."

So, he said, "Yes, ma'am, I am. Right now." He took his cell phone out and called Grace's number. After several rings with no answer, he left a message for her to call him back. Luray stood there witnessing the call, staring at Noah, when he said, "Okay? I'll keep trying." Luray turned and walked back to the counter. During this interchange with Luray, Noah had instinctively put his hand in his pocket and grabbed his arrowhead; it always seemed to soothe him and make him feel better.

He was wondering what might be wrong with Grace, as he was absently rubbing the smooth edges of the arrowhead when Catherine walked in the café. He instantly smiled as she walked over to him. She extended her hand towards Noah, in greeting, and he reached to take her hand when they both realized he was still holding the arrowhead. He quickly put it back in his pocket and took Catherine's hand, thinking, *Whew! How did that happen?*

Catherine smiled back at him, as she held his hand, thinking, *Yep . . . there's something going on with that arrowhead that he doesn't want to tell me about.* However, she kept those thoughts to herself, for the time being. They were, by now, very comfortable with their friendship and the conversations included everything imaginable, from life in Moab to life on other planets—and everything in between. Finally, it was time for Catherine to leave for work and for Noah to get back to his job, which really couldn't be described as work at all. He loved what he did.

As they rose to leave, Catherine asked, "Would you like to come over to my house tonight for dinner? It won't be much but I can throw something together."

Noah was surprised. He had been thinking of asking her out to dinner sometime soon, but this was even better. He smiled and answered, "Yes, of course I would. Thanks so much, what can I bring?"

"A nice bottle of wine might be nice. You choose. See you about 7:00, okay?"

Noah was beaming as Catherine walked out. He started to leave as well but noticed Luray standing behind the counter staring at him. He said, "I'm calling her back . . . don't worry." Then he walked outside and down the street to his Jeep when he started thinking, *A nice bottle of wine? How do I know what that is?*

42.

HE STOPPED AT THE GROCERY STORE on the way home and went over to the wine section. The only thing he knew about wine was that the red stuff tasted terrible and the white stuff almost as terrible. There must've been a thousand bottles of wine to choose from. How in the world could he pick one that Catherine would approve of? A moment later, a grocery store employee came down the aisle pushing a cart to restock some shelves with. Noah stopped him and asked, "Excuse me. I need to pick out a good wine for dinner tonight that would please a lady friend. Do you have any suggestions?"

The young man, who had a name tag on that identified him as Jon, said, "I think that one over there with the picture of a windmill on it looks pretty cool." Noah nodded and thanked Jon, then decided to Google wines on his iPhone instead. He knew the Sonoma Valley area of California had a good reputation, and that Catherine was from California, so he found one that looked impressive-- at least its cost was impressive. He waited until he got home to call Grace again. She answered on the first ring this time, "Noah, what's wrong?"

"Nothing's wrong, Grace. I was checking on you."

"Checking on me for what?

"Luray asked me to call. She said you needed someone to talk to. Are you sure you're okay?"

"Yeah, I'm okay. I've got some 'woman' issues, but I don't think you want to hear about that, do you?"

Noah had to think quickly. Does he want to know? Even if he did know, could he help? So, he settled on, "Is there anything I can help with? Do you need me to come down there?"

After a moment or so of silence, Grace answered, "Only if you can tell me if I'm pregnant or just late with my period."

"Pregnant?"

"I knew I shouldn't have said anything to Luray. Y'all worry too much. I'm probably only late. Just let it go."

"Grace, if you're pregnant . . . "

She interrupted him, "Let it go, Noah! I'm probably just late."

Noah thought quickly. He didn't want to ask this next question, but he couldn't help himself, "Who is the father? I didn't even know you were seeing anyone."

"I'm not really seeing anyone."

"Not seeing anyone? So, you just woke up pregnant one day?"

"I meant I'm not dating anyone. Me and this guy from another band just hooked up a couple of times, that's all. I haven't even seen him since then. Heck, I really don't even like him. He just . . . you know .
. ."

Now Noah interrupted, "No, I don't know, and I don't want to know. What are you going to do?"

"Soon as I wake up and have some coffee, I'm going to the drug store and get one of those pregnancy tester things. Then I'll know for sure."

"Call me as soon as you find out. Okay?"

"Sure, DAD."

"I mean it, Grace! Call me as soon as you find out. You promise?"

Noah

"I'll call you, Noah . . . jeez!"

Then, he had to end the call by telling her, "And until you're sure, no beer, no alcohol of any kind, no smoking, and no doobies--I mean it, Grace, no doobies."

Grace was silent. She enjoyed a late-night doobie after the shows. But she finally said, "Okay, Noah. I promise. I'll phone you later. And, Noah . . . thanks for calling."

●●●

Noah tried to answer some work emails, but he quickly abandoned that. He was too nervous about his "date" tonight. After he got ready and paced around the house for an hour, he went out to his Jeep at 6:45 for the five-minute drive over to Catherine's place. When he drove up, she must've been nervous too because she was standing at the door and waved for him to come in. He walked in and she asked, "Did you bring any wine?" He cursed himself worse than any sailor had ever cursed his commanding officer--he had forgotten the wine. Catherine laughed at his slip but assured him she had a couple of bottles in the kitchen. When she said "in the kitchen" and not "in the refrigerator," he knew he was in trouble; that meant she had room-temperature, red, dry-tasting wine. Why were the gods always against him?

Dinner was great: Catherine had prepared a roasted chicken dish with vegetables that Noah truly enjoyed. She quickly deduced that red wine was not his favorite, so she produced a bottle of Michelob Ultra, which was almost better than the chicken. After dinner, they sat on the couch, close but not quite touching, and talked about everything: politics (without arguing), books, travel, music (she liked Joni Mitchell, Norah Jones, and Linda Ronstadt--older stuff). She also talked about what movies she liked, which left Noah as only a listener since he knew very little about movies, and told him about living on the California coast and how beautiful it was. Before either of them realized it, the clock read 11:45.

Noah walked to the front door and opened it, with Catherine standing closely next to him. Catherine looked deeply in his eyes and said, "Thanks for coming, it's been a lovely evening."

Noah, who wrote for a living and could talk about anything with anybody, was tongue-tied, or enamored, or something, because he only stood there, silent, staring into those beautiful blue/gray eyes he found so irresistible. Catherine then leaned slightly toward him, inches from his face, and Noah said, "The chicken was good."

Catherine was a bit confused, but replied, "I'm glad you liked it."

Noah smiled and nodded, then finally said, "Okay, well I guess I'll see you later then." And he turned and walked out to his Jeep. Catherine, being very confused, watched him get in the Jeep, then closed her door. He sat there, looked back at Catherine closing her door, and said, "The chicken was good???"

 For the second time that evening, he was cursing himself! This time, he was cursing so badly that he missed the turn-off to his home. When he finally arrived and pulled in the driveway, he turned the motor off and sat there muttering to himself, "The chicken was good??" Over and over, he kept repeating that insane comment. However, what he didn't know was that he and Catherine were on the same wavelength . . . she also stood in her living room, repeating that same sentence over and over, "The chicken was good?" While wondering deep and mystical thoughts about the man she had such high hopes for.

The next morning, Noah arrived at the coffee shop early, so he wouldn't risk missing Catherine in case she came in early. They didn't have a standing date or anything; it was just something that had morphed into a pleasant and regular expectation and presumption in each of their minds. He ordered his coffee but waited to order his bagel until Catherine arrived. As he sat down, Luray walked over and asked, "Did you have fun last night?"

"What do you mean?"

She smiled and repeated, "I mean, did you have fun last night? You went to Catherine's house, didn't you?"

He wasn't sure why, but beads of sweat popped up on his forehead. Had Catherine told Luray about his insane comment, "The chicken was good?" Luray continued to stare at him, waiting on an answer. He finally said, "I guess so."

Luray shook her head slowly and disgustedly muttered, "Men!" as she went back to the kitchen. Noah drank his first cup of coffee, then his second cup, and had ordered a third cup when Luray came back over to his table, saying, "You know she's not coming, don't you?"

Noah fondled his arrowhead and said, "Who's not coming?"

Luray rolled her eyes, then said, "She's gone to a conference over in Cedar City, won't be back until Friday. Didn't she tell you?"

Noah felt a little disappointed and a little relieved. At least he wouldn't have to explain his "The chicken was good" comment this morning, for which he really had no explanation. So, he looked up at Luray and lied, "Yeah, I knew." He felt it best to forego his morning bagel and leave the coffee shop as soon as he could. After paying for his coffee, he started walking down the street when his phone rang. It was Grace . . . he had forgotten all about her.

"Hello"

"Noah, I'm pregnant."

Silence . . . more silence . . . and more silence. Noah reached his Jeep and opened the door, then sat and rolled the window down. Still nothing. He didn't know what to say and worse, he didn't know what she wanted him to say. Finally, Grace asked, "You still there?"

"Yeah, I'm here."

"Do you hate me?"

"No, I don't hate you, Grace."

"I don't understand how this happened. We only did it twice . . . well, three times, if you count doing it twice that second night. But only two nights, Noah. This isn't fair." Then she started crying and didn't stop for several minutes. Eventually, she regained enough composure to say, "Noah . . . "

He knew . . . so he cut her off and answered, "I'm on the way. I'll call you when I'm close."

He went back to his place and quickly packed his bags. He thought of trying to call Catherine--she had given him her cell number--but he decided not to. What would he say? If he drove straight through to Las Vegas, he could probably get there by eight or nine o'clock that night. Then, he remembered that this was a weeknight; Grace was supposed to be singing at her new job every weeknight. He called her right back and she told him that she had called in sick for the night, and that she would be home when he got there. He grabbed his laptop and his other stuff and took off. It was going to be a long trip: no stopping in Zion today, nothing but driving and stopping for gas and snacks.

Usually, he enjoyed the drive because the scenery was exquisite. Not today. His mind was swirling from Grace to Catherine and eventually back to where it always seemed to end up . . . to Dorothy. Why Dorothy? He didn't know. He knew she was a dead end, but he kept remembering the old Woody Allen quote, "The heart wants what the heart wants." So, he drove onward in a ubiquitous fog . . . thinking of everything, thinking of nothing. On one long stretch in the Utah hinterlands, there was an open prairie on both sides of the highway. It was late afternoon and off to his right-hand side, he spotted a herd of about eight or ten deer running parallel the road. He took his foot off the accelerator to get a longer look at them and wondered why they were running as they were. As far as he could tell, nothing was chasing them. Maybe they were running because God made them able to run . . . who knows?

Just as he put his foot back on the accelerator, the entire herd started veering left, toward the road, the road he was on. Again, he took his foot off the gas pedal but didn't apply the brakes. At the speed they were running, and the direction they were headed, he and the herd of deer would intersect in about ten seconds. Still, it was daylight and they could see him. Then, five seconds, they were still coming so he started blowing his horn: BEEP, BEEP, BEEP! They never veered and never changed direction. He suddenly tried braking, but it was too late. Three of the deer ran in front of his Jeep. One other deer jumped across the hood, its hoof grazing the paint, but one deer ran

Noah

directly into the side of Noah's Jeep, knocking off the rearview mirror and putting a large dent in the door.

Noah closed his eyes and cringed as it all happened in about one second's total time. He heard the thud of the deer hitting his door and looked in his mirror to see the dead deer rolling over and over down the highway. He stopped as quickly as he could and ran back to the deer. Why? He didn't know. Even if it hadn't already been dead, what could he have done? It was a lonely deserted stretch of highway. No other cars came in either direction. Just Noah, by himself, staring at the dead dear.

He did have enough forethought to grab the deer's hooves and pull it off the road so no one else would hit it. He knew by mid-day tomorrow that the vultures would have the bones all cleaned and this deer would only be a memory to all the other deer who ran away. But not to Noah. This deer meant something to him. A symbol that his life could be over in an instant. A revelation that he must live, he must love, and must never forsake that which he really wants. Now, to him, the question that eternally begs is: Noah, what DO you want?

43.

BACK ON THE ROAD, IT TOOK A LOT OF MILES to forget what just happened. Plus, his right side mirror was dangling by a wire down in front of the large dent in his Jeep. He came upon the exit for Zion National Park but kept on going; however, he would have to stop for gas and a bathroom break soon. The little town of Springdale was a good stopping place; it had all he needed and it was just before he drove onto the interstate for Las Vegas. He pulled off the little two-lane road into the convenience store parking lot that he'd always used on previous trips, right next to the first stoplight in town. He filled up and noticed that the prices had risen slightly since his last visit here. He tried to do something with his broken right-side mirror, but it was beyond repair.

He bought a Diet Pepsi, some BBQ potato chips, and a small bag of salted peanuts to help pass the time down the interstate toward Vegas. Back in the car, he checked his phone, but there were no messages. He was hoping for something from Catherine. As soon as he pulled out of the lot, his phone rang--Grace. He reached over to get it at exactly the same time that an official park SUV was meeting him from the opposite direction. The driver of the official park SUV was almost certain she recognized the driver and the Jeep. She only saw him for a half-second . . . can anyone be sure of something in a half-second? She quickly looked in her rearview mirror to see if the license plate was from Utah. It was. If anyone ever tells you that your mind can't process a thousand different thoughts at once, they're lying! It can. The problem is that it's almost impossible to decide which of those thousand thoughts is appropriate and which of the other 999 are simply crazy. The driver of the official park SUV decided that her thoughts had to be one of the 999 crazy ones--after all, what are the odds? So, she kept driving.

Noah answered, "I'm getting on the interstate; shouldn't be too long now." In the background, he heard Kai crying. Then he heard Grace crying, no words, only crying. He continued, "Try to get some rest, I'll be there shortly. I'll stop and bring us something to eat, too. Okay?" No answer, only some deep breaths. "Get Kai a bottle and you both get some rest. I'm on the way." She hung up without saying a word. She didn't have to; she knew Noah would take care of her.

When Noah finally arrived, there were no lights on in the house. He had a key so he went in, carrying a bag of food, and found Grace and Kai asleep in Grace's bed. He didn't wake them. He went into the small kitchen and wrapped the food, then stuck it in the refrigerator. He looked for something to drink but only found milk and tonic water. Bed seemed like the best alternative for him as well, even though it only just before 9:00 at night. He had no problem going to sleep, especially after the long drive and the deer incident. He woke in the morning to hear laughter and then he smelled bacon cooking. He dressed, went to the bathroom, splashed some water on his face, and went into the kitchen to find Kai and Grace giggling about something and a plate of freshly cooked bacon on the table, next to a steaming hot cup of coffee. He had finally hit the jackpot in Las Vegas!

After a day or so, Grace had come to grips with the reality of her situation. She was fine now. Having Noah there just made it better. She went back to work that night and had no problems. Noah stayed on until Friday morning so Grace could finish her work at the club that week; she was off Friday, Saturday, and Sunday. Noah left her Friday morning, in good spirits, and almost looking forward to having another sibling for Kai . . . almost. At least she was Grace again. He wasn't looking forward to another eight-hour drive, but he needed to get back. He'd made an appointment to have his car worked on Saturday, to try to get the dent and mirror repaired. There was also the big question of Catherine. He didn't even know what the question was, but it was there and it bothered him all the way home.

●●●

It felt good to be back home. But he was behind with his column and needed to catch up quickly. He spent a couple of hours Friday night answering questions, ending with these three:

"Noah: I've been dating my girlfriend for nearly two years now. She wants to get married. It's not that I don't want to, but . . . what do you think of marriage? I mean, what do you REALLY think of marriage? Signed, David."

"David: Since I've never been married, I'm not exactly qualified to answer that question. However, my best friend who is married once told me that he and his wife were happy for 20 years. Then they met."

"Noah: You don't seem like you're the kind of person who avoids controversial subjects. If you're not, then tell me what you think of birth control and abortion. Signed, Lydia."

"Lydia: Have you ever noticed that all the people in favor of birth control are already born?"

"Noah: I check the astrology charts every morning before work. Help me understand you a little better--what sign are you? Signed, Pam."

"Pam: I don't believe in astrology, but I'm a Libra and we're skeptical."

Saturday morning, he took his Jeep to the repair shop after learning that his insurance would pay for everything--except the deductible, of course. While he was waiting for them to bring around a loaner car, his phone rang. He assumed it was Grace but it wasn't; it was Catherine. He answered and she said, "Hello Noah, it's Catherine. I've been out of town a few days and wondered if you'd like to join me for brunch at the coffee shop if you're not busy."

He tried to act cool, but couldn't pull it off as he almost yelled into the phone, "YES! Tell me what time and I'll be there."

Noah

"Twenty minutes okay with you?"

"Great, I'll be there." Then, he found out that his loaner car wouldn't be ready for thirty more minutes. He quickly called Uber and had them on the way in ten minutes. Catherine was there waiting on him but hadn't ordered yet. He went in and sat down and they looked at each other with a quiet awkwardness still lingering from the comment about the chicken being great. Noah finally broke the silence and said, "I'm sorry about the other night, I was just . . . "

She bailed him out by saying, "It's okay, I'm glad you liked the chicken." With that sentence, they both burst out laughing. She then laid her hand on top of his hand and everything from that point on was smooth sailing. They made a date for dinner that night at a local restaurant as Luray was trying her best to overhear what was going on. After Catherine left, Noah decided to walk back to the repair shop: It was only about two miles away and he needed a little exercise. He hadn't even walked three blocks when his phone rang. It was Grace and it worried him that something was wrong and she might need him to come back to Vegas.

He answered and Grace asked, "What time is your date tonight?"

It took him about three seconds to figure things out, then he said, "Tell Luray to mind her own business!"

Grace laughed and said, "Well, don't get her pregnant." And she hung up before Noah could respond.

●●●

Noah's loaner was a Smart Car although he didn't feel very smart driving it, especially in a western, desert town where most men drove jacked-up, revved-up, pickup trucks. He barely fit in the ridiculous little car. He pulled the sunshade down and put on a hat and his sunglasses, hoping no one would recognize him. He made it to his home okay, but as he was getting out of the car, two teenagers rode by on bikes and stopped beside him. They stared at the car, then started laughing. Noah pulled his hat down lower and went inside. He looked back out the window to make sure the two teenagers didn't pick up his Smart Car and carry it away, then he thought to himself, *I've got to pick up Catherine in that thing.*

He drove over to her house that evening and knocked on the door for their dinner date. She opened the door and looked even more gorgeous than he thought possible. Her eyes were luminous and her hair had a glow to it, plus she was wearing a rather short skirt, only reaching several inches above her knees. She grabbed her purse and locked the door as they both walked outside, then she stopped dead in her tracks. Noah thought something had happened to her, so he looked over and asked, "Are you okay?"

She pointed at the Smart Car and said, "Is that yours?"

"Well, my Jeep's in the shop. It's a loaner."

She looked at Noah as if she wanted to say, *Are you serious?* She didn't; however, she didn't move either. He completely understood; heck, he felt the same way. He asked, "Do you wanna take your car?"

"Would you mind?"

"Heck no! I'd love it."

So, Catherine grabbed her keys from her purse and handed them to Noah and said, "You drive."

The dinner was lovely and they were seated in a rather dimly lit corner of the restaurant. They started holding hands before the waiter even brought the menus over. At that point in time, Noah wanted to forego the dinner and get to the "taking her home" part of the date. From the way Catherine was looking at him and acting, she wanted the same thing. However, they ordered steaks and red wine for her and a gin and tonic for Noah. They each barely ate anything, especially since it was difficult to cut their steak while holding hands. They politely skipped dessert and hustled back out to Catherine's car for the ride to her house.

Noah opened the car door for her and they walked up the steps to the front door. Catherine unlocked the door and turned the knob, then turned to face him and asked, "Would you like to come in?"

Well, he certainly wasn't going to answer, "The chicken was good." He said, "Yes if it's okay." They walked in and she told him to have a seat on the couch while she visited the powder room. He was so excited he could barely sit down . . . but he did, with great expectations. Catherine returned in a slight change of clothes. She had changed from her short skirt to an ankle-length skirt, which initially disappointed him, until he saw her sit next to him and cross her legs, revealing a slit up the side of the dress that revealed the entire length of her legs.

She picked up a clicker from the table and dimmed the lights, then another clicker and soft music started to play. To Noah, this was all an incredible dream, or like something from a movie; but it wasn't a movie, it was real, and he was living it. Their legs were touching; his arm, which was on the back of the couch, had inconspicuously moved down to her shoulders; and their faces were only inches apart as he gazed into those beautiful blue/gray eyes. Seconds later, they kissed. Not long, but not short either. He wanted this to be the best kiss in the history of kisses . . . but it wasn't. He couldn't describe it, he had never experienced anything like this before, and was totally bewildered . . . but the kiss was not good. In fact, it was bad.

Catherine must have felt the same thing because she pulled back and had a quizzical look on her face like, "What happened?" They leaned back a little, then looked around the room as Catherine straightened her skirt to hide her exposed legs. Noah cautiously removed his arm from around her and sat motionless. Neither of them moved for about three hours, or so it felt; it was probably only a minute or two. Then Noah said, "Well, I have an early day tomorrow, I'd better be going."

Catherine jumped up and went over to the door and said, "Yeah, me too . . . thanks for dinner, Noah." He went to the door, stopped momentarily to look at her face, then continued out into the yard to his Smart Car, which seemed a whole lot smarter than he did at the moment. He drove away and went straight home. He turned the motor off and sat there wondering what in the world had just happened. He had no clue! He had a beautiful woman in his arms, lights were low, the scene couldn't have been any better--until they kissed. That changed everything. It just wasn't there. Whatever "it" is was missing. Noah had never experienced anything like that before.

He didn't understand it, he couldn't explain it, and he couldn't contemplate or rationalize the implications. But he totally understood the result: He and Catherine were not meant to be.

It wasn't only Noah. Catherine stood at the door when he left and didn't know whether to cry or laugh. She had always heard that sometimes all it took was one kiss to define a relationship. She never imagined it would happen to her in the opposite way. But it did. Like Noah, she couldn't describe or understand it, but she knew it would never happen again.

44.

NOAH WENT A WEEK WITHOUT VISITING THE COFFEE SHOP in the mornings. He'd visit the Moab Brewery and Fiddlin' Fish in the evenings, mainly because he knew Catherine never visited these two places. But for breakfast, it was now him and his Keurig, and a pack of bagels he bought at the grocery store. He missed what he had with Catherine for breakfast, but it is what it is. He was working on his column, answering questions from the good people of Salt Lake City, when he came across this one:

"Noah: Why have you quit coming to the coffee shop? Did I do something to make you mad? Signed, Luray."

He finished all the other mail and then when he felt like Catherine wouldn't be there, he drove down to the coffee shop to see Luray. He first walked past the window and looked in to make sure Catherine wasn't there, then he went in. Luray saw him and stood there staring at him with her hands on her hips--never a good sign when you're going to talk to a woman. She said, "What's wrong with you?"

"Nothing's wrong. I've been busy, that's all." From the look on her face, he knew that she knew he was lying. He continued, "Have you heard from Grace lately?"

"Don't Grace me! What happened? Catherine has been in here every day and you haven't. She sits here drinking that awful tea and looking out the window."

That news surprised him, but he had to change the subject. "Why did you email my work address?"

"Cause that's the only way I knew to get in touch with you. I need to know what's going on here!"

"Why didn't you call Grace and get my phone number? And, I can assure you there is nothing going on here."

Luray answered, "I tried calling Grace but she wouldn't give me your number. She didn't want me getting involved in your personal life."

Noah smiled and said, "Good for her."

"No, not good for her. I don't necessarily care about YOUR personal life, but I do want to find out about my friend, Catherine, who just comes in here now and stares out the window. What did you do to her?"

Heck, he can't even explain to himself what happened with Catherine, how could he ever explain it to Luray. So, he didn't even try. They talked about Grace and Kai, then Luray tried to get some more information from him but he was silent. However, he did sit down and have a cup of coffee. He liked his Keurig, but he loved Luray's blend much more. After a trip to the grocery store, he finally got back home and noticed he had a text message--it was from Catherine. Oh, my. It read: "Noah, I miss our breakfasts together. I know we can't 'date,' we both understand that. But can we just be friends and do the breakfast thing again--I really enjoyed our conversations. Let me know. But I'll understand if you don't want to. Catherine."

Wow, Noah was floored. He, too, missed the morning meetings--not the other stuff-- just the morning conversations and talks about books and music and current events. He texted back and told her he'd love to. They met the next morning, and after the first couple of minutes, everything was back to normal. They never discussed the "kiss" and they never would. This is what they both wanted from each other-- someone to talk with. As much as Luray tried to pry into their business, neither one of them would ever tell her anything. Grace knew something had happened but Noah was silent with her as well. But, the difference with Grace was, she knew Noah; she knew he was lonely, and she knew he had a hole in his heart. And she also knew who the only person in the entire world was who could fill that hole . . . Dorothy.

Catherine and Noah became almost like brother and sister. They met every morning at the coffee shop and occasionally for lunch--never dinner. It's fair to say they quickly became each other's best friend. He even explained a little of his history with Ana and Dorothy; not all of it, but some of it. Through his past several visits with Grace, Noah had also explained his relationships, or lack thereof, to her. He especially liked those nights at her house when Kai was asleep and they'd sit around talking. Grace had talked with Luray about Noah and Dorothy and what could be done. Grace was not the type of person to let a small detail like not knowing who Dorothy was or where she lived deter her.

She did have a few details from conversations with Noah: She knew Dorothy was a park ranger, that she was about Noah's age, that she had a college degree, and that she had at one time worked at Death Valley National Park. However, she didn't know if Dorothy was still a park ranger and she didn't know what college she attended. She did verify that Dorothy had worked at Death Valley; unfortunately, they wouldn't tell her anything else--privacy laws. Since Grace was off Friday, Saturday, and Sunday each week, she had plenty of time to investigate. She took it as a personal challenge to find this woman!

She started by listing all the national parks in Utah, Nevada, California, and Arizona. Noah had told her that Dorothy loved the West and always wanted to remain in one of those states. Nevada only had 1 national park, Arizona had 3, Utah had 5, and California had 8. She quickly found out that national park administrative personnel don't like to give out much information. None of her phone calls helped at all. Not one park would verify or deny that Dorothy worked for them, all saying they couldn't give out any personal information without the approval of that particular ranger. She pretty much ruled out the park in Nevada . . . who would want to live in Nevada? And she could rule out Death Valley since she knew Dorothy had left that place. That left her fifteen parks to somehow figure out if the girl of Noah's dreams was working there. It might take time, but Grace was determined.

Noah worked on his column every day. He met Catherine for coffee, tea, and bagels every morning. He usually went to the Moab Brewery or Fiddlin' Fish each evening--not so much for a drink, but rather for the enjoyment of being around people and the social aspect of it. Most people work in offices or plants or stores or wherever, but they're all around other people--Noah wasn't like that. He worked on his computer in his home. He missed the social interaction. He missed seeing pretty girls, ugly guys, old men, and nice women. He missed it. That's really why he went to the Brewery and the Fish. And, there was always the slight, minuscule, microscopic chance that he could actually meet a lady one time--there was a chance!

He spent a lot of days hiking by himself out in the remote wilderness areas of Canyonlands National Park and in the vast uncharted regions that surrounded Moab. He would usually drive his Jeep out to some back road, then take the first dirt road he saw and take that until it dead-ended, then begin his hike. In his opinion, the region of southern Utah was the most beautiful place in the world. Every so often, he would hike out to the exact place that he and Dorothy were when he found his arrowhead. He'd sit on a rock and hold that same arrowhead in his hand and dream. Great dreams! Very great dreams!

Once or twice he ran across his old flame, Vicki, at the Brewery. She had mellowed a little and didn't seem to harbor any grudges against Noah any longer. But she didn't try to jump his bones either. Sometimes he would meet his other friend Sandy for a drink and a burger as well. She would try to work her way into Noah's bed, but it never happened. He wasn't that bad off. Then, every month or so, he'd make the long trip down to Las Vegas to check on Grace. But if the truth were revealed, it was Grace who was checking on him, not the other way around. She was starting to show a little bit and she seemed very happy about it. She loved her job and the owners told her not to worry about the pregnancy, everything would be fine.

Noah always made time to stop for a few hours and explore some trails in Zion when he was traveling to Las Vegas. But he and Dorothy never crossed paths again. Zion is a large place. He also stopped at the same convenience store to gas up on every trip. Dorothy drove past that store each day on her way home, but they never saw each other there either. Dorothy finally did date a few guys, but no one more than twice. She just didn't seem interested. The rumor mill kept insinuating that she had to be gay. She would visit Shirley and Shirley would visit her, but no more blind dates were on the horizon. Life was just trickling along for everyone in its tame, tedious, tiring fashion when one day, things changed.

● ● ●

Grace had finally figured out a way. She mailed each of the fifteen national parks with this same letter:

"Dear Sirs:
I recently visited your beautiful park and had a little trouble. One of your female rangers really helped me out and answered all my questions for me. I'd like to send her a thank you note if that is possible. Unfortunately, all I remember is that she was a young woman with dark hair, who was very pretty, and that her name was Dorothy. If she still works there, could you please let me know so I can send her a thank you note?
I would very much appreciate it,
Grace"

Grace liked her idea. She wasn't asking for any personal information; she was only trying to "thank" someone for helping her. She wasn't trying to obtain any personal information or prying in any way. She mailed all fifteen letters and hoped for the best. After all, how many female rangers, young and pretty with dark hair, named Dorothy, could there be?

After three and a half weeks she had received responses from all fifteen parks. Great news! The bad news was that there were four park rangers named Dorothy. One in Arizona, one in Utah, and two in California. Grace then wrote each of these four thanking them for their help: Rangers help hundreds of people each month so there was no way they would find this strange. Then, she had the coup de gras for her plan. She ended her thank you note to each of the four Dorothys with this sentence: "By the way, you looked very familiar to me that day. I think I saw you once at Death Valley National Park. Did you used to work there?" She knew this would work.

Grace received her first response about a week later. It was from Yosemite National Park and this Dorothy had never worked at Death Valley. The next day she received a letter from a Dorothy at King's Canyon National Park who told her that she did work at Death Valley once, about fifteen years ago. The third response came two days later and this Dorothy didn't remember the incident where she helped out but was very happy to see that everything ended up well. And, yes, she did recently work at Death Valley. Bingo! She currently worked at Bryce Canyon National Park in Utah.

Grace was so excited that she screamed, scaring Kai, and almost wet her pants. What to do? Should she call Noah? Should she drive up to Bryce Canyon and talk to this Dorothy? Her mind was racing. She called Luray; she had to talk with someone. After explaining everything to her and what she'd found out, she first made Luray promise not to say a word to Noah. Then, she asked Luray what she should do. Luray advised her to take a day and drive up to Bryce Canyon National Park and see this girl, Dorothy, just to make sure. If it was indeed Noah's Dorothy, then explain everything to her and see if she would still want to see Noah. Hopefully, she wasn't married or involved with someone. This made sense to Grace. Her first off-day, she would take off for Bryce and finish her project.

Two more nights performing at the club, a little morning sickness in between, then, Friday came. She packed Kai in her car seat and took off on her journey. It's about a four hour and thirty-minute drive for normal people. Grace wasn't a normal driver, plus, she was excited. After passing nearly every car on the interstate, she ended up at the entrance to Bryce in three hours and forty minutes. She first drove to the park headquarters and visited the restroom, then changed Kai's diaper. She figured and hoped that since it was a Friday, most park personnel would be working. She walked to the information desk and asked the young male ranger if he happened to know a lady ranger named Dorothy.

The young man said, "Sure, everyone knows Dorothy. She's great."

Grace's heart was about to explode, "Is it possible I could talk to her? Or, can you just tell me where she's working today and I can drive out to meet her."

Noah

The guy smiled and said, "You don't have to drive anywhere, she's back in her office. Hold on, I'll go get her."

Grace's mind was whirling, *Okay, what do I say first? How do I explain my part in this? Do I tell her about Noah right away?* Before she could confuse herself any longer, the young ranger came walking back up the hallway with another ranger, an older, stern-looking woman, at least twenty years older than Noah.

The lady ranger said, "Hello, can I help you?"

Grace looked at the name tag pinned on her uniform and it read "Dorothy." She then asked her first stupid question of the day, "Are you, Dorothy?"

Certainly, with all her vast number of years in the park service, she had been asked hundreds of stupid questions, but this one was right up there. She glanced down at her name tag and answered, "Yes, I am."

Grace was stunned. How could this be? She looked back and asked her second stupid question of the day, "Are you sure?"

"Well, I was when I woke up this morning. Is there something I can help you with Miss?"

Then Grace asked her final stupid question of the day, "But, you're not young, are you?"

Ranger Dorothy showed a lot of restraint and experience and understanding as she replied, "I guess not."

Grace started to turn and leave, then finally some common sense seeped into her head and she said, "I'm sorry, I'm just very confused. I'm so sorry."

Both the ranger Dorothy and the young male ranger nodded as they watched Grace walk out of the Welcome Center. She got back in her car and turned out of the park. All that driving and she never saw a glimpse of the beauty that was Bryce Canyon National Park. She made it back to the interstate in a fog. She started driving trying to understand what went wrong. She was so sure. Then, blue lights were flashing and she heard sirens all around her. She was startled back to reality and quickly pulled over to the side. The sirens had upset Kai and she was wailing her lungs out. The trooper came over to Grace's door; she rolled the window down and the trooper immediately looked in the back to see what was wrong with Kai. He asked Grace for her license, then said, "Do you know how fast you were going, Miss?"

Grace had no idea. She did know that the speed limit here in the desert was probably 75 or maybe even 80. So, she answered with a question, "80?"

"No, ma'am. I clocked you at 105 mph." Then he looked back at Kai who was only screaming louder now, and said, "Is she alright?"

"She's fine officer. I'm so sorry, it's been a hard day. I had no idea I was going that fast. I'm so sorry."

He started scribbling in his notepad, then handed her license back to her and said, "I'm only going to give you a warning. I shouldn't, but I am. Watch your speed, okay?" He smiled at her and walked back to his car. Grace gave Kai a bottle to calm her down, then started back on the interstate. She did notice that the trooper followed her for about fifteen minutes before turning off.

She thought to herself, *What a day.*

45.

GRACE AND KAI WERE WORN OUT FROM THEIR ROAD TRIP; they both slept late on Saturday morning. Noah and Catherine were at the coffee shop discussing the merits, value, and importance of country music versus pop music. Luray was upset because someone didn't set the oven at the right temperature and burned a batch of muffins. Sandy was just now waking up and wondering who the person was lying in bed next to her. Shirley was looking for a bottle of extra-strength anything to help with the effects of one-too-many glasses of red wine the night before. And Dorothy, well, she finally decided to mail back the response she'd received a couple of weeks ago from someone wanting to know if she had previously worked at Death Valley National Park. She'd laid the letter on her desk and had forgotten about it.

After mailing the letter, she drove out to the wilderness area on the other side of Zion National Park, parked her car in an old abandoned picnic area, and starting hiking into the unknown. She had a backpack full of snacks, water, and a book she'd started reading; and a mind full of regrets, sorrows, pity, anguish, and heartache. She hiked three or four hours, generally in the same direction so she could find her way back easily enough, then found a large juniper tree to sit under and have her lunch and read for a while. She had started the book, *Firefly Lane*, by Kristen Hannah, and was enthralled by it so far. Of course, it could turn out like her life: exciting, energetic, and full of hope in the beginning, and then morph into despair, disappointment, and depression at the end. She was hoping the book and her life did not have a parallel osmosis going on.

She read until her eyes became tired, then she leaned back against the tree and napped for an unknown period of time. She didn't wear a watch because, well . . . she didn't really care. She dreamed of days gone by, of emails sent and received from someone special, and of hikes in the wilderness with that someone. She didn't want to dream those thoughts, just as someone doesn't want to have bad dreams--you just seem to have no control over what your emotions and mind carry forth. She woke to find a large, black wooly-worm crawling next to her leg. She'd never seen one of these creatures out west. She thought they only lived in her home state of North Carolina. It slowly crawled away and she repacked her stuff and started back to her car for the drive back to her lonely home in Springdale, Utah.

What if Dorothy had never mailed that letter? What if? What if? What if? But she did and three days later, Grace opened it in Las Vegas, Nevada. It confirmed that, yes, she had also worked at Death Valley National Park, not long ago either. Everything in the letter seemed to confirm what Grace was hoping for. But that's what she thought with the other letter. She needed to think.

Grace finished another week at work, which gave her several days to think about what she should do regarding the letter from another Dorothy. This Dorothy worked at Zion National Park, which wasn't nearly as far away as Bryce was. Maybe a three-hour drive, if she didn't speed too much. She thought about it all week but knew, in her mind, she had to go. She owed it to Noah. So, Friday morning she dropped Kai off at a babysitter, so she could speed without too much guilt, and started north for Zion National Park. She remembered this place from when Noah drove her through it before. However, the beauty of the park wasn't what she was interested in; she was solely concerned with a young lady ranger named Dorothy. Was she the one and only person in the world holding the key to Noah's heart?

She arrived at the park headquarters around 11:00 to find the parking lot full and tourists roaming around everywhere. Her pregnancy created the urge for her to quickly find a restroom. She took care of that, then went to the Visitor's Help Desk and stood behind two other people asking about camping sites. The ranger at the desk was a middle-aged man who seemed as though he'd rather be home sleeping. Grace asked him if he knew a ranger who worked there named Dorothy.

This particular ranger was in the group of male rangers who thought Dorothy must be gay because she had never wanted to date any of them. So, when a young female tourist came inquiring about Dorothy, he put two and two together, in his own warped way, and deduced that this young lady must be a girlfriend of Dorothy's. He said, "Wait just a minute, young lady; I'll be right back." He went down the official hallway to another office, stepped inside, and said, "Lance, come out here. I got one of Dorothy's girlfriends at the counter looking for her."

Lance immediately stopped what he was doing and said, "What? Are you sure?" Lance had asked Dorothy out a couple of times and she always turned him down.

"Yeah, I'm sure. Come out here and take a look at her. I think she might be pregnant, too."

Lance had started to get up from his desk when he heard the word pregnant. He said, "Pregnant? How could that happen?"

"I don't know. You know they do the artificial stuff now or get donors or something like that. You coming out or not?"

Lance followed him out and walked up to the counter where Grace was waiting. He asked, "Can I help you with something, Miss?"

Grace answered, "Yes, I hope so. I need to see Dorothy if she's here."

Lance said, "Let me check on that for you. Would you like to sit down while you wait? Looks like you might be expecting." He knew this was probably rude and, at the least, none of his business, but he had to know.

Grace was semi-shocked. Was she showing that much already? But, she answered, "No, I'm okay, I just need to see Dorothy."

The two rangers went back down the hallway and Lance said, "Yep, she's pregnant and I bet Dorothy is going to be the father, or mother, or whatever." They both nodded in the way that men do when they don't know what to do next. Then Lance asked, "Is she here?"

"Who?"

"Dorothy! Is she in her office?"

"Oh . . . no, she's out on patrol. Probably won't be back until after lunch, maybe not till quitting time."

They both nodded again, then Lance walked back out to the counter where Grace was and told her, "She's not in right now, ma'am. In fact, she might not return until the end of the day. Is there something I can help you with?"

But Grace didn't hear what he said. She had her eyes and focus on a set of pictures against the far wall of all the rangers assigned to Zion. Dorothy's picture was third in line. That picture was exactly like Noah had described her: very pretty, fairly young, with long dark hair, and a beautiful smile. Grace had hit the jackpot. Then she realized the two rangers were speaking to her, so she replied, "Excuse me?"

"Is there something we can do to help you with?"

Grace couldn't wait around all day, so she said, "No, you've been a great help. Thanks."

As she started to leave, Lance called to her and said, "Can we tell Dorothy who was here looking for her?"

Grace only turned and smiled at them both, then kept walking.

When Grace got back in Vegas and picked up Kai, she went home and called Noah just to verify some things. No answer. She waited fifteen minutes and called again--nothing. Now, she was frustrated! Where was he? She waited twenty more minutes, no answer. Then, she fed Kai, put her to bed, took a shower herself, and ate something. Then called him again, "Hello."

"Where have you been?"

"And good evening to you, Grace. I'm fine, I hope you and Kai are well. It's been a beautiful day, hasn't it?"

"I've been trying to call you for over an hour. Why haven't you picked up? It could've been an emergency!"

"Was it an emergency, Grace?"

"No, but it could've been. You need to always carry your phone and answer when I call. Do you understand?"

"Yes, mother. Can you read me a bedtime story now?"

"Noah, sometimes I'd just like to wring your neck."

Noah thought for a couple of seconds, then asked Grace, "Do you even know what it means to wring someone's neck?" Grace thought about that question, then started to say something, but wisely changed her mind. Noah continued, "What's up? Why are you calling so late? Is Kai okay?"

"Yeah, we're fine. I just wanted to talk . . . is that okay?"

Grace sounded a little strange to him, but he played along. "Alright, go ahead, what do you want to talk about?"

She started talking about her job, the club, how much she misses Moab, about how Luray was doing, what was happening with him and Catherine . . . everything except what she really wanted to know. She did not want him to think that the only reason she called was to ask questions about Dorothy. Finally, after Noah filled her in on all the other so-called news, she got to the point: "Anything new with your old flame, Dorothy?"

He knew she was beating around the bush for something; however, he didn't think it concerned Dorothy. He answered, "Nope."

"I forget what you told me. Where did she move to when she left Death Valley?"

251

"I told you, Grace, I don't know where she went. She disappeared. Why are you asking about her, anyway?"

"No reason, I was just curious. She was about your age, wasn't she?"

"More or less. Why do you care?"

"And she had long, dark hair, right? Kind of a pretty girl?"

"Grace, I'm not answering any more questions until you tell me what's going on."

"I'm just curious, Noah. I'd like to see what sort of girl got you so hot and bothered. Do you have a picture of her?"

He knew something was up but he couldn't figure it out. "If I did, I wouldn't show it to you."

"Noah, don't be like that. I'm just curious, that's all. So, you don't have a picture?"

"Grace!!"

"Okay, grumpy. Is she still a ranger?"

"No more about Dorothy. She's gone and everything will be better as soon as I can forget all about her. So, all of your inquisitions here are not helping, okay?"

"Alright, sorry. Don't get your panties in a wad. You still lusting over Vicki?"

"I'm going to bed. Kiss Kai goodnight for me, and if you don't mind, look in the mirror and slap yourself for me. Goodnight."

Grace hung up, not quite satisfied, but feeling more confident that she had indeed found the Dorothy of his dreams. Now, to execute the next phase of her plan.

46.

GRACE DIDN'T BRING UP DOROTHY IN ANY CONVERSATIONS with Noah over the next several weeks. She wanted him to forget that she had any interest at all in the ghost from his past. Then, when she hinted that it might be time for Noah to come and visit her again, he committed to driving down the following weekend. On that phone call, before she hung up, she said, "Oh, Noah, remember that place we visited in Utah? I don't remember the name of it, but we drove through it and it was really pretty?"

It took him a moment to understand what she meant, then he remembered they quickly detoured through Zion National Park on their trip to Moab. He answered, "Yeah, that was Zion National Park. A beautiful place."

"I'd like to see it again. Do you think we could drive up there, just you and me? I could get a sitter for Kai. What do you think?"

This request struck him as really odd because Grace was not at all the outdoor type and had never shown an interest in anything of that nature. But, being the good friend he was, he said, "Sure, we can go. It's a gorgeous place, I'm sure you'll like it."

"Great, and can we go this Friday? I can't get a sitter all day on Saturday."

"Sure. I'll drive down there Thursday evening and we can leave early Friday for Zion."

So, it was set. Grace knew that Dorothy worked on Fridays because that's when she was there before. She would let Noah take her to Zion, then she would "accidentally" arrange to have them meet. Finally, after all this time of him helping her, she was going to be able to do something special for him.

He arrived in Las Vegas around 9:30 Thursday night. Grace had taken Kai to the babysitter's house and was eagerly waiting on him to pull in the driveway. She met him on the steps and was talking non-stop. Noah had never seen her this excited before. Something seemed a bit "off" to him but he couldn't decide what it was; Grace just seemed to be overly-Graced. Her constant talking was hard for him to take so he made an excuse of being tired and headed off to bed. They agreed to leave in the morning for Zion no later than 6:00 AM. That would give them all day to see the sights, and for Grace to find where Dorothy was working.

Noah did the driving; Grace did the talking. He tried tuning her out but she was overbearing at times. He had never seen this side of her. Seeing Zion National Park obviously wasn't the cause of her weirdness, but he had no other explanation. Just as they arrived at the park entrance, his phone rang. It was Catherine: "Hey, where are you?"

"We're here at the entrance to the park. Where are you?"

"I'm here at the coffee shop sipping tea and eating one of your bagels. Hope you don't mind."

Noah laughed and said, "Help yourself, young lady. See you Sunday morning, okay?" Catherine missed her morning meetings with Noah; she just wanted to touch base and let him know that she missed him--in a friendly way.

Grace rolled her eyes at this entire conversation and when Noah ended the call, she asked, "You're not dating her again, are you?"

"No, we're just friends. Trust me, that's all it is."

"Good."

He thought that was an odd response, so he asked her, "Why is it GOOD that I'm not dating anyone? It doesn't seem GOOD to me."

"I just meant that it's good you're not dating HER. That's all." He knew something was up but he still couldn't figure out what Grace was doing. She insisted they stop at the Visitor Center to visit the restrooms and get a snack, which was fine with him. When Noah went to the bathroom, Grace went over to the counter where the same ranger from before was stationed. He remembered her and smiled when she walked over. Grace asked him, "Is Dorothy working today?"

"Yes, ma'am, she is. She's out on patrol right now. Not sure when she'll be back."

Grace nodded and thanked him, then wondered what she should do next. There was only one main road through the park, so maybe they'd just drive that road, stop at some turnoffs, and she'd keep an eye out for an official park SUV. Noah came out from the bathroom and asked if she was ready to go. She said, "No, not yet, I need to go to the bathroom." He wondered why she hadn't already gone. What was she doing? He knew something was up. When she returned, she said, "Let's go."

He asked, "Don't you want something to drink? Or a snack?"

"No, let's go." So, they left. Every time Noah wanted to take a pull out for a scenic view, Grace would say, "No, not here." Then, the next scenic area, "No, keep going."

Finally, he was fed up with this whole thing and he pulled over, despite her objections, and asked, "What's going on here? You're acting weird and you don't want to stop and see anything. Tell me what's happening, Grace."

"Nothing's happening, Noah. I'm enjoying seeing this beautiful place. It's great, just like you said. Now, pull out, and let's keep going." Then, she suddenly yelled, "No, stop! Pull over, Noah!" This sudden change startled him. First, she said to keep going, then a park SUV pulls in the lot and she says to stop. He looked over at her and she was staring down at the official park vehicle. A park ranger opened the door and an older looking man got out, put his hat on, and started walking away. Then Grace looked back over at him and, "Okay, we can go now."

They drove all the way through the park, then back again, taking each scenic turnoff on the way, but Grace never wanted to do any short hikes or exploring. He assumed it was probably because of the pregnancy. After several hours of driving through the park, they had arrived back at the park Visitor Center, where they had started. Noah parked his Jeep and said they were going in to get something to eat. He first visited the bathroom again, which gave Grace a chance to go back to the counter and confront the young ranger, "I didn't see Dorothy anywhere! You told me she was working today."

"She's on duty, ma'am, but she could be anywhere: helping a hiker, checking on some wildlife issue, doing paperwork; there are hundreds of things she could be doing. Heck, she might even have taken off early and gone home. I don't really know."

Grace asked, "Where does she live?"

"I can't give out that information, ma'am, you know that."

"Well, what can you do? I need help!"

Noah had walked up behind her and said, "What kind of help?"

"Oh, Noah, umm, you know, woman issues sort of help. It's okay, I'll be fine. Where are the bathrooms?" Without waiting for an answer, she hustled away.

Noah looked at the ranger, who looked back and sighed, "Women." Noah nodded and went toward the small cafe to wait for Grace. She sat on the toilet trying to figure out what options she had, which were basically none. She gave up hope for this trip, but she wouldn't give up hope totally. They had a small snack and decided they should probably start back for Las Vegas--they told the sitter they would be back before 10:00 to pick up Kai.

Suddenly, Grace's entire demeanor had changed. No more constant talking at all, she just sat there staring out the window as they left the park. Noah decided to stop at his favorite little convenience store in Springdale to gas up before hitting the interstate. He stopped at the gas pumps and looked up to see what the price per gallon was that day before he put the nozzle in. On the other side of this gas pump island was an official Zion National Park SUV, with a long, dark-haired, beautiful woman pumping gas.

Initially, Noah thought he was dreaming, or hallucinating. It only took about three seconds before this long-haired beauty looked up herself and saw the man she had been dreaming of her entire life, staring back across at her.

●●●

Do fairy tales really come true? Do dreams ever materialize? Does love ever win?

Sure, why not?

THE END

Friendship is a rare and elusive gift in this shattered, chaotic, frantically moving society of ours. I'm blessed and lucky enough to have a few good men who are my friends; one of them edited this book for me: Larry McRacken.

But you can call him Lance, he won't mind at all.

www.ingramcontent.com/pod-product-compliance
Lightning Source LLC
Chambersburg PA
CBHW070814180626
46818CB00001B/265